THE JADED SPY

OTHER BOOKS BY NICK SPILL AVAILABLE AS E-BOOKS AND PAPERBACKS

The Jaded Kiwi
Part One of the *Jaded Trilogy*

Reluctant Q
with George Spill

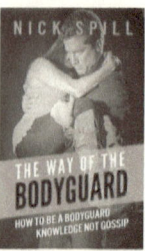

The Way of the Bodyguard

The Palace in TriBeCa

Dolphin Kicks Cactus Pricks and K-129

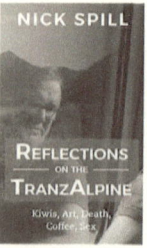

Reflections on the Tranzalpine

THE JADED SPY

The curator who lost Captain Cook

PART TWO OF THE JADED SERIES

NICK SPILL

The Jaded Spy, Nick Spill – 1st US Edition

The Jaded Spy

Library of Congress Cataloguing-in-Publication Data

Spill, Nick
Crime – Fiction Mystery- Fiction
Action and Adventure–Fiction
Thriller–Fiction
New Zealand–Fiction
ISBN-13: 978-0-578-56937-6

Book Cover: Angie Alaya
Interior book design: 52 Novels
Author photo: Leon Smith

More information about The Jaded Spy can be found at
http://nickspill.com
and
http://nickspill.blogspot.com

WARNING

"If you publish this story, you can never return to New Zealand. You're finished. Too much rings true and relates to real people and events. Some very important people are going to be pissed!"

"I know. But it's fiction. I have a disclaimer. The dates are different. The names have been changed. It's a story. A good yarn, I hope, but it's still fiction."

"You're deluding yourself. You have no idea what they could do to you. You were once one of them."

"You're forgetting an important fact. Four people knew about me—Muldoon, the Prime Minister; Alan Highet, the Minister of Internal Affairs; Richard Catelin, the Under-Secretary; and me! I'm the only one still alive."

"For now."

"Diplomats and intelligence agents, in my experience, are even bigger liars than journalists, and the historians who try to reconstruct the past out of their records are, for the most part, dealing with fantasy."

MALCOLM MUGGERIDGE,
Chronicles of Wasted Time: Number 2: The Infernal Grove.

"This inability to distinguish between the fiction and the reality of the intelligence world is ironically appropriate, because that was how it all began—in fantasy."

PHILLIP KNIGHTLEY,
The Second Oldest Profession: Spies and Spying in the Twentieth Century.

Portrait of Captain James Cook, circa 1780, England, by John
Webber. Gift of the New Zealand Government, 1960. Te Papa
(1960-0013-1)

PROLOGUE

There is a large crater off the Southern Motorway close to Drury, once a busy petrol station. On the edge of the charred moonscape is a memorial, a slab of dark marble two meters tall with the names of the victims of the largest and deadliest explosion to occur in New Zealand six months ago.

Among the names are Terry Turner, the leader of the Auckland underworld, and John Eustace, his feared henchman. It was rumored Turner's wife, Barbara, donated the money for the memorial.

North of Auckland, at the entrance to the track where the Titirangi shootout took place, is another memorial. The names of the five dead officers are inscribed on a large block of granite. Above is the badge of the police. Five native trees were planted behind the memorial and are fenced in to protect their roots.

The memorial was unveiled a month ago and the Police Commissioner, dignitaries, the entire command staff and many of the rank and file attended the unveiling. The road was blocked off and they were bussed in from the shopping center a few miles south. It was a somber affair with deference to the grieving widows of the slain officers. The Commissioner, Ian Thompson, declared that the individual police sacrifices were not in vain, that valuable lessons had been learned from the shooting. The war on drugs had started.

CHAPTER ONE

Alexander Newton squeezed the shutter release with his left hand and kicked out his right leg, spilling the milk bottle full of pee. Yellow liquid flowed across the floor into his new Italian loafers. Through his telephoto lens touching a hole in the black paper, he spied the red-haired Soviet diplomat in a tan trench coat hand a newspaper to the doctor. Inside the Toyota van the Nikon motor drive sounded like a machine gun.

The Soviet kept walking and the doctor, who wore a similar coat, entered his house, a couple of doors from where the photographer was parked. Through a crack in the black paper, Alexander could see an ordinary-looking man in a dark suit on the other side of the street. The man kept glancing across, as if the Soviet diplomat might disappear. The Soviet waved at the ordinary-looking man as if he knew him. The man kept walking till he reached the van. Alexander lost sight of him. He held his camera and tripod to his chest. He wrapped his raincoat over his six foot three frame and sank into the Chesterfield, closing his steel grey eyes. He heard the thermos break beneath him and stuck out his square chin in a grimace. He knew the ordinary man would press his face into the windscreen to peer inside. He resisted the temptation to run his hands through his short dark hair and held his breath.

Alexander had parked between the lights, on a street lined with restored Edwardian and late-Victorian wooden villas in an inner-city suburb. A green Ford Escort had cruised past him and parked around the corner at the top of the hill. He had taken a few shots of the two men inside but did not know if their faces would show. Now the ordinary man, who was not so ordinary, tried to force the driver's door.

The van started to rock. Alexander opened his eyes and reached out with his right foot to stop the empty milk bottle. He wanted to leap out and hit the ordinary man. Instead, he breathed out his aggression, relieved to be in control. He had been fired from his part-time job at the *Listener* after he called his editor an ossified turd. They had argued over one word. One word out of a thousand, in an article he had written on a "School of Nicolas Poussin" painting he had discovered tucked away in the basement of the National Art Gallery.

He heard the man walk away, the whine of an engine and squealing brakes. Alexander sat up and aimed his telephoto lens through the windscreen and managed a couple of shots of the Escort as it screamed downhill. The van stank. His feet felt like ice. Yellow ice.

Alexander had researched his target. Doctor Cedric Winter had been an advisor to four prime ministers, was an avid Labor supporter and, now semi-retired, held the prestigious title of Emeritus Professor of the Economics Department at Victoria University. He had headed the New Zealand delegation at the United Nations to save UNICEF against the United States's opposition. Dr. Winter was writing a memoir of his political life. He was described as a socialist and a true patriot by his political peers and enemies. Labels he did not dispute. The week-long spy trial had gripped the nation. Found not guilty of espionage, he had walked out of the courtroom a free man, much to the consternation of the National government and the Security Intelligence Service, known as the SIS. Several Soviet diplomats had flown home before the trial.

Four weeks ago, Alexander had been summoned to the office of his real boss, Richard Catelin, the Permanent Under-Secretary of the Department of Internal Affairs. Catelin inhabited, rather than occupied, a huge office on the second floor of the old Government Building on Lambton Quay. It was the second time he had been in Catelin's office. The first, more than a year ago, had been a formal interview for the exhibition curator's position at the National Art Gallery, which was administered by Catelin's department.

The Permanent Under-Secretary rose from his high seat and walked around the massive desk piled with papers, books and folders with government crests to greet Alexander with a firm, dry handshake. In a new single-breasted grey suit, white shirt with a white pocket square and a thin black tie, Alexander looked more like a playboy than a curator.

"Alexander, so glad you could make it at such short notice." Catelin's neatly trimmed mustache and goatee, the wave in his full head of dyed black hair and his Prussian-blue floral waistcoat lent him an air of a 19th-century aristocrat rather than a 20th-century antipodean bureaucrat. He reeked of power, persuasion and pipe tobacco.

Catelin motioned to the other side of his office where three large black leather chairs and a matching sofa were arranged around a low marble coffee table, stacked with newspapers, magazines and books. Alexander realized the seating was a test. He chose the most comfortable armchair but not his boss's. He adjusted the knife-edge crease in his pants, admired his shiny black loafers, and settled down so as not to tower over his boss. He made a mental note to look into purchasing floral waistcoats, although the French cuffs and gold cufflinks were not his style.

Catelin eased into his seat, next to a large telephone set. He pressed a button and summoned his secretary. "Would you like a drink? Coffee? Tea? Something a little stronger?"

"Coffee would be marvelous." Alexander noted a well-stocked cocktail cabinet against the nearest wall, surrounded by maps, photographs of politicians shaking Catelin's hand and paintings with familiar metal labels on golden frames. He watched Catelin find a pipe on the table and inspect it before using a small penknife to scrape ash from the bowl into a large marble ashtray.

The secretary appeared in the doorway. "Mavis, two coffees please and the usual. Thank you." She was in and out of the office without a word.

Catelin finished cleaning his pipe and filled the bowl from his leather pouch. "How are you finding the gallery?"

Alexander leaned forward, stuck out his jaw and fixed Catelin with his intense grey eyes. So, he was not to be fired or reprimanded. "Great. I'm sorting out the inventoried works and organizing a few new shows." Keep it short and confident. Don't give anything away, he had told himself.

"Good." Catelin found a box of matches on the table, inspected it, and started the ritual of lighting his pipe for the first time. After a certain amount of puffing he turned to Alexander. "You like photography." It was not framed as a question.

Alexander smiled. He had no idea where this was going.

"Do you have a camera?" He inspected his pipe and relit it.

"Yes." Alexander placed his hands on his thighs and breathed out.

"What type?"

"A Canon A1, couple of lenses, and a Leica, an old 3 series from 1937. Has an amazing lens for color."

"How would you like to use a new Nikon with an extra-long telephoto lens, a tripod of course, and a fast motor drive? It's almost a movie camera."

"What for? Something to do with the gallery?"

"Not exactly. It's for some candid photos." He let out a cloud of smoke, looked at Alexander and broke into a smile. "I might as well lay out all my cards. I trust whatever I say to you here will not be repeated, ever, outside these walls? Not even to your ex-girlfriend." He looked around as he puffed on his pipe.

Alexander frowned. He thought his break up was a secret. Without thinking he replied, "I'm far too curious to say no."

"That's a yes?"

"Yes."

"Here goes, then. The minister is concerned about a certain someone, a well-known man, who might be meeting with a diplomat, who might be something else. Do you see where I'm going?"

Alexander nodded. "All the way down the garden path."

"Not quite, I hope. You see, the minister wants photos of the target, to keep an eye on him, very discreetly of course, and get evidence of a contact. You know what a contact is, don't you?"

"You mean passing national secrets? Envelopes stuffed with production figures of wool and butter?" Alexander did not mean to sound sarcastic. He brushed his hair away from his face, a gesture that worked when it was longer. He smiled.

"Along those lines. But just the photos would be enough here. It's like art, or a performance. Context is so important."

"I think I get it." Alexander nodded and leaned forward again.

"Well?"

"I cannot resist." He held up his hands and kept the smile on his face.

Catelin placed his pipe on the ashtray. "We'd loan you the equipment. You could develop the film yourself, right? You have a darkroom at home."

It was not a question. Alexander did have a darkroom no one, he thought, knew about.

"I have high-speed film, paper and instructions on developing for you, I'm sure you already know all that, and you would furnish us with all the negatives and prints. Everything. Very simple, really. We'd give you a couple of weeks to complete the assignment. Then we'll see. There could be more work. But if you get into any trouble, we would know nothing. You'd get no help from anyone, officially, but we can always work it out. Do you understand?"

"Yes. I think I do. And you can rely on my discretion."

"Absolutely. Don't even tell your girlfriends." He paused. "You cannot tell *anyone*."

When Alexander was a pimple-faced teenage virgin, he had read Ian Fleming. He had dreamt of being a spy. He did not have enough time to think about what Catelin had said. He had thought he was going to be fired, then the comment about his break-up and all his girlfriends put him at a disadvantage. What girlfriends? Then he was offered a job as a spy. Alexander did not have the foresight to consider why he was being chosen for this assignment. He should have asked "Why me?" But he only thought about the interview much later, and by then it was too late.

Instead he asked, "Where's the camera?"

CHAPTER TWO

Alexander developed the Tri-X film in the darkroom he had in the tiny bathroom of his one-bedroom flat in Thorndon. First he ran a test strip to make sure he had the right calculation, before pushing the 400 ASA negatives to 1600. The contact strip looked promising, if a little dark. The 8" x 10" black-and-white prints were grainy, but he could make out the Soviet, the doctor and the Russian newspaper. The two SIS men were captured. The ordinary-looking man was older, dressed in a dark suit. The younger man had a lighter suit jacket with a wide-open shirt collar. Alexander could make out the long sideburns and swept-back hair. With the prints drying on a line over his bath, he thought about Catelin's comment, "Don't tell your girlfriends." What girlfriends? He had moved out of his girlfriend's flat months ago and had not dated since. He was too busy with the gallery and now his night job consumed his spare time.

He developed two copies of every correctly exposed print. In the morning, he would return the gallery van, fold up all the black paper for another time and store the Chesterfield in the loading bay before delivering the original prints and negatives to his boss.

Alexander reminded himself he did have one girl-friend, or rather a sauna friend, a sauna platonic friend, to be precise. On Sunday nights he went to a private sauna party held at a Swedish diplomat's Victorian home in Oriental Terrace, a double-story wooden villa nestled against a hill. There was a tiny garden in the back with an ice-cold pool they could skinny dip in, one at a time, after sweating in the sauna with other naked strangers. Kathy, as his guide, had instructed him to put $5 in a Chinese vase on the mantelpiece. She was the best friend of one of the shadow minister's daughters. On one of their long walks back across town late on Sunday night, towels over their shoulders, she had confessed her affair with the shadow minister. Alexander had felt embarrassed and hoped she never brought up the topic again.

Then last week as he walked with her down the steps to Oriental Parade, Kathy had asked, "Have you ever had anal sex?" Alexander had been concerned where she was going with the question. It was a long walk to her apartment in Thorndon.

"He started with one finger. You know? Then he put in two. Next thing I knew he had his entire dick up me. It hurt at first, but I got used to it and now I can't get enough. He's an animal. Politics must be a big aphrodisiac. I mean, I've never had anything like it before," she gushed.

Alexander did not know how to respond as he tried to keep a straight face. Why was she telling him the gory details? He did not understand. He kept walking along Cable Street, next to the harbor. There was no wind or rain to shield him from his friend's confession. He looked out over the harbor and only desired to appreciate the unusually mild weather, the lack of traffic and noise and the fresh sea air. "He turns you on?" was all he could finally muster.

"Yes! Exactly. It's amazing."

Alexander walked her home and was careful to not say another word or move too close to her. He assumed Kathy wanted to confess her sins, like the good Catholic girl she wasn't, and she knew he never gossiped to her and therefore her secret was safe. When she got to her front door, he thanked her for the evening and quickly walked away.

CHAPTER THREE

Wiremu Wilson pushed his chair away from the wooden table, stood up and held a newspaper clipping in front of Moana and Rawiri. He was so big he knocked the bare lightbulb back and forth above the table. "Captain Cook is coming to Auckland." He paused. "And we are going to kidnap him. For Maori land!"

"What?" Rawiri, his older brother looked up. "You're planning the crime of the century?" The light played shadows across his lined face.

"Yes," Wiremu whispered. He sat down and looked at their expressions of astonishment. The family kitchen had seen better days. Cobwebs were thick in the corners of the ceiling and papers and crumbs lined the cracked linoleum floor.

Moana scratched her head. "Isn't he dead already?"

"How long have I been out?" Rawiri asked.

Wiremu had come across the article in the *Herald* the previous week and had been thinking of a plan to steal the most valuable painting in New Zealand, the symbol of colonial dominance. He had been monitoring the new seedlings growing in hidden plots in remote areas around Hokianga, on the south side of the harbor in native bush. Having lost his entire crop in February, he was determined to cultivate and sell the biggest harvest Auckland had ever known next year, and cash in on another expected marijuana drought. The Captain Cook caper might appear a distraction but both plans concerned Maori land rights, and Wiremu believed all the land marches and sit ins and protests and letters to the editor would amount to nothing. Only hard action would produce results. Only hard cash would buy back their lands.

CHAPTER FOUR

Two days before, at seven o'clock in the morning, Rawiri had been let out of his cell by a Corrections officer. On the landing he said goodbye to everyone waiting to be unlocked at seven thirty. It was obvious he was popular and respected. A powerful presence with his wide shoulders and barrel chest, he looked taller than he really was as he followed the officer through the sally port to a long corridor and the receiving office. He was handed his clothes and property in the canvas bag he had when he was incarcerated four and a half years ago. He was escorted past Central Control and along another long corridor to the last sally port, and the stairs and through the metal grille. A young Maori woman in a short red floral dress waited for him in a small office, accompanied by two more Corrections officers. She was on her toes to press noses with him; as he bent down so her long black hair fell over his shoulders.

"Hey, cuzz!" he said.

The two walked over to the visitor's carpark. He heard the click of the big metal lock behind him and grimaced.

He looked at the sky and was blinded by the sunshine. He squinted and saw his cousin walk up to a 1974 cream Holden Kingswood. "Your car? Christ, Moana!" he exclaimed.

"It's my boyfriend's. He let me borrow it for the weekend."

"Let's go. I want to get away from here." He swung his bag into the back seat.

Moana planted her foot on the accelerator and the eight cylinders growled. She slipped into first gear and eased up to the boom, the V8 rumbling. She roared through the barrier as it was raised and turned left onto Paremoremo Road. All that was left in the prison parking lot was a cloud of smoke.

Rawiri had one hand on the dashboard, the other on the door handle. "The Chinese guy I heard about, with the bomb?"

"He's a third-generation New Zealander and his name's Ricky, Ricky Wong. How did you know about the bomb?"

"Nothing we don't know in there."

"Ricky bought the car after what happened to his brother and his cousin." Moana expertly steered through tight corners and blind bends as they made their way along a tight two-lane road lined with bush.

"How is Wiremu?"

"He's good. Sends you his best. Dying to see you, but knows you have to make your journey first." If Rawiri turned around he could catch glimpses of the sunken fortress of concrete and barbed wire they called Parry amid fields of green grass and mature trees.

"Yeah. Let's not talk about it now. And I have to see my probie within twenty-four hours."

"In Kaikohe?"

"Yeah." Moana accelerated in the straights then braked hard at each corner. Rawiri held on with both hands. He looked at the green hills, the intensity of the light. He kept squinting; the colors blinded him.

"Above you." She pointed to his visor.

He pulled the visor and a pair of wraparound sunglasses fell into his lap. "Cool! Now I can rob a post office!"

She jammed on the brakes and Rawiri almost hit the windscreen. She glared at him.

"Just kidding, Moana. It's all I've heard about from some jokers. You'd think they'd learn."

"Well, we all have to learn. I was naive." Moana stepped on the accelerator and Rawiri held onto the dashboard and the door handle again. She turned to Rawiri. "A little country girl seduced by the big city."

Rawiri pointed to the road and Moana swerved to miss a dead opossum.

He had been sentenced to seven years for cultivating and dealing in cannabis. Harvested, cured and distributed from secret plots on Crown land. Rawiri never admitted to the crime and never implicated anyone else. He had been arrested driving a large truck full of high-quality marijuana. At least 100 kilos.

Originally classified as a security risk, he had been sent to D Block in Paremoremo maximum-security prison but had been a calming influence on other Maori inmates. He had applied for and earned a BA in English literature, and successfully petitioned the classification committee to let him stay in Parry till his release this morning. He had at least two years to go, on probation, before his sentence was finished. Once he had reported to his probation officer he was to enroll at a Department of Social Welfare office and look for a job. His brother, also a graduate from Parry, whom he would live with, had promised he would help. There was the problem of associating with, let alone living with his brother, an ex-felon but Rawiri was sure Wiremu could smooth that out with his probation officer. All the other general and specific conditions he could manage—apart from not drinking alcohol, especially all the beers he was looking forward to. He thought such a restriction impractical and unreasonable.

"We're gonna take the main highway and go across 12 to Dargaville, okay? We can go past Waipoua forest."

"You're driving. The big kauri tree. Too much excitement for a poor little Maori boy like me. Shit! I haven't been in a car for years!" He gazed at the green paddocks with cows before him, a big smile on his face. "Hey, can we get a burger and a shake? I'm starving."

Moana turned left when she got to the junction of State Highway 12 and 14, otherwise she would have missed most of the town. She doubled back to Victoria Street where a takeaway shop was open. Dargaville was a collection of one-story shops along the main street: what had once been a thriving center for gum traders and kauri-timber merchants was now a quiet farming community that seemed stuck in the 1950s. Rawiri ate two cheeseburgers and drank three passionfruit milk shakes at the takeaway. Moana paid for them. When they came out of the shop the sky turned dark as if all the color had gone out of the street.

In the time it took Rawiri to wind down his window, Moana had left the town. He burped several times, looked at his driver who ignored him, and breathed in country air: grass, trees, cows, cow dung, truck exhaust. He leaned his head out of the car and enjoyed the wind blowing through his hair.

"Still the same colors, the same smells. Nothing changes here." He looked back at the town, the muddy Wairoa River and the narrow road north.

"What do you mean?"

"Been away such a long time and now I'm out and it's like, everything's the same."

"What do you expect? Another planet? It's Dargaville. New Zealand."

Rawiri adjusted his sunglasses. He looked out at farmland, large flax plants pointing to the grey sky, the sheer green of the grass covered hills. An occasional totara tree standing alone in a field surrounded by sheep. Squashed opossums by the side of the road. A harrier hawk riding the thermals. Pukekos, fat swamp hens, with their distinctive walk in paddocks next to the road. Everything looked familiar but different. He took his sunglasses off to squint in the sunlight and reassure himself the colors were so intense. He put his glasses back on and turned to Moana. "What's your boyfriend going to do now? Rebuild the Hungry Wok? It had a reputation in Parry."

"Really? Nah. Too awful. Think he's going to concentrate on his martial-arts supplies and his other business. You know? Needs to clear his head. It'll take time. And get the insurance company to cough up the dough. Greedy buggers."

Moana concentrated on driving for a few minutes. "The Hungry Wok? They knew about that?"

"Yeah. Lots of boob-heads ate there. If they weren't talking about scores they were talking about food, or, you know."

Moana swerved to miss another dead opossum. She adjusted her steering and kept her eyes on the road. "Boob-heads?"

"Yeah. Lots of slang inside. Want to leave it all behind." Rawiri turned and studied Moana. "My little cousin. You've turned into some young woman, girl." He sighed and kept looking at her. "I haven't heard from Wiremu since Hone."

"He's keeping quiet. Lying low. A social worker for the local council, would you believe? He's not his former self. It's like he's lost his mana."

"And all his pot and plans."

"Yeah, it was a huge shipment. The best Hokianga weed ever, from what I've sampled. Would have bought a lot of land with the drought and all."

"Do you have seedlings growing?"

"Do we ever. It'll be a bigger crop. All tucked away in places no one knows about, let alone cops in helicopters."

"Can't wait to see it!" Rawiri rubbed his hands. "After I've spoken to my probie. Do you have a radio? Any music?"

"Wondered when you'd ask." Moana switched on the radio and the car filled with the sound of "Bohemian Rhapsody". She floored the accelerator and Rawiri held onto his arm rest.

CHAPTER FIVE

Mark Rose stopped at the junction as a cream Holden roared past. He adjusted his long black hair behind his ears as he leaned on the steering wheel to get a better look at the car. It looked familiar. His city drug dealer had a similar model, though the driver wasn't the Chinese guy, Ricky, but a young Maori woman he hadn't seen before, together with a huge Maori he didn't recognize either. New Zealand is a small country, he mused, and wondered what Ricky's car was doing here. Why would Ricky lend his car to a Maori girl? He would have to find out. Not for a moment did he think Ricky had had his car stolen. No one in their right mind would steal anything from Ricky. Not after what had happened to his brother and the Hungry Wok. Mark had heard a rumor that the explosion on the Southern Motorway was somehow related to Ricky and his relatives in Pukekohe.

Anyone who messed around with explosives had to be taken seriously. He should know. A few years ago, he had a 44-gallon drum of gelignite in his living room for a week, as his comrades plotted to blow up various targets around Auckland. The gelignite was old and starting to break down into the unstable nitroglycerine. The sweating drum gave out the most obnoxious fumes. His visitors got headaches, and none of his student girlfriends would come over to his Parnell flat, so he figured a way to put the drum onto a rowing boat and tow it out to the Devonport naval base. He had estimated the current would draw the boat to a docked ship and cause a large explosion. The boat sank in the harbor. He decided gelignite was unstable. The small quantities they had used previously had made little damage but had created enormous headlines. He had learned a valuable political lesson here, how small, random acts of violence, however poorly planned and imperfectly executed, could send the authorities into absolute panic and confusion. And Mark Rose had endeared himself to Nikolai Raganovich, a Soviet diplomat.

Ricky was not only skilled in explosives, Mark reasoned, but he grew the most mind-blowing pot Mark had ever smoked. Mark did not grow such potent sensimilla at his commune, and his brand was well known, and expensive. He would have to find out what Ricky Wong and the Maori girl were doing.

Mark Rose, peace-loving activist and general busybody, pushed a favorite old cassette into the new audio tape machine he had fitted into his truck and turned up the volume to hear Bob Dylan play "Maggie's Farm". This tape had a special meaning to him, as he'd had to rethread it with a pencil after it had become unspooled. He thought that was a metaphor for his life. He had become unraveled, and now he had found a woman who made him feel wound up again, whole—Annie, the earth-mother Samoan nurse he was dating. He looked forward to seeing her again but couldn't remember a Dylan song featuring Annie, otherwise he'd have played it. He slid into first gear and started his journey home with a big smile on his face.

CHAPTER SIX

"What's happening, Wiremu my brother?" Rawiri hugged Wiremu. They were the same size, same solid build, tight black curly hair, sharp brown eyes, wide shoulders.

"Rawiri! It's good to see you. You look older. I hope you are wiser. I swore to myself I would never go back, you know, and so far it's working. I pray it will be your way as well, little brother."

"You know how many relatives have said that before they were arrested again?" Moana muttered but neither brother heard her nor paid her any attention. They were too busy staring at each other. "I can't get over how you look!," said Rawiri. "There were rumors you were defeated. You'd lost your mana. I'm telling it to you straight, brother. I would never say anything behind your back I wouldn't say to your face."

"I appreciate your honesty. It's been a tough year and I've been worrying about seeing you again, and what you have become. But I see from your presence, your mana, you are ready to get into the fight."

"Parry was designed to break the spirit of the Maori. It failed."

"We can't fail on our mission, can we, brother?"

Rawiri shook his head.

They walked across the metal road down the paddock to the edge of the harbor and the stone beach. Two harrier hawks rode the thermals. The brothers watched the birds, the tide going out and bubbles surfacing from shellfish. There were no boats on the water, only the sound of small waves. Wiremu explained how he had spread rumors that he had lost his drive, his ambition to reclaim their lost land, he had retired from growing marijuana, he had abandoned the huge plots spread over Northland. Instead, he committed to helping young Maori find themselves and their place in the changing world. How young Maori could realize what they could do for their iwi, and their power within tangata whanua and how Pakeha and Maori could live together.

They returned to the porch that overlooked the harbor. The house, a one-story wooden villa built in the early 1900s, used to belong to their mother, Whina Wilson, who in turn told the story of an aunt who had inherited it from a kauri-gum trader she had married and who had died shortly afterwards. When Rawiri turned eighteen, he discovered that Whina had left it to her three sons, Rawiri, Wiremu and Hone. With filigree carvings and fretwork around the front porch, the house still looked majestic despite not having seen a paintbrush or a hammer for a long time.

Wiremu had two beer bottles in his hand. He bit the top off one and handed it to Rawiri. "There was a young samurai lord," he said, "who was brilliant and had a quick tongue. But when he came to court, he realized what a dangerous place it was and how many potential enemies he had. So he acted dumb. He never said anything to anyone and pretty soon the court forgot about him. One day, after a court uprising and all the other courtiers were fighting each other, the quiet one stepped forward and declared himself the leader. He fought two of the top men and he became their new lord."

"Are you going to fight me, boy?" Rawiri screwed up his face.

"No! Are you playing stupid now? I'm telling you the story because I've been lying low and playing dumb, at least to outsiders. I don't want any attention. I got interviewed by a whole clam-bed of cops who came here and blew bubbles but didn't do anything. They just sank into the sand when the tide turned."

"Hey, that was the pipi bed? Can we go at low tide, what, in about an hour or two?"

"And a couple more beers!"

.   .   .

Moana had walked down to the beach at low tide to fill a reed basket full of pipis and all the mussels she could find. She let them soak in a bucketful of seawater to spit out their sand and grit. She gathered a pile of dry manuka branches and started a fire, spread out an old blanket on the grass and waited for Wiremu and Rawiri to walk to the beach with the beers. She had the pipis on long thin manuka sticks she adjusted over the smoldering wood. "The manuka gives them a smoky flavor," she said. "Only in Hokianga, eh?"

Wiremu grinned and turned to Rawiri. "Did you see your probie?"

"Yeah. We're good."

"It's George?"

"Yeah. He seems laidback. Lot of things I can't do. Like drinking." Rawiri lifted up his large brown beer bottle and clinked it against Wiremu's.

"You're at home. You're safe. He's on our side. And we have a full-time job for you, tending all our new plants hidden away."

They both laughed. "Then what did you do?" Wiremu asked.

"I went to the marae. Paid my respects to our whanau. Stayed up all night. There were elders there. It was good to be with them. Made me feel real again. Like I belonged. No better feeling."

Wiremu nodded. "Yeah."

"Remember we used to think the elders were just sitting around, doing nothing?"

"Yeah. Now we know better." Wiremu lowered his head. "And we are in the right place."

Rawiri laid on his back and pointed out the meteors shooting across the sky on a moonless night. He was home, he was a free man.

·   ·   ·

The next morning Moana brewed tea while Rawiri made pancakes. He was proud of his thin, sweet crepes cooked to perfection on a thick iron skillet with butter. They were smothered with manuka honey. A recipe he had learned in prison. They ate in silence until Rawiri got up from the table to look for more bread.

Wiremu glanced at Rawiri as he finished a slice of bread he had found. "Do you ever stop eating?" Wiremu asked.

"Talking about conspiracies makes me hungry."

Wiremu waited until Rawiri had finished licking his fingers before he told them of his plans, and they read the newspaper clipping.

"The City Gallery?" Rawiri had risen from the table to look for a crust in the bread box.

"Yeah. Captain Cook will be there. Hanging on a wall, ripe to pluck."

"He's been dead almost, what, two hundred years? What's the big deal?" Rawiri buttered the last crust and took a knife full of honey to spread over it.

"It's a big exhibition about colonialism and how the Pakeha found us. If we kidnapped Captain Cook, it would be a big deal."

"Like we would steal his mana?"

"Yes. And we would trade him for land rights. The perfect non-violent crime. A political gesture heard around the world. It would capture everyone's imagination. Especially all the lefties and socialists here. They would love it. And it would anger the right-wing government. They wouldn't know what to do. Look at the Hikoi. Look what happened there. Nothing. The politicians haven't changed their minds."

Rawiri nodded. "Yeah. We talked about that a lot, you know? But I don't know what happened after. It made some people think they were doing something important."

"You said it. Nothing happened. But Captain Cook—that's different. They couldn't sacrifice Captain Cook. He's a symbol of their Western dominance. Their conquering hero. Their icon. It's why he's in their exhibit. He's the man!"

"You think we could use him as a bargaining chip?" Rawiri's eyes moved from the manuka honey jar to the bread board and the crumbs. "Isn't it kidnapping? I mean, it's a painting but it's the same thing."

"Stealing Captain Cook would have more of an impact than any march." Wiremu didn't tell Rawiri he had been talking to a friend in Auckland who had the contract for additional security at the Auckland City Art Gallery and had extra security uniforms. Wiremu would keep every-thing compartmentalized. No one would know the entire plan. No one would be able to betray him like Hei Hei had.

Rawiri licked his fingers and smiled. "Steal the painting. Hide it and demand a ransom. You have a plan?"

Moana turned from one to the other, noting how Wiremu changed as soon as he was with Rawiri.

"Have to be really well worked out. Who could organize it all?" said Rawiri. "How do you steal a painting worth millions, and have no violence? Where's the fun?"

Wiremu sighed. "Now I know why you're my favorite half-brother."

"I'm your only half-brother, unless there are more. Are there more?"

CHAPTER SEVEN

Police Commissioner Thompson had his secretary book the twilight special with his favorite inspector, Bernie Grimble. They were the last on the course. The hum of traffic seeped between the tall pines and birds sang in the twilight. The commissioner wore a cap to control wisps of white hair and a police-issue blue nylon jacket that barely contained his stomach. Grimble's tweed jacket with leather elbow patches made him look more like a country squire than an Auckland city detective inspector. His hair had turned the color of steel since the shootings and he now kept it a short uniform length. His eyebrows almost came together and with his dark hazel eyes he looked intense but calm.

They played the first few holes in silence, like a prayer for the dead, the dead policemen they were both thinking about.

After Grimble managed to putt his ball into the fourth hole, the commissioner started to talk. He had given up keeping score several games ago. They wheeled their trundlers to the next tee and in hushed tones talked about the funerals they had attended for the fallen officers. "Lucky for you I didn't have to attend your funeral," said the commissioner. "How're the headaches, by the way?"

"Not as frequent now, thank you, sir."

Grimble concentrated on his game. At the fifth hole, the commissioner started to talk again. "The way we shaped the police inquiry lessened the political consequences. We have greater powers. The rules of engagement for armed police officers were too strict. Even if the Maori had a gun pointed at us, we still had to identify ourselves and command them to drop their weapon. And wait for them to disarm. So, we got killed. In reality, our procedure was sheer fantasy. We now have more relaxed rules. If we are in fear of our lives, even if we don't see a weapon, we can shoot to stop the threat. It's more real-world. And we don't have to shout any commands the brown bugger holding a gun at us is not going to hear, let alone obey!" He took a deep breath. He was red in the face now. "As I said in the hearing, you cannot negotiate with a gun aimed at you, let alone a bullet coming at you. It only happens in movies and TV and those silly mystery books my wife reads."

Grimble nodded and wheeled his trundler behind the commissioner as they came to the sixth hole. In the pines on either side of them were invisible tui, birds with dark, almost black plumage, offset with a white collar. They made a mocking sound with their honks, he thought, as if deriding him and his golf game. "I think it's changed all of us. No one is the same," he said.

The commissioner selected an iron and lined up his next shot. He made a practice swing before he hit the ball onto the next green. Grimble admired the commissioner's technique. "At least we could claim we destroyed the Maori gang bringing all that marijuana into Auckland. At a terrible cost, mind you. A terrible cost."

The commissioner pointed to the iron he thought Grimble should use. "Those bloody Ngapuhis! Spoiled my knighthood." He had managed the crisis and deflected most of the criticism—but when you control the press with a few phone calls to your friendly editors at the *Herald* and the *Auckland Star*, you would not expect otherwise.

Grimble copied his boss and made a few practice shots before letting loose with his swing. The ball sailed between the two lines of trees and landed at a respectable distance from the green. His luck, like the light, had not run out yet.

Commissioner Thompson was to retire at the end of the year and expected to become Sir Ian in the Queen's Birthday honors list. He looked forward to the time when he would be relatively powerless and content. It would be a relief to wake in the morning and know the growing gang problems and the breakdown of family values would no longer be his responsibility. If his golf handicap were his one problem, he would be happy. And he would be able to play with better golfers than Inspector Grimble.

The commissioner had always seen his job as an elemental battle between good and evil. As head of the good guys, all the laws were stacked in his favor. The courts co-operated in putting away criminals, even with inadequate evidence. With a strong "law and order" lobby in a National government he was assured of adequate funding. New Zealand had more police per capita than any other western democracy. The last study he saw stated there was one policeman for every 540 citizens. He had the new multi-million-dollar Wanganui Computer Center, touted as being able to keep extensive records on every man, woman and child in the country. Even the Soviet Union did not have such a computer system or such thorough records. There was a joke he had heard that the inmates in Paremoremo told, that because New Zealand was such a small country the inmates knew who had committed a major crime before the media found out. So why was he, the Police Commissioner with so many advantages, so out of touch with what was going on? Not for a minute did he think he was winning the war on drugs. They had been ambushed in a huge gun battle in the forest, reminiscent of the Maori wars of the 19th century; drugs were plentiful on the street; and the prisons were getting more dangerous.

Grimble made two more shots before he sank his ball. He looked at the commissioner, who seemed preoccupied.

"We played the same position in the First Fifteen, didn't we? What, sixteen years apart? Got to give you credit. At least you can play rugby."

The two policemen were Mount Albert Grammar old boys and shared a common bond. The commissioner liked to recall the good old days when winning was clear and simple, the rules did not change, and you always won because you went to the right school.

"Correct. Right wing." Grimble humored him, anticipating the conversation from their infrequent meetings. "You scored eighteen times. I got seventeen."

"But we won the championship."

"That's the important thing."

"Exactly. Now, there is something else I want you to do for me, Grimble. We'll make the next one our last hole."

Grimble watched the commissioner's ball sail to the next green. It was a par three shot. He would be lucky to complete it in six. "Do you mean follow up on Wiremu Wilson? Superintendent Jarvis told me to lay off after the shooting."

"No. In a way you took care of the Wilson problem, didn't you? It's one of our victories."

Grimble took two practice swings. Grass flew. The commissioner groaned as Grimble's ball veered off into the trees. "Were you aiming at the tui? He seems to be mocking you."

The commissioner allowed Grimble to place another ball on the grass far from where he had lost his original. Several strokes later Grimble sank his putt, bent over to retrieve his ball, and walked to his bag without looking at his boss.

As they pulled their trundlers to the clubhouse the commissioner said, "There is a rare and valuable painting coming to Auckland. It's Captain James Cook. Well, three quarters of him. The government is extremely worried about the security. Even the Army is being recruited for its transport. I want you to keep an eye on things. You'll have full authority. The Auckland police will have control. I just wanted you to hear your orders from me."

"Yes, commissioner." Grimble attempted a smile.

"A hotshot curator is bringing it on a plane and escorting it to the Auckland City Art Gallery. You can co-ordinate with him." The commissioner fixed Grimble with his stare. "And I don't want a body count."

CHAPTER EIGHT

"Today we're going to work on holds, when someone grabs you, from the side, in front or like so, behind you. Come here, Annie." Dr. Mel Johnson in bare feet wore tracksuit pants and a T-shirt, like her students who trained in their street clothes. The dozen students she had led through her usual nonstop bodyweight exercise regime were gathered around her in a wide circle. She looked relaxed as her curly black hair fell over her wide shoulders. She had perfect white teeth and amber eyes that could turn golden in bright sunlight but were now dark in the overhead light. The dojo was a bare room with rubber mats on the floor above a clothes shop in a two-story wooden building on Ponsonby Road, across the street from her women's clinic. Like a gym, it had the familiar smell of sweat and body odor but mixed with women's perfume.

Annie, her training partner, was a large, well-proportioned Samoan, with long black hair, big eyes the color of coal, and a wide smile. A good three inches taller, she grabbed her teacher in a bear hug as sweat dripped onto Mel's T-shirt.

"Any time an attacker grabs you, treat it as a gift. They've given you a hand, a finger, any body part you can use against them. Here." Mel twisted her hips slightly to the left, dropped her left shoulder and dug her elbow into her partner's ribs while stomping on her toes. She took her opponent's left middle finger and bent it backwards. Annie loosened her grip and Mel twisted a little more while keeping control of the finger as she grabbed and twisted her partner's wrist. Annie tried to step away but stumbled, as Mel continued using her momentum and her opponent's loss of balance to force her to the ground. "I still have her wrist, her whole body." She changed the direction of the wrist lock and Annie was forced to move in the opposite direction, still under Mel's control, on the ground.

"She can't get to me. And I'm not using much force. It's not about brute strength, it's about body mechanics, natural body movements." Mel kept smiling at her students who paid close attention as Annie tried to get up, but Mel eased her hips down and applied more pressure on the wrist. "If she moves, she hurts herself. Whatever she does to get out of my hold, I still control her."

All the movements were fluid—Mel made it look easy. She was not perspiring but looked coolly detached from the swift violence she had inflicted on Annie. "We train slow and easy because we want to use our training partners again. If you are too aggressive, it's gonna come back at you." The class laughed. Mel kept a straight face. She had had new students injure their partners. She called it working out their aggressions on the wrong person.

"Now split into pairs. Nice and easy. Remember, we all walk out of here in one piece."

Once her students had completed their routines, changing sides, altering the speed and angles of attack, under her one-on-one direction, she had them form another circle around her. "There are lots of ways to defend yourself, based on who is attacking you, your physical makeup and limitations. Oh yes, we all have limitations. But we are talking about possibilities here, and I want to stress the positive and keep it simple. So here, Annie."

Anne put her outstretched hands around Mel's neck, her thumbs digging into Mel's throat.

"I put the hands up, she loosens her grip and I stab with my thumbs in her eyes, or I can claw at her face. But I am getting in her face." Laughter. "Note, I don't actually claw her." She went through the routine again, not as slowly. "What do I do?"

"Finish him off?" one of the smaller students asked.

"What if he's down and there are witnesses and you are in a public place?" Mel countered. "I don't teach aggression. I teach self-defense. It's different."

Another student put up her hand. "Run. Run like hell."

"Yes. That could be your best option. Get the hell out of there. Wherever you are, run. Before he recovers and counterattacks or his mates join in. Why stick around?" She was quiet for a moment as she remembered situations she had been involved in and how she had retreated as fast as she could. She did not want to share them with her group, or anyone.

An older larger student broke the silence. "What if it's in your own home?"

"All the more reason to leave. Run to the neighbors and call the cops. Don't expect him to be nice to you after you've defended yourself. I know every situation is different, but leave the scene. Nothing good can come of you staying. And if you have kids? Take them too. Probably listening in the other room scared stiff. Grab them and go."

The group nodded in unison and Mel walked them through another sequence, one move at a time. She wanted them to be able to move, grab, kick, poke and punch with confidence, and know their own capabilities: when to defend themselves as effectively as possible, and when to run.

Mel dismissed her students and watched them leave. She threw Annie the one towel they had, and Annie wiped her face and hands.

"Are you up for a little sparring?" Mel asked.

"You got something you want to work through?"

"We can talk later. You ready? Not full on, but don't expect me to hold back too much."

"Bring it on, sister." Annie put up her hands but kept them open as she stepped back enough to force Mel to advance and show what she was going to do with her footwork. Mel in turn took her time moving around Annie, looking relaxed, almost bored.

"Come on, Mel," Annie shot out but regretted her remark when Mel feigned a roundhouse kick with her right leg by sliding her left foot forward. Annie knew Mel favored her right leg and at the last moment Mel shot out a left side kick that Annie did not see. She fell over and Mel leapt on her, grabbed her left arm, dropped to the mat and put her in a leg lock she could not escape from. Annie tapped out. Mel untangled herself and helped her partner get up. Annie shook her head. They had sparred enough together that they knew the other's favorite techniques—but Mel kept coming up with new moves Annie had not seen before.

"Should have known you'd do something like that." Annie tried to grab Mel by stepping to her left and sweeping her leg behind Mel. Mel made a small adjustment and put Annie in a head lock that saw Annie lose her balance with Mel's knee in her back. Annie tried to reach back but fell onto Mel, who locked her legs around her. Annie had to tap out again.

"Do you see what you're doing?" Mel asked. "Once you commit to a technique and your opponent does something else to thwart it, you have to change. Like last time. You should have moved with me instead of against me, used your weight and balance to trip me the other way. Don't rely on your strength and height. Here, I'll show you, nice and slow first."

Mel went through the routine twice then they continued sparring again until Annie called it quits. They retired to the back room, and a small bathroom with a cold-water tap that had not seen a cleaner for several years. Mel changed into her work clothes, a white shirt, black trouser suit and Doc Marten 1460 combat boots. She adjusted her hair and picked up her work out bag. "Do you think they're getting it?" she asked.

"Yeah. They love the physical stuff and the sense they can handle themselves with a few simple techniques."

"You don't think I'm giving them a false sense of confidence, do you?"

"You in your Doc Martens? You couldn't look more kick-ass!"

"Seriously. I don't want to lead them on. Fighting someone bigger than you is very different from what we do in the dojo."

"They understand."

"When violence happens, it's usually random, unexpected or just so damn fast, not like here, the way we train."

"Yeah. But tonight's lesson was built on last week's, so they're getting more used to this. Don't overthink. It's just fighting. So, what about Henry? You don't seem to talk about him so much."

"Oh, Henry," sighed Mel. "He's in Wellington. Applying for a job at Victoria Uni, in their physics department. He doesn't think he'll get it. Been out of the country too long. No connections here. You know how it is."

Annie pushed curls from her face and started to zip her leather jacket. "No, I don't. I thought you flew to New York to bring him back. In fact, I remember having a similar conversation like, what? Six months ago? What happened?"

"I really don't know. After our little adventure, he went cold. He seems to think about his science problems all the time. I don't think I know him anymore. It's weird."

"So, what are your plans?"

Mel shrugged. "We were like two love birds. But now he can be attentive, the next minute, remote."

"Another woman?"

"I don't see how. He never goes out or does anything without me. I'm thinking I'll take him up north for a holiday. Maybe a break will do him good. He's been very hard on himself. What about you?"

"I'm seeing someone new. Well, he's been around forever, old student activist, but he's charming and very attentive. A girl needs attention."

"Yes, we do," Mel smiled. "Do I know him?"

"Mark Rose. Been arrested umpteen times, he admits. Anti-Vietnam war protester. Runs a commune in Hokianga and comes here a lot. He makes me laugh."

"The student with the long hair and megaphone? In that anti-Vietnam War photo? That's who you're dating?"

"Don't sound so surprised. We're almost the same age. I think."

"Is he well behaved?"

"What have you taught me?" Annie struck a pose, her legs in an attack stance, her fists up.

When Mel laughed her curls shook.

CHAPTER NINE

"It's okay to borrow the gallery van, isn't it? I had to kit it out. I have no idea if my director knows. Does he?"

Holding a large brown envelope Alexander sat in his favorite seat in Richard Catelin's spacious office. He wore a dark blue single-breasted suit with a plain white shirt and a narrow grey wool tie that brought out the color of his eyes, though he was unaware of the effect. He looked at his old Oxfords that needed a shine—he was still annoyed he'd had to throw away his Italian loafers—and then at the paintings and drawings borrowed from his gallery. He wondered if there were any records of them on loan. He had discovered a set of original Dürer woodcuts gifted to the gallery in the 1950s. They had been forgotten in a set of old steel drawers. He was getting them framed and ready to exhibit, but he didn't want to tell Catelin about his find as it might reflect badly on his director. He felt he was in enough trouble proposing new shows that had nothing to do with his director's interests or research.

"Oh no. As long as you return it in the morning." Catelin eyed Alexander. "Has anyone been asking questions about the van?"

"Just the carpenter, who's wondering what I'm doing. He's an old trade unionist and suspicious of anyone in a suit."

"The director specifically was told to let you use the van whenever you needed it, even overnight, no questions asked."

"Here they are, negatives and all." Alexander handed over the envelope with both hands. Catelin pulled out the 8 x 10 black-and-white prints and scrutinized each one. He counted the negatives versus the prints he had in hand.

"A few were too dark to see anything. They're all there." Alexander watched Catelin compare the prints to the negatives. "The white negatives couldn't be printed." He scratched his head and checked for dandruff on his jacket. He had been so consumed with this new project he hadn't had time to shop for shampoo lately—or anything else.

As a precaution, he had printed an extra set of photos. He had no idea if or when he would need them. He couldn't imagine giving them to a newspaper. He thought he could not trust anyone, let alone Catelin, with these secrets. He had hidden the prints in a sealed plastic bag under a floorboard in his bedroom.

Today Catelin was all business: no coffee or stronger drinks were offered. "How many times did you go out there?"

"Since our last meeting, five times. SIS were there as well. Tried to break into the van."

"Did they see you?"

"No, but they would've run the plates on the van and traced it to the gallery."

Catelin looked up and smiled. "Don't overestimate them. It's why the minister wanted you, to have a fresh set of eyes."

Alexander should have challenged that last comment. Had the minister specifically asked for him? How did the minister even know he existed? Looking back later at what happened, he realized he should have asked questions, not been so willing to believe. Catelin's comment about the SIS's inability to check license plates should have been a red flag.

Catelin lit his pipe then held it in his left hand. In his other hand he held the grainy photographs and scrutinized them one at a time. Alexander waited for him to come to the last set.

Two nights ago, he had parked the van earlier than usual in what had become his regular parking place, across from Winter's front gate but between two lamp posts. He was not sure if the black paper he had stuck on the side and rear windows would be as effective. He walked around to check for any gaps. To anyone spying on him, it would appear he was checking the tires and the panel work for any scratches. He had previously driven up and down the street and had not spotted any surveillance cars. He had the side door open when he spotted a full-figured woman with a mass of red hair walking towards him, carrying a large shopping bag. He couldn't remember where or when he had last seen her, but she recognized him.

"What a surprise, Alexander! What are you doing here?" Her scarlet wool coat was open to reveal a low-cut red cotton outfit with buttons about to burst.

Alexander tried not to stare at her chest. "I'm working on something, actually. Do you live nearby?"

"Right there." She pointed to the next house, across from the doctor's.

His head started to spin. "I'm doing a sort of performance piece with photos, but I was looking for a better vantage point." He lifted his head to the windows of the semi-detached house, and she followed his cue.

"It's a flat, but you'd have a perfect view of the street."

"Do you think I could set my camera there?"

"Sounds exciting. I've just bought a bottle. Do you like cab sav?"

"I'd love anything you're offering."

Her wicked grin told Alexander he had underestimated his mystery acquaintance. Then he remembered her name. "Look, Deborah, let me bring my bag of stuff inside and my tripod. Can I help you with your shopping?" He was trying to be gallant, but she had already opened her front door. Alexander noted the street was still deserted. He locked the van and followed her, mesmerized by her swaying hips as she climbed the stairs.

"I'll show you the view of the street. You must tell me all about your project, it sounds radical." She dropped her shopping bag and showed him the bedroom. He walked over to the windows and saw he had a perfect angle to observe Winter's gate and the walkway to his front door. He wondered if he would be able to see across to Winter's bedroom or whatever it was used for opposite Deborah's.

"I'll get the wine while you, oh, help yourself."

Alexander screwed his camera into the tripod. He had focused the lens on the doctor's entrance when Deborah returned with two full goblets. She had curtains and lace over the windows. He could not be seen from the street provided she kept her lights off. He would have to change the timing as it grew darker, but the aperture was as wide as he could get. He had his extended release in his hand as she handed him his wine.

"Delicious, Deborah. And you look wonderful as well. We've never had a chance to get to know each other." He took another sip. "I know it sounds contrived, but it's true. Amazing, bumping into you. I'm doing a piece on the gentleman across the road. Do you know who he is?"

Deborah bent over and looked through the viewfinder then back at Alexander who was staring at her bottom. "Should I?" she asked.

"Well, it doesn't matter. The entire piece is based on randomness. You know, indeterminate images taken at different times and locations. It's rather complicated, really."

Alexander thought she had not grasped what he said. He was making it up as he went along. And where was he going? He was already in her bedroom, drinking wine. He threw his heavy rain jacket on the floor next to his camera bag. "You know I'm on my own again."

"Yes, I heard."

"You did? It's not like I've told anyone."

She smiled. "Small town. Word travels fast. Especially a man like you on the market again."

Alexander did not know if another button popped open on her dress, but she looked more accessible, more enticing. "Moved out from my ex-girlfriend." He shrugged, hoping his shyness would not show.

"You do have a reputation about town. Did you know?"

"I have?"

"Alexander A. Newton. Everyone knows you put together hot new exhibitions at the National. There's that article about you in the paper. And you're always being seen with beautiful young women. But I don't care," she sighed. "I can't resist those cheekbones and those deep grey eyes."

"What beautiful women? How about beautiful woman." He was still trying to process what she had said.

Deborah took a step nearer. "You make me smile. I feel very lucky."

Alexander breathed in through closed teeth. He should have leaned over and kissed her, but he was confused about the idea of having a reputation. Wellington, being the political capitol, did thrive on rumors. But he was the subject of gossip? Was he so isolated? So ignorant of what was going on around him? Seen with beautiful young women? Who were they? He would like to know, as he never went out. And if he thought about himself at all, it would be as a spy with a camera who worked alone.

He rummaged around in his bag. "Here, I have to check my meter and make adjustments." He had a light meter but rarely used it. He had an instinctive feel for Tri-X film, setting it at 400 ASA, but pushing the negatives in the dark room to 1600. He toyed with the idea of taking photos of Deborah. Get her to undress and pose. But he had three rolls of Tri-X with him and didn't want to waste sensitive black-and-white film on a woman who screamed for deep rich colors. Oh god, I bet she's a screamer, Alexander fantasized, although he was still disturbed by his reputation as a ladies' man. How did he get such a title? Was it a good thing or a bad thing? He did not want to ask Deborah.

Alexander had his extended shutter release hang beside the Chesterfield loveseat draped in crimson velvet fabric. He focused on the bedroom for the first time and saw Gustav Klimt posters. There was *The Kiss* on one side of her bed and *Danaë* above her bed. The resemblance to Deborah was striking. There were gold and red fabrics draped over furniture. Her bedroom was lush and sensuous, as was Deborah, as she sipped her wine, eyeing him.

"Alexander Arkadyevich Newton," she said after she emptied her glass.

"You know my middle name?"

CHAPTER TEN

"Now the last photos are interesting. You took them from inside a house?"

"Er, yes." Alexander could feel his cheeks turn red.

"And what is the Russian handing the doctor?"

Alexander recalled how in the morning Deborah had woken him at five. He wondered why she had wound her alarm clock before they slept. He had not realized she wanted another session before going to work. If they hadn't done it over the loveseat he would not have seen the milkman. When he spotted the Russian, on the street with a milk bottle, approach the doctor, he squeezed the shutter until he ran out of film. He didn't think Deborah could hear the loud motor drive, with her face buried in a pillow, her moans kept time to his rhythm.

"God, I'm going to be late for work. Do you want coffee?" she asked.

"I'll have whatever you're offering."

"You've already had it." She hobbled to the bathroom. Alexander, naked, his legs quivering, started to put his equipment away.

"Looks like a bottle of milk," he told Catelin. "There is a milk van goes by at about six in the morning. The Russian or the Soviet, or whatever you want to call him, gave his bottle to the doctor, as you can see. It's just a bottle of milk."

"What do you think is going on, Alexander?" Catelin had never used his first name before. He did not know whether to be flattered at the more intimate tone, or wary of being led into a trap.

"I don't think there's much spying going on. The Russian knows he's being watched by SIS. They are not too subtle, you know. He's playing them."

Catelin blew out a huge cloud of smoke from his pipe and smiled. Alexander felt compelled to continue. "The photos don't tell the whole story. It's all in the body language. The Russian is courting him. It's like a seduction. But they're not passing secrets one way or the other. I mean, what secrets does New Zealand have? What do the Russians need for their security? The number of sheep born last month? The bank rate next month? What Mr. Muldoon said to someone last night? What the minister thinks of his wife?" Catelin was still puffing away on his pipe, content to listen. "He's keeping his hand in. Maybe the doctor was a spy once and they are keeping him close, but the Russian has his hand in."

"How can you be sure?"

Alexander Arkadyevich Newton took in a deep breath and let it out. He decided not to explain his family origins to the Under-Secretary. "First, I've been watching them for three weeks. Second, I know how Russians think. I was almost seduced by a gorgeous Russian woman called Natasha. She was more aggressive than a Kiwi girl, a little on the plump side but she had amazing intense blue eyes. She tried to seduce me right in front of my girlfriend. She did it to keep her hand in. It's what she does. She couldn't care less about my girlfriend or about me. It was about the conquest. She was practicing. The Russian is doing the same. And we're falling for it."

Catelin raised his eyebrows as he inspected his pipe. "He's just going through the motions?"

"Never underestimate a Russian trying to screw things up for everyone else. It's what they do. What Marxism ends up doing."

"You have read *Das Kapital*?" Catelin kept a straight face. "But it's really Lenin, isn't it? Anything is acceptable if it advances Communism and is moral by definition. Even murder and sabotage."

Alexander couldn't tell if Catelin was mocking him or making a joke. There was more to Catelin than just an older man behind a huge desk in the upper reaches of government, with a rack full of pipes.

"I think the Russian is playing a game, a complex one, keeping Moscow happy with his contact reports, taunting our security services, implicating a respectable member of our establishment, creating havoc here, and of course as a bonus, upsetting the Americans." Alexander paused to gauge his words. "It's all part of their plan to undermine us, sow confusion and conflict. It's what the Soviets have always done. And isn't he succeeding? Look at the trial. What happened there? Acting as a spy is safe here in little New Zealand. He gets to file reports to Moscow while our government, present company excluded of course, hasn't the balls to deport the spy."

Catelin held his pipe in the air and looked at his young protégé. "You got all this from Natasha seducing you?"

"Well, for a start she didn't succeed. Thank god! But she taught me a valuable lesson."

Catelin scowled and sucked on his pipe before letting out a cloud of smoke. "You're probably aware that we have finally reestablished diplomatic relations with the Soviets. There is a new ambassador in Moscow we do not want to jeopardize. And there are other matters involved here, including trade, so don't go jumping to conclusions that may sound good but are false. Do you understand?"

Alexander nodded.

"I've been meaning to show you something." Catelin walked over to his desk and picked up a book with a bright red cover. He handed it to Alexander who read the cover: *KGB: The Secret Work of Soviet Agents.* "Never underestimate your enemy. Predators go after the weakest. The Soviets think our little country is the weakest. They've stolen codes from us we use with our allies, they've procured passports from willing accomplices in other consulates, and they've built alliances with fellow travelers, those sympathetic to their agenda, so they have done a lot of damage you would never hear about. And we know Nikolai Nikolaevich Raganovich is the Soviet resident. It's why we treated Dr. Winter's case so seriously. And he's still here. The other two who were involved fled the country as soon as Winter was detained, but Raganovich remains for some reason." Catelin frowned. "They are dangerous, so don't underestimate them. Here, read the book. And let me know what you think."

Alexander did not want to admit to the Under-Secretary that he had read John Barron's exposé of the Soviet Union's secret security service. He had a collection of non-fiction spy books. He was fascinated by the Tsar's Okhrana, the Soviet Union's Cheka, NKVD and all their variants, right up to the KGB. And he knew what a resident or rezidentura meant. Alexander Arkadyevich Newton, New Zealand's latest KGB spy hunter, appreciated being told what he presumed was the real government position on Raganovich. He was about to stand, but Catelin reached for another pipe from the rack on his desk, and motioned for Alexander to stay. Catelin started to fill his pipe from his leather pouch as if it was the most important task in the world. "You mentioned another project?" he asked.

"Oh. Yes." Alexander placed the book on the table and put his hands on his knees. "It involves your boss's counterpart in the other party. The shadow minister." He told Catelin the details of his conversations with Kathy and how she would see the older political boyfriend after their sauna on Sundays.

"How do you know she meets him?" Catelin asked.

"She told me."

Catelin placed his pipe on the table, and he went to his desk to select another from his rack. He picked up one, inspected it, then took another pipe which he started to clean with his small pocket knife. Alexander kept his eyes on the ritual, intrigued by the movements. He thought Catelin was stalling for time, to think what to do next.

"Can you use the camera again?" Catelin finally offered. "We need something where there is no doubt. Say, by next week?" He stood.

Alexander leapt to his feet and said "Yes." Holding the red book, he strode out of the office, on top of the world.

.   .   .

If Alexander had been a real spy, he would have positioned himself by the Cenotaph at the corner of Bowen Street and Lambton Quay to watch Richard Catelin, bundled in his black double-breasted trench coat, cross the Quay and walk up Molesworth Street with his executive briefcase. He would then have observed Catelin march across the grounds into the neo-classical Edwardian Parliament building smiling broadly despite the typical bitter August wind blowing through the city, and rain falling horizontally. It was the same area where the Maori land march leaders had camped out to protest the year before. Next door, the Beehive was rising up to its full ten-story height, like a giant wedding cake rather than an actual beehive, but without a bride and groom stuck on the top layer.

Once inside, Catelin headed to his boss's office. He breezed past the minister's secretary and handed the minister a large brown envelope from his briefcase. The minister offered him a seat and Catelin sat in his wet coat which he had unbuttoned, eyes on the minister. The desk was not as big as Catelin's; only a large leather-bound diary lay open on its shiny walnut surface. There was no ash-tray. The minister had given up cigarettes, and hated pipe smoke.

"Well, how is our new man doing?" the minister asked.

Catelin unclenched his teeth. "See for yourself. He got them."

"Our new man" was an interesting turn of phrase from the minister, Catelin thought. Was he presenting it to the Prime Minister as his own successful project? Catelin was a civil servant and a cog in the wheel. He kept his face neutral, as hard as it was without a pipe sticking out of his mouth.

The minister opened the envelope and looked at the photographs. "Better than what our boys did."

Catelin nodded.

"And here? It's a milk bottle?"

"Yes. He had rather a good vantage point for what was playing out, two mornings ago I think."

"What is going on here?"

"Our man"—Catelin stressed the *our*—"thinks it's a simple passing of a milk bottle. No message in the bottle, so to speak."

"Does Winter get milk delivered?"

"I don't know."

"Well, get him to find out and see if it happens again. It might be important, it might not, but I'm buggered if we're going to leave any stone unturned. Not after we've been humiliated with the trial and the bloody jury. How soon can you get more photos and report on the doctor's milk supply? And why don't the others know?"

"I'll check with them first, then send out our man."

"Good. Anything else?"

"Yes. A couple of things. He thinks the Soviets are trying us on. Sort of giving us the run around and at the same time keeping close contact with the doctor. He also thinks they have history. The doctor has had previous contact with the diplomat. An old spy who is being kept warm."

"Sounds like a Graham Greene novel. *Our Man in Wellington.*" The minister breathed out and changed his tone. "We're still recovering from the damn trial. How could the jury find him not guilty? I don't see how they could find him not guilty. It's as if they didn't believe us. We must be missing something. But we can still end the whole sordid affair."

When the minister looked at him, Catelin gripped his thighs.

"What does he know that we don't? Maybe Winter was a Soviet spy in the Fifties and Sixties and our predecessors missed it. I've said it before, but the damn SIS denies it, because they don't know, never knew, and will never admit they were wrong. Well, that, that is chilling."

Catelin fidgeted but kept his hands on his knees. He was silent as the minister eyed him. The damp from his trench coat seeped through his suit.

"You said a *couple* of things?"

"Yes." Catelin hesitated. "He has a source who reliably informed him your counterpart is having an affair with one of his daughters' girlfriends. He can get you photos."

The minister scratched his chin. "Hmmm. What does he want?"

"I'm not sure. He hasn't asked for money, yet. He seems to get a thrill out of the operation."

"And you encourage him, of course."

"He does seem enthusiastic about the gallery. Lots of plans."

"I heard he wants to organize a traveling Maori exhibition," said the minister "Contemporary artists, carvings, sculptures, paintings. Sounds expensive."

"The director isn't exactly supportive," said Catelin.

"He's a product of the Courtauld. He can't help himself, but times are changing. I'm having lunch with the chairman of the Arts Council tomorrow. We'll talk. They could fund it and bring him on as the organizer. If we get those photos."

"Should keep him happy." Catelin wanted to rub his hands together but thought better of it.

"Let me know as soon as you get anything." The minister rose to shake Catelin's hand. No small talk. No invitations. And no notes of their unscheduled meeting.

As he trotted out of the building in his wet coat Catelin understood why the minister was handling this case rather than the Prime Minister, who was in charge of the security services. Catelin was the cut out, just as he was using other personnel for his operation.

CHAPTER ELEVEN

The FBI legal attaché special agent who was known as the Legat, from the US Embassy in Wellington, asked Henry Lotus for the third time what happened to him in the hotel room in Manhattan. They faced each other across a metal table in a room high up in the Auckland Central police station on Vincent Street. To one side was a policeman Henry never wanted to see again. He was unnerved by the close-set eyes that bored into him. But Henry did not want to show any weakness. Inspector Bernie Grimble, wearing a dark checkered sports jacket and Mount Albert Grammar School tie, kept his customary deadpan expression. Mr. FBI appeared spectral in his plain black suit and thin black knitted tie with a gold tie-pin set against his bright white shirt.

Henry, a good ten years younger than his interrogators, was dressed in a white T-shirt, navy blazer and blue jeans. His straight black hair was almost to his shoulders and he had the habit of running his right hand through his hair when he was nervous. He was taller than either policeman and kept his back ramrod straight, despite his obvious impatience. "You must have the NYPD reports."

Mr. FBI, who without his jacket would have no shoulders, looked over at Grimble then asked Henry, "What did you do with the notebooks?" He sounded patient but wary.

"I burnt them. After what I went through I decided it was too dangerous to keep them. Anyway, I've changed my line of inquiry. I don't want to put myself in harm's way again. Would you?" Henry ran his hand though his hair.

"Can you wait? Can I get you a soda?" Mr. FBI rose from his chair and stretched his arms that seemed to reach the ceiling.

Henry shook his head. The two policemen left the room. Mr. FBI looked drained.

"Are we being played?" Mr. FBI asked Grimble after they entered the adjoining room and looked at the tall scientist who sat motionless in his chair, his eyes searching for them through the mirror.

"I think so, but it's not like he's a criminal mastermind." Grimble squinted at Henry Lotus who ran his right hand through his hair again. "He's mirroring me, though. That's what's disturbing."

"What do you mean?" Mr. FBI asked.

"He mimics my body language. Whatever I do, he does as well. I think its deliberate."

"You think he has the notebooks?"

Grimble nodded. "He's got them. He's lying."

Mr. FBI looked at Henry again. "Could be, but he's supposed to be a brilliant physicist. I've been told to go easy on him, but something's bugging me about him. He told the same story, only the last time it was more elaborate."

"Well, ask him again in a few weeks. He's not going anywhere. And see if he really did destroy the notebooks. You've been instructed to retrieve them, haven't you?"

"Yes."

"Do you know what's in them?"

Mr. FBI shrugged.

"The Soviets want them, don't they?"

Mr. FBI did not shrug again, just sighed.

"And you want them too," Grimble stated. "What happens if you don't get them?"

"To me? My next stop is Africa."

"I know how that works."

CHAPTER TWELVE

"You think the threat is real?" Richard Catelin relit his pipe as he sat in his leather seat in his office. An office he knew to be at least twice as large as the commissioner's. He was a lifetime civil servant. The commissioner was appointed for only two years.

"Oh yes." Commissioner Thompson crossed his legs and looked at the whisky he held in his left hand. His white hair was under control with a tight combover and he wore a white shirt, and a dark green tweed suit with a matching tie. He looked more like a retired farmer than the top policeman. He twisted his feet and looked at his shiny brown brogues.

"How did you find out?" Catelin kept his pipe poised in mid-air, anxious for a real answer, not one of the commissioner's tedious lectures.

"Every empire has its intelligence networks. Ears and eyes. Sources and methods. It's how we gather information. Might sound a little clichéd, but it's the truth." The commissioner adjusted himself on the leather sofa and surveyed the office. "An odd comment here, snatch of a conversation there, someone seeing someone at an odd time or place. We weave it together. It's never as complete as we like. Lot of guesswork involved, call it intuition if you like. But we put together a case, for what it's worth.

And the so-called experts are wrong most of the time. But life isn't always clear-cut, is it?"

"You bugged a few phones and heard about the Cook painting?" Catelin asked from a cloud of pipe smoke.

"It's part of the puzzle. We have our suspicions about radical elements in the so-called Maori land movement. And there are links."

"Who knows?"

"We've kept it very close, considering how we got the information."

"What do you want me to do?"

"I hear you have a new man working for you. Maybe you can get him to keep watch over the painting. You're going to get a memo soon." The commissioner eased himself out of his seat. "Didn't know you had such good scotch. I would have come here sooner."

CHAPTER THIRTEEN

Dr. Mel Johnson and Henry Lotus were at the tiny shopping center in the small town of Rawene on Monday morning. A line of cars and trucks were lined up to wait for the ferry. Mel peeked through the shop window at Wiremu Wilson as he sat at a desk. Henry rang the doorbell. Wiremu unlocked the door and looked his guests up and down. He wore a red plaid shirt, green army pants and spit-shined black boots. He had kept his hair short, but his eyes did not reflect light—you could not look at them for long.

Henry and Mel wore matching white shirts and blue jeans. Mel was almost as tall as Henry, but her shoulders looked wider. They looked like a couple and their rosy checks and big smiles showed their relaxed adventure up north was going well.

"Good to see you." Wiremu hugged Henry and held him close. "It's been a while. How are you both?" Henry, never one to hug back, did his best to reciprocate but looked awkward. He tried to smile but could not match Wiremu's wide grin or tight grip on his arms.

Wiremu turned his attention to Mel and, rather than hug her, shook hands then made a joke about her strong grip by holding his hand as if it had been crushed. Wiremu and Henry laughed. Wiremu acting the clown, rather than a drug dealer.

"What brings you here? Are you moving? Finally?" He faced Mel and expected a retort from her. She did not smile, too tired to take the bait.

"Remember your letter?" She looked around his narrow office.

"Oh yes. Here, let me make you tea. We have very nice government-issue Lipton's."

Wiremu charmed his visitors with how he helped young Maori and provided them guidance and connected them with jobs in the community, if not college or other schools further south, in Whangarei or even Auckland.

"Look how tiny this is. I have no budget. They barely pay me, but it's what I can do for the kids is important." Wiremu smiled. "And my brother and cousin are here, so I have family."

"Brother?" Henry asked.

"Yeah, Rawiri. He is a little older, and wiser than me."

"And cousin?"

"Moana. She was in Auckland. She returned to look after the family home. Bright girl, though she goes to the city at times." Wiremu smiled.

"You kept your short hair," Henry said. "No more afro?"

"Yeah. Being respectable. I must invite you out tonight, after work. Cook up a feast and have a few beers."

"Or a lot."

Wiremu beamed. "Hey! My Henry!"

.　　　　　.　　　　　.

They parked in a field next to an old wooden house not unlike Mel's in Mount Eden. Mel carried fresh bread and a box of local pastries. Henry had a couple of bottles of Cold Duck in a bag. Mel took Henry's hand as they crossed the metal road and walked through a paddock to a small beach on the estuary. The temperature had dropped, and Mel wore her old red-and-navy checkered Swanndri wool shirt she had had since her Otago Medical School days, Henry his blue checkered bushman's jacket. They saw the outlines of two large Maori men standing near the water wearing army boots, green trousers and black pullovers. The sun had set and the thin lines of clouds over the mouth of the harbor were streaks of purple and blood-red. The green hills were painted with thick black outlines. All they could hear was the crackling of a fire and the sounds of cicadas.

Moana's face and long black hair were illuminated by the embers. She had a bright red shawl draped over her shoulders. In the fading light they watched her place a container of mussels over the smoldering manuka sticks.

Wiremu introduced Moana and Rawiri to his two guests, and they sat on blankets Moana had laid out on the grass next to the fire. They looked out over the harbor and the darkening hills on the other side of the water. The grass felt damp.

"We went to Waipoua forest." Mel could not see glasses for the wine, nor a corkscrew.

"Tane god of the forest is awesome," said Henry. "It's just breathtaking how it stands there. No branches for seventeen meters?"

Mel turned to Henry. "You read the sign."

"I can read. I'm a scientist." Henry gestured to Mel to open the wine.

Wiremu offered Henry and Mel beers. Henry used a bottle opener. Mel declined and saw there were no knives or forks. She laid the large loaf of bread on its paper bag, on top of the blanket.

Wiremu and Henry stared at each other. The silence was punctuated by the crackling of the fire as Moana tended to the shellfish.

"Tell me, Henry, where is the Tear?" Wiremu asked. Henry had worn his shirt buttoned up at the office, and now wore his jacket.

Henry ran his hand through his hair. "Your grandmother gave it to you, didn't she? You never told me her story or anything about your mother and father. I know nothing about your family. Tell me now, then I'll tell you about the Tear, but you have to be honest with me. None of that happy-go-lucky Maori shit you pull."

Wiremu took a deep breath. "Wow, Henry. You're usually so reserved. What's got into you?" He held a new bottle of beer and took a swig.

"It's the pendant, I think, but you go first." Henry ran his hand through his hair again and glanced at Mel.

"Okay," Wiremu said. "Hone, Rawiri and I have the same mother. She died here a long time ago. Whina Wilson." She had died giving birth to Hone and there had not been a doctor or even a nurse to help her. The mortality rate for Maori babies and their mothers in country areas were far higher than for their Pakeha counterparts in cities with adequate hospitals and doctors. The brothers had talked about their family history a long time ago and come to peace with what had happened. Wiremu did not talk about it.

"I'm sorry for your loss." Mel said.

Wiremu nodded. "Our grandmother was Elsa Wilson. Elsa we remember well, eh Rawiri?"

Rawiri nodded. They had not started to eat, even though Moana had the pipis and mussels ready.

Wiremu finished his beer with a long swig. He looked out over the water and everyone was quiet. "It was Elsa who gave me the Tear of Tane. Her father was a tohunga. He wore it. He gave her instructions. She passed it onto me before she died. I was young and always getting into trouble, so I gave it to you. You saved me from going to jail the first time."

Henry lowered his head. He did not know how to react. He felt ashamed and overwhelmed. And guilty. He had been given so many opportunities in his life compared to Wiremu.

"Let's eat!" Moana exclaimed. "The pipis will get rubbery and everything's ready."

Mel noticed how Moana gave Henry furtive looks as she served pipis and mussels on plates to her guests. They tore hunks from the loaf Mel had brought to soak up the juices, and ate in silence, but for the moans of Rawiri and Wiremu who were noisy, enthusiastic eaters.

When they had finished, Wiremu turned to Henry. "Anyway, Henry, enough about us. What happened to the Tear?"

Henry wiped his mouth, glanced at Mel, and reached into his jacket pocket and held a small package, wrapped in tissue paper. "Having worn the Tear, I feel like, well, no one ever owns it." He unwrapped the pendant and held the dark greenstone to the light of the fire. "I had it for what was an important time in our lives, and it feels like we were connected. But now I am thinking of returning to the States and it should stay here. It should be in New Zealand. I am giving it back to you, Wiremu."

Wiremu accepted the pendant with both hands. His face was as hard as jade. He let the pendant hang from its long leather cord and watched it start to rotate.

Mel stared at Henry, a look of shock on her face. Henry kept his head down.

"Are you sure you want to return it?" Wiremu asked. "It's taonga." He watched the pendant's dark green reflect the flames as it slowly spun. It glowed. Rawiri and Moana were transfixed. The cicadas had stopped: the only sound came from the fire. "I gave you the Tear and never expected to see it again. In a way, it was too much responsibility for me. I would have lost it, or it would have been confiscated by the police. Something bad would have happened to it. But you kept it safe and saved me again."

"I was a keeper of the Tear and now I return it to you, the rightful owner. I'm leaving anyway. "

"What? You're telling me now?" Mel whispered.

"The FBI has been talking to me here," Henry continued. "It's been getting a little weird. An FBI agent and a cop, an Inspector Grimble, questioned me at Auckland Central police station. I think the FBI want the notebooks I had in New York."

Wiremu lowered his voice. "The FBI and Grimble?"

"Yes. We all know him, right?" Henry added as he glanced at Mel who glared at him. His attempt to change the subject had not succeeded. She looked angry.

Wiremu rubbed the pendant with both hands before placing it around his neck with his eyes closed, then took a deep breath. No one said anything for some time as the new moon appeared on the cloudless horizon. The cicadas started again, and Moana poked the dying embers of the fire with a stick.

"How is your clinic, Mel?" Wiremu asked. "Are you treating Maori girls?" He stretched his arms above his head and Mel saw the pendant against his black pullover.

"Yes. Everyone. I specialize in general medicine for women. I leave the baby stuff to other doctors and midwives." Mel smiled. "There is a lot to do."

"What about abortions?"

"Oh, you know they are illegal. A crime." Mel sighed. "Lots of young girls can't seem to come to grips with an unplanned pregnancy. They certainly need counseling. The hypocritical thing is rich white girls can fly to Sydney on Friday night, get an abortion on Saturday and return Sunday and no one is the wiser. But poorer girls don't have any options." She placed the two unopened bottles of wine into her bag. Henry was still sitting, legs outstretched, gazing into the night sky.

"Can you recommend poor girls to get an abortion here?"

"Wiremu, it's illegal. Last thing I want to do is lose my license. Even if it was legal I don't think I could do one. Our clinic might, if there was a demand. Maybe we'll get a more enlightened government."

"Don't hold your breath," Wiremu muttered.

Moana kept her eyes lowered and tightened the shawl around her body. Ricky had introduced her to an old Chinese woman who had given her special herbs. She had endured impossibly painful cramps for one night. It was if she had shat it out of her body, she had described her miscarriage to Ricky the next morning. She had cleaned herself and dumped the remains of the embryo in the garbage, wrapped in plastic. It looked like a lizard, a monster, which was how Moana had remembered the father.

"Where are you guys staying tonight?" Moana asked to break the silence as she kicked dirt over the fire to put it out.

"We have a room at a hotel in Rawene." Mel stretched her legs again and prodded Henry, to get him to stand.

Henry rubbed his thigh and said, "Next time you are in Auckland you should drop in."

"I might just." Wiremu stomped his boots. "Planning on going to Auckland soon. Would be great to see youse guys."

Mel kicked Henry harder when Wiremu turned his back.

CHAPTER FOURTEEN

When Alexander received the call from Catelin to take more photos of the milk bottles and discover if the doctor ordered milk himself, he had an excuse to see Deborah again. He didn't have her phone number and couldn't recall her exact address, but there was only one Deborah working at the Turnbull Library.

"I'm really sorry I haven't called you again," he said when he got through, "but my job is keeping me busy. When I get to my tiny apartment late at night, I haven't got a phone. They say another three months."

"Oh, okay. I've been very busy."

Alexander thought he detected a certain reluctance in her voice. How busy could she be, arranging books on shelves?

"Actually, I've been meaning to call you but have been too embarrassed." Groveling might work, Alexander thought.

"Look, I'm at work."

"Yes, I know, but the photos didn't turn out as good as I hoped. I was preoccupied. Can I come over again and we could, you know."

"I have to put you on hold." Alexander could not see her rise out of her office chair, execute a little dance before she sat down again and picked up the phone.

"When?" He could hear anticipation in her voice, and she was out of breath.

"What about tonight?" He waited for a response. It worked with artists when he asked to come to their studio with no notice. He heard her deep breathing.

"Oh. Let me check my diary. Hmmm. I might have to cancel something. Can I call you back?"

"Yes, of course. I'm sorry for the rush but I've got a lot happening, I'll tell you all when I see you." Alexander repeated his office phone number to her and prayed she would call before 4.30 when the switchboard closed.

Deborah called at 4.25 to make him pay for not calling her sooner, Alexander thought, and he couldn't blame her. He felt hopeless, or was it helpless? He didn't know when to call, what to say, how long to wait till you could call again. What were the rules? Were there any rules? He was confused about women, and apprehensive about Deborah. She was voluptuous but also unpredictable. He wondered if she would cause problems later if their relationship ended. Although he was unsure what constituted a relationship with regards to Deborah. But she was a redhead. He had dated a redhead in high school and she had run off with an older boy. Well, a young man with sideburns, a cigarette dangling out of his mouth and a large American car with a noisy muffler. It would take more than a noisy muffler to get rid of Deborah.

He arrived with a bottle of Blue Nun, take-out from the local Indian restaurant and Southern Comfort in case they needed extra inspiration.

"So, what are you doing in Auckland? What's the big secret?" Deborah asked after dinner.

"Well, I shouldn't tell you but, as you are a certified librarian and keeper of the nation's secrets and upholder of the sacred Dewey system, I'm taking Captain Cook to the Auckland City Art Gallery for a show and I'm getting army and police escort. They seem to be real worried. As if anyone would steal Captain Cook." Alexander savored his Comfort on the rocks. He felt relaxed and doubted if he could stand, let alone perform in bed again. The second time Deborah had bent over the loveseat by the window and Alexander could watch for the doctor and his Russian mate. Concentrating on getting the perfect photo had made him last longer.

He saw them, at the most inappropriate time, as Deborah was demanding more and yelling obscenities at him. Deborah had graduated from being a moaner to a screamer. He was distracted from using his shutter release. If he didn't get the money shots, he would have to return. Still, there was no downside to that.

Later, as they laid in bed exhausted, Deborah said, "Talking of secrets, I hear Muldoon has hired four ex-army guys, you know, Special Forces, and they're doing dirty tricks. Taking photographs, blackmail, political subversion. It's what the Soviets do. Counter-revolutionary stuff. It's very disturbing."

"More government gossip," Alexander sighed. "You said four guys. How did you hear that?"

"I'm a librarian. I hear things. Somehow it's related to the spy case. The one the government failed to convict, the economist fellow. Don't follow the news, too disturbing."

Alexander wasn't sure he believed her. The tone of her voice sounded odd. But then he noticed the turntable and two small speakers beside her bed and faint piano music. "Can you get me more Comfort? Is there any more curry?"

"You ate everything."

"Yes, I did." He tried to pull a pubic hair from his teeth.

She returned with two full glasses and shook her breasts as the ice clinked. He clapped his hands in delight as she returned his wicked grin. He was drunk enough to enjoy himself and forget about her tone.

She handed him a glass and slid back into bed.

"What are you playing?" he asked.

"Erik Satie." She sipped her drink and adjusted the sheets to cover her chest.

Alexander sat upright and inspected the turntable. "Trois Gymnopédies?" he asked in a fake French accent.

"Non! Gnossiennes, cinq!" she said after another mouthful of Comfort. "I thought it might slow you down."

"Well, it's still French, which reminds me." Alexander lifted the sheet and started to kiss her again. When he reached her stomach she giggled. He righted himself, picked up his glass and swirled the ice around. He looked at her seriously. "We have to stop meeting like this."

"Why you!" She playfully slapped his shoulder and he almost dropped his drink.

"No. We have to go out and do something. I just can't come over here and climb into your bed. Unless you want that." Alexander looked into her eyes. "Do you?"

"I would like to go out with you very much."

"Good. And I still don't understand the rumors. I go out with lots of women? I mean, you're the only woman I know."

"Come here." Deborah removed his drink and pulled him towards her.

Later, Alexander watched her set the alarm for five o'clock. He hoped all the strenuous activity would prevent a hangover.

. . .

Alexander looked across at Mount Egmont. The volcano reminded him of Mount Fuji in the Japanese print he had seen recently. Where? Oh, yes. Deborah's bathroom. He had gazed at Mount Fuji as he tried to pee. He had been in such pain from all the, what was it? Friction? Stronger than friction. Stranger than fiction. He let out a sigh and relaxed. He closed his eyes and thought of Deborah. Thinking of mounts, Egmont stood at over 8000 feet and with the light coming from the east it looked majestic. He patted the wooden crate leaning against the window seat next to him in the front row of his Air New Zealand flight to Auckland. Which seemed more than ironic because it was Captain James Cook who was the first European to see, and name the smoking volcano, after a Lord of the Admiralty who had supported his voyage around the world. What was his name? Of course, Egmont! Here he sat at 30,000 feet in air-conditioned comfort, next to the famous portrait of the explorer. He wondered if any of Cook's crew had had similar soreness after their nights with rapturous and wild Polynesian women. Not a topic for serious art historians or sociologists, but Alexander thought he was in good company, at least with Cook's sailors. Captain Cook, Alexander had read, was not one to cavort with the ladies.

Alexander had been accompanied by two policemen from the National Gallery's loading dock to the airport. A rare perfect day in Wellington, for the sky was blue and there was no wind as he wheeled the crate on a cart to the plane on the tarmac. A uniformed stewardess greeted him by name and had him seated in the front. Seat 1B. Captain Cook was in 1A. Or rather the crate was leaning against the seat. A tight fit. But no one seemed to mind where the Captain sat. He made an ideal travel companion: silent, easy to handle, and commanding instant respect.

But when Alexander went to place his left hand on the crate again, containing the only three-quarter portrait of Captain James Cook in existence, he had a premonition. His trip to Auckland was going to go terribly wrong and he would be responsible, or at least blamed for the catastrophe.

Two days before, he had entered Under-Secretary Richard Catelin's large office with two manila envelopes. Even the circumspect civil servant could not contain himself when he saw the black-and-white photos they contained. The shadow minister's hand squeezed the young woman's rear as they stood kissing, no, snogging would be the correct term, Alexander explained to Catelin. The photos told a story, from the first intimate kiss outside her front door, to a series of embraces, to the couple disappearing inside, and the shadow of the shadow minister.

In the other envelope were what he called the "extra milk bottle" photos. "Are they good enough? I had to push the film."

"I can see." Catelin was clearly trying not to smile.

"I've been thinking. We can talk about the doctor and the Russian spy all we want and the milk bottle. And by the way, the doctor doesn't get milk delivered in the morning. I checked with the milk delivery as well. So, one mystery solved. Though they did see each other again yesterday morning. It's like I said, the Russian is courting him. Keeping him warm." Alexander paused to see if Catelin would respond or reach for a pipe. His boss did not move. "But the photos. They are dynamite. Real election-changing stuff. I mean, what if they leaked? Or *Truth* or the *Dominion* got hold of them?"

"You haven't shown them to anyone, have you?" The Under-Secretary sounded near panic.

"Mr. Catelin, who do you think I am? We have an agreement. I work for you. And I would not break it for the world. Now, let's get back to the photos. If certain people saw them, wouldn't it change everything? If his wife saw the photos, she would divorce him. His own party would disown him. All sorts of things could happen we can only speculate on. One thing we do know, though — it's a game-changer. An election-winner. So I need something from the government in return." Alexander was careful not to make it personal. He knew the National Party would pay for the photos. "For a start, I need a significant salary increase. What I earn is way too low and not commensurate with what I have achieved so far and the shows I am planning. And second, I want, what can I call it? A finder's fee."

Catelin reached for a pipe and started the process of checking it, cleaning the bowl out with his penknife, and filling it from his leather pouch. "We could accommodate you, up to a certain point," he puffed eventually. "We would have to account for the expenditure." He waved his pipe, and smoke whirled around his head. "But I am sure we can come to an arrangement. It might not be what you would expect but it would be much better than you are getting now." He got up from his desk. "You have your ticket to Auckland, correct? And you have a place to stay?"

"I think so. An old friend." Alexander had written to his friend, and called her a few times, but she was never home.

"Good. You will meet with an Inspector Grimble from the Auckland police when you arrive. Follow his lead. Once the painting is safely delivered, the handover and paperwork are very important. It will be the Auckland Gallery's responsibility and the police's, after they sign the papers. But I want you to do something else. And your director agrees."

Alexander froze.

"I want you to stay for the opening of the exhibit and be in Auckland for a few extra days. The government is very worried about the security of *Captain Cook*. It's a very valuable painting and they are concerned. Bring the camera and stay alert."

Alexander understood his new role but was intrigued by Catelin's choice of words. Who would steal it on the way to the gallery? Or rip it off the wall once it was in Auckland? It wasn't an episode of *The Sweeney*, his favorite English cops-and-robber's TV show. Kiwis did not steal old paintings and they did not nick old Captain Cook.

"The army is helping out as well. Expect to see them. But I have no idea what they have planned as they won't tell us. Operational security. And here are your expenses." Catelin handed him a thin envelope. Alexander did not want to open it in front of him. Was the money in five-dollar notes, tens, twenties? He was concerned that he did not have to sign for it, like a good government bureaucrat. He rushed to his office at the National Art Gallery and counted ten $20 notes. It wasn't as much as he'd hoped, but he had his airline tickets.

CHAPTER FIFTEEN

The plane came to a complete stop before the terminal. Alexander saw a row of army Jeeps and trucks on the runway as if they were expecting an invasion. Serious army men with bad haircuts and big rifles were running around shouting at each other. Alexander was amused by the display of force for a dead British navy captain who had been murdered by natives on a faraway island almost two hundred years ago.

The front cabin door was opened by the stewardess, and Alexander carried his crate down the gangway to the tarmac. She carried his camera bag and suitcase behind him. An army major saluted him and walked with him to the second Jeep. Alexander placed the crate behind the front seats and took the suitcase and his camera bag from the stewardess. "Good luck, Mr. Newton," she smiled. Alexander nodded, pleased he had chosen his blue suit with a white shirt and narrow blue tie.

They roared off in a convoy. Four motorcycle cops were in front with their lights and sirens on, then the lead Jeep with four armed soldiers. Alexander followed in his Jeep with the major in front directing the procession by radio. Two more Jeeps were behind with more soldiers. Two canvas-covered trucks worked through their gears to keep pace. Inside, soldiers sat across from each other holding their rifles as if ready for an ambush. Alexander turned and saw more police motorcycles behind him. He felt like a rock star with a police and army escort. Sirens and lights. If he had kept his hair longer, it would be blowing in the cold wind. But he was a respectable curator, and an unknown spy, with a mute *Captain Cook* and half the New Zealand army for company. The government had underwritten the insurance to cover the risk of moving such a valuable painting from Wellington to Auckland.

At the receiving dock of the gallery, the police motorcyclists blocked one end of Kitchener Street while the two trucks blocked the other, and a phalanx of soldiers with their rifles allowed the major to usher Alexander into the gallery out of sight of any passers-by. Inside, a tall plainclothes policeman stood almost at attention, and the major saluted him. "Major Sinjin Mainwaring."

"I'm Inspector Bernie Grimble and I officially take control of the painting. Thank you, major. Can you sign here, please."

"I'm Alexander Newton, the curator," Alexander said but the major and the inspector ignored him as they eyed each other, and what they held in their hands — paperwork.

"Of course. And if you could sign here too, please." Major St. John Mainwaring signed at the bottom of what was a quadruplicate form and presented Grimble with another set of papers documenting that the major, as a designated representative of the New Zealand Army, was relinquishing control of the aforesaid painting to the designated representative of the New Zealand Police.

Grimble tore off a copy and handed it to the major. The major did the same with his set of papers. Each held the requested signed copies, and for a moment there was confusion as to who had signed what. The major tucked his signed copy and the other copies into his jacket. "Best we be on our way. Pleasure to do business with you." The major saluted, swiveled around and marched outside to his jeep. He whirled his right hand above his head and the entire group of soldiers and vehicles came to life and formed a straight line behind him.

Grimble gave copies to the gallery's curator then Alexander carried the crate upstairs to the conservation room. The curator followed with Alexander's camera bag and suitcase. "I'm Colin McMillan, by the way," he said. "I'm supposed to open the crate, inspect the painting and install it right on the wall. The entire space is closed off, but do you want to see it?"

Alexander nodded. He could not determine the curator's age. Colin had scraggy hair to his lean shoulders, and a long nose like a beak. He wore bell-bottom jeans and a crisp white lab coat that accentuated his thinness. Alexander followed him, with Grimble close behind.

Colin used his electric screwdriver to open the top of the crate. He removed the painting slowly. "Oh, I love the old frame. He's not even full size."

"Yes, a three-quarter Cook," Alexander replied.

"Are you happy with the way the canvas is attached at the back? The frame?" Colin inspected the back of the painting and with his white gloves pressed the canvas against the frame. "We do this differently. More secure." He moved the canvas back and forth and glanced at Alexander.

"That's how he came. You see a problem?"

"Not my painting." Colin looked back at Grimble, who was out of earshot.

Alexander shrugged.

Colin said no more and carried the painting to the wall where it would be displayed. He placed the mounting wire on a set of hooks already screwed into the wall. The wire was snapped into place with clamps. He adjusted the frame and asked, "Is it level?"

Alexander looked at Grimble who nodded his approval. "Perfect. Just the right height too. And secure?"

"It conforms to Lloyds of London's stipulated security guidelines for securing valuable paintings," said Colin. "Besides, who would want to steal old Captain Cook?"

Alexander and the policeman exchanged glances.

.   .   .

"I didn't want to say anything in front of the cop, but you looked nervous about the painting. What's going on?" Colin asked after escorting his Wellington counterpart to his office where Alexander's suitcase and camera bag were secured.

"Oh, they all seem so guarded about Captain Cook as if someone might steal it." Alexander shrugged. "But as you said, who would?"

"Beats me. But I don't lie awake at night thinking about robbing banks and post offices either."

"The hooks and stuff in the back look secure, but the actual canvas seems not as tight as it should be in the frame."

"I'll look at it after the opening. We can take it to our lab early Monday. We should have done it before, but there's no time." Colin smiled. "Anyway, we're having a party on Saturday. It's costume, if you want to wear something different."

"Great, thanks. Now, Colin, do you have a darkroom? I want to take photos here, around the exhibit."

"Sure, I'll show you. You have a camera in your bag?"

"Yes, the latest Nikon and a great telephoto lens."

"Cool. I thought it was a Tommy gun."

"Oh, they haven't issued me one yet."

CHAPTER SIXTEEN

Alexander knocked on the blue door of a wooden two-story house at the bottom of Grafton. He breathed in the sweet smell of witch hazel, or was it the camellia shrub next to the large casement window? Auckland, or at least this valley, appeared shabby and damp with its Victorian and Edwardian architecture despite signs of an ugly future with high-rise insurance buildings downtown and the carved-out earth of the new motorway near Tsara's house. He felt uneasy back in Auckland. Called Sin City by those who never visited, it was bigger, noisier and far less hospitable than he remembered.

A young woman opened the door and looked blankly at him. At first Alexander feared she would not recognize him. She occupied a long granny dress and had a black overgrown pageboy haircut. Even without makeup she had large round eyes that looked charcoal black, thick dark eyebrows and thin red lips. A car raced down Grafton Road and skidded, but they both ignored it. She finally broke into a smile.

"Tsara! I tried calling. Did you get my letter?" He felt like a refugee at her front door with his suitcase and camera bag.

"Yes. And here you are." She spoke softly as she looked at him from under her fringe. They had first met in Introduction to Art History at the university, kindred spirits in art appreciation, protest marches and late-night talks in the university coffee bar, but they had never kissed or even held hands. "My god! You look so different. Come in."

Tsara looked exactly the same as Alexander remembered her. "Can I take you out to dinner? There's a pretentious French restaurant in Parnell. What is it called? Antoine's, I remember. I just got into town, and—"

"I've made peppermint tea and I have cake." Tsara wafted into the kitchen and Alexander followed, noting her effortless grace, her relaxed nonchalance. "Are you staying?"

"I didn't want to assume anything but if I can, it would be great. The gallery doesn't like to spend any money on little people like me."

"You're not little." She looked him up and down and not for the first time Alexander wondered if she was playing with his expectations—or, rather, the lack of them.

They sat across from each other in the kitchen. She poured tea and cut a slice of homemade fruit cake with walnuts. "What made you shave your beard off and cut your hair?"

"I'm a professional curator now."

"Goodbye to the student rebel. And I heard you broke up with your girlfriend."

"What? You know as well? How?"

"Word gets around. Are you seeing anyone?"

"And I was going to ask you deep questions about your photography and your current work with a Diana camera."

"We can talk about that, but I asked first."

"Well, if you must know, I'm seeing someone. Strange relationship, really."

"How did you meet?"

"I bumped into her on the street. We got talking and…" Alexander gestured vaguely.

"Were you drunk? I thought you were shy around women. More important, was *she* drunk?"

"No. She's a librarian. A little on the voluptuous side and older than me but a great sense of humor. I think." Alexander pulled a face and had a flash of insight about Deborah. He started to see her with Tsara's eyes, and he was disturbed. *Did* Deborah have a sense of humor? Was she as uninformed as she claimed about her neighbor the alleged spy? Did she know what he was really doing? He shook his head to get rid of these thoughts and put on a smile. If Tsara knew he had taken surveillance photos for the National government, she would throw him out of her house and never speak to him again. He looked around, nervous. Fabrics in red and gold in the living room reminded him of Deborah's bedroom.

Unsure now how to react, Alexander resorted to his standby phrase when visiting an artist's studio: "Show me your latest work." Was he really shy around women? He must be. He couldn't remember the last time he had asked someone out on a date.

Tsara picked up her Diana camera, that took 120 film and had a pinhole lens, she had bought at Woolworths. "I use tape as light leaks in. It's low-tech and makes great images."

He gazed at the moody, out-of-focus portraits she had on one wall. They made him feel sad and on edge, but he kept his impressions to himself.

Tsara placed two pillows and a blanket on the sofa in the living room. She put *Songs of Leonard Cohen* on her turntable and disappeared into the bathroom. He knelt down and flicked through her collection including the latest Cohen, *New Skin for the Old Ceremony*. He wanted to hear it but didn't know what to make of the cover, two naked angels in an embrace. The merging of the conscious and subconscious? He would have to sleep on it.

He changed into a T-shirt and got under the covers. As he slipped into a semi-conscious state, a track on the album caught his attention, "The Stranger Song". Was he the stranger seeking shelter? Too tired to think, he was asleep before Tsara waltzed passed him to her bedroom.

He woke at three and did not know where he was. The sofa was uncomfortable, but he could stretch out. He thought about all the changes in his life since he had last seen Tsara, and could not reconcile how much he must have changed in her eyes. If she only knew.

Alexander awoke to see that Tsara had made him tea and marmalade toast. There was a comfortable silence as they ate their breakfast together. Later he had a bath, a shave and dressed. He sat beside her on the sofa. He had forgotten how serene she could be. He felt unmotivated to rush to the gallery, so he gazed at the back cover of the new Cohen LP and wondered about the devout brunette in chains devoured by the fires of purgatory. Was this a message? Or was the other cover with the lover angels meant for him? His life had been so busy he had not thought about what he had been doing, and the moral and ethical implications. Staying with Tsara, he was reminded of his strong student beliefs. What had happened to his anti-establishment protests? His sense of rebellion? They had left him, he realized, along with his long hair and full beard.

Alexander had sent Tsara a letter about his trip, with a black-and-white print he had developed in his own dark-room. He saw the photo in a frame near the kitchen and was reassured that she cared enough about him to see the print every day.

She had a new book she had been reading earlier, *Against Nature* by J.-K. Huysmans. He looked inside. "A government functionary, eh? And he died in 1907 so he missed all the horrible parts of the twentieth century, which is most of it, but lived through La Belle Époque. Government functionary is a nice way of saying a flunky. There might be hope for me yet."

"How come?"

"I feel inconsequential at the gallery. I have no control or say over the security, and they are rather worried about Captain Cook."

"He's already dead."

"Yes. But they are worried about him being stolen."

"Why would anyone want to steal him?"

"Beats me, but what do I know? I'm just a government functionary."

They drank their tea. Tsara was playing a Procol Harum album with a sailor on the cover. Alexander heard a celeste and listened carefully to the lyrics. He knew he would never forget this moment—it was both sweet and melancholy. Tsara was engrossed in her book about a government functionary. He was relieved they did not engage in any political talk. He looked down at her sandals sticking out of her long dress and remembered she didn't shave her legs.

CHAPTER SEVENTEEN

Wiremu parked the rusted Holden by Mel's house, sat in his car, windows down, and listened to bird songs and his radiator grumble. Mel's BMW was not present, and he couldn't hear Henry's hi-fi system. The property extended to the reserve, an extinct volcano nearly seven hundred feet high, once a terraced Maori fortress that dominated the entire isthmus and allowed for unrestricted views over the Waitemata Harbor and Hauraki Gulf and, to the west, Manukau Harbor and the Tasman Sea. He noted how well maintained her house looked with its wooden slats painted a dark green and the windows and shutters a rusty grey, compared to his similar but rundown house in Hoki-anga. Her front garden was full of flowering shrubs and he remembered the grapefruit tree in the back.

The owner of the security company had told Wiremu he would be the last to leave the art gallery after the opening and would make sure the front doors were left unlocked. He and his partner would sign off with the elderly night watchman, who would then be the only one left in the building. The watchman was very slow and always took the elevator to the top floor then worked his way down, checking all the rooms and turning off any lights before returning to the entrance again. He wouldn't think it un-usual that the front doors were left unlocked after a party.

All Wiremu had to do was time his arrival at the gallery, take the painting and carry it down the stairs to the foyer. The frame was securely fastened to the wall but the canvas itself with some persuasion could be separated from the frame. Now Wiremu had to find a hiding place, and what better location than beneath Dr. Johnson's house? He banged on the door and when he got no reply he walked to the rear and looked at the steps to the kitchen. Making sure no neighbor could see him he bent down and opened a small wooden door. He removed his leather jacket, took out a flashlight and squeezed inside.

Wiremu crawled to beneath where he thought the kitchen was, based on all the pipes. He was searching for a space between the joists where he could hide a painting wrapped in a plastic bag, 43 inches by 27 inches. Wiremu thought in feet and inches, pounds and ounces. He didn't like the new metric system.

He went further under the house and spotted a black lump stuck between the joists. It could only be seen from where he was lying. He felt around with his hands and it came loose. The black plastic package could be drugs. Heroin? Hashish? It did not smell, but then it was sealed. Once outside, he carefully latched the small door again and brushed off the dirt from his plaid shirt and army trousers. He put his leather jacket on, the package secure inside.

Wiremu shook himself again and walked over to the tree to select a grapefruit. A small green bird on the tree, with distinct white and silver eyes, watched him. Wiremu ate the grapefruit on the steps and stared back at the bird. It was a tauhou, and reminded him of the piwakawaka he had seen in Hokianga at the beginning of the year. After encountering the tiny fantail his life had changed in ways he could not have imagined, and he wondered if this small waxeye was another omen.

He debated whether he should take the package to Moana's, then shook his head, stood and brushed more dust off his pants. His curiosity got the better of him. He threw the peel into a garbage can, started up his car and made his way to Grafton.

CHAPTER EIGHTEEN

At lunchtime Colin and Alexander walked through the exhibition again. Colin introduced him to the director of the gallery, Thomas Jones, who barely acknowledged him, and the director of security, Peter MacIntosh, who shook his hand vigorously. Both had large stomachs that projected in front of them, and mustaches to complement their balding heads. The gallery director had a thin waxed mustache, pointed to the sky, making him appear wildly optimistic; the security director possessed a bushy mustache that drooped, giving the appearance of ill humor.

Alexander led Colin towards the Cook portrait. "Do you think it's secure enough? I noticed the inspector wasn't concerned, and I didn't want to say anything in front of him." He held the frame and pretended to lift it off its hooks. "I can't rip it off the wall, can I?"

At the far end of the room Cadd, the new gallery security guard, was staring at them. He looked younger than the other guards, in better shape and far more menacing. With a broken nose and cauliflower ears he had to be a former rugby player. Front row, Alexander assumed. Not someone you would want to upset. "Don't look now," he said, "but he's a cop, put here to keep an eye on the painting. No, don't look. God! Why is it when you say, 'Don't look,' everyone automatically looks?"

"Sorry. Couldn't help it. He is unfriendly, like a cop. Usually new employees quiz me on everything. He seems standoffish. Now, you should bring a date to the party after the opening. Do you have any costumes? Uniforms?"

"Well, no. I'm bringing Tsara Burton, you know, from Elam?"

"Oh, yes. Saw a show of hers. Polaroids mounted on black. Very mysterious. She has talent. Here's the address." Colin slipped him a piece of paper in such a way that Cadd could see.

"You said uniforms. Do you mean fancy dress?"

"You could say that. Some of us have military uniforms. It's dress up, call it fancy dress if you like. Goes well with alcohol and when we put on our uniforms it gets crazy."

"Crazy good or crazy bad?"

Colin smiled. "Depends on how much we drink!"

Alexander put the paper in his trouser pocket and looked back at Captain Cook. "Can we secure the actual painting better? We can't screw the frame into the wall, and it won't help if someone takes a knife to the canvas."

"You can't lift it off the hook, even if it looks like you can. Same as all the Goldies here, and a few other valuable paintings. It's stipulated in all our loan agreements, but you saw Terry Thomas and Mexican Pete. They don't seem to know what they're doing. Which is fine by me, as long as they leave me alone to do my job."

"Mexican Pete?"

"Well, technically he's Scottish, from the Met Art Fraud squad, he claims, but we think he's Mexican. Check out the mustache."

"And Terry Thomas?"

"After the old English actor, had a waxed mustache and was frightfully British in a ridiculous way. Like our director."

"I was not impressed. He doesn't seem to be all there, and I hardly know him."

"Join the club. He's rather aloof. They seem to work well together. Matching competencies, like the Peter Principle."

"I've never heard of him till now."

"He was the director at the Australian National Art Gallery in Canberra. But the rumor is they faked his recommendation to get rid of him. Pass him off to the Kiwis. Sick joke."

"Didn't you get references and call them? Talk to people he worked with before?"

"No, it was done by the city council. The art committee. Full of experts. They didn't need to call. They *knew*. Also, overseas phone calls are expensive. No budget. No common sense."

"Incredible." Alexander shook his head. His gallery was paradise in comparison.

CHAPTER NINETEEN

Mel parked her BMW on the street. From her gate she could hear Henry's sound system but did not recognize the song. In the living room Henry was spread out on her sofa, a letter in his hand. He hadn't showered or shaved and didn't smile when he saw her.

Mel turned off the amplifier and picked up the empty album cover. Bob Dylan's *Blood on the Tracks*. She held it to his face. "Are you trying to tell me something?"

Henry sat upright and ran his hands through his hair. She put the album down and sat next to him. There was a university crest on the letterhead.

"I'll never get a job here," he said. "It's a small, petty, jealous place. When I left, I closed the door for good. And now there are rumors. I'd been fired. I was a troublemaker. I couldn't hack it. I couldn't make it overseas. You know, the classic overseas experience gone wrong. So it was my last try. I don't think anyone will accept me now."

Mel took the letter and read aloud, "Much as we are impressed with your work and experience in Long Island, we find we cannot offer you a research position within our department. Your qualifications do not fit in with the focus of our academic and research goals. We therefore regretfully cannot accept your application." She put the letter down. "Aren't you forgetting you announced to Wiremu you were going back to the States?"

Henry grimaced. "It was a spur-of-the-moment thing. Not sure I agree with what I said. I'm just going through a tough time and I'd appreciate your support. I'm sorry for what I said, but I don't know what to do now. Honestly."

"You seem to be drifting away from me. Is it just because you can't get a position here?"

"Yes, that's it. It's as if they all got together and copied each other's rejection letters. They're almost all the same." He looked up at her as she stood. "Oh, I get it. You think I'm rejecting you and I don't want to live here anymore."

"Henry, I'm not feeling any love. You've been distant lately and then that announcement out of the blue? And you're listening to that morose album about Dylan leaving his wife?"

Henry eased himself off the sofa, ran his hand through his hair again and straightened up. "You know about that?"

"I know people who know about all this stuff. I listen to people all day."

He took a step forward and held her by the waist. "You never cease to amaze me. And I've been an ass. I don't know what's come over me. It's the job thing for sure, but giving back the Tear also affected me in a way I could not imagine. You know?"

"No I don't." She put her hands on his waist and held him in her gaze. "You don't say much, do you? And you're terrible at expressing your feelings."

"Well, I'm a man. Aren't we supposed to be inarticulate? Unable to tell the women we love how we feel?"

Mel raised her eyebrows. "Women we love?"

"You know what I mean. You, of course."

"Okay. Annie from the dojo gave me invites tonight to the opening of a new show at the Auckland City Art Gallery. 'The Two Worlds of Omai'. Well, technically her boyfriend got them, but if we get ready now we can make it. It'll cheer you up."

Henry grunted. "Do I have a choice?"

"No. Get ready now!" Mel released her hold on him and raised her right leg as if to kick him but put her foot down. Henry straightened his shoulders and marched to the bathroom.

CHAPTER TWENTY

Inspector Grimble, in a dark grey suit and wide red tie, arrived an hour before the opening to oversee the security arrangements. Alexander greeted Tsara with an awkward kiss on the cheek at the entrance. She offered her other cheek with a wry smile and Alexander was obliged to kiss her again. She wore mascara, dark red lipstick and a long, red velvet dress that hugged her figure and was dramatically different from her usual granny dresses. With black stockings and pumps she did not look like the hippie student he had known. He wondered what she thought of his change in appearance with his short hair, dark blue suit with narrow lapels, sharp white shirt and a blue knit tie. He was no longer the hippie activist, but a government-hired provocateur. How would Tsara feel about his new role?

When Grimble and Alexander went to check the front entrance they saw two new security guards in identical black blazers accepting invitation cards. A young assistant with long blonde hair held a clipboard with the guest list and directed guests to the foyer where they could check their bags and coats and wait for the opening ceremony. Grimble openly looked her over, her high heels, her miniskirt, her long eyelashes.

Alexander shot a couple of photos of the unsmiling guards then continued photographing guests, either shooting from his waist where the camera hung on a strap, or manually focusing on a scene, a group of people.

"How do you not draw attention with your camera?" Grimble asked.

"Oh, just act natural and shoot," Alexander smiled. "You never know." He had learned a lesson in Wellington in the gallery van, and in Deborah's bedroom, he would not forget: the more you shoot, the more you see.

When the important guests had assembled in the foyer, there was a powhiri, a traditional Maori welcoming cere-mony. A large bare-chested male in a piupiu, a flax skirt, challenged everyone as he expertly wielded his taiaha, a long spear-like club with carvings and feathers at one end. Grimble later described to Sergeant Cadd how a handful of older males had performed a haka, but it was so differ-ent from how he had performed a haka at the start of his grammar school rugby game. Cadd had been upstairs all the time, standing next to the three-quarter length portrait of Captain James Cook, circa 1776, painted by John Web-ber (1751-1793.) The artist had completed the painting after Cook's untimely death on February 14, 1779. Webber had painted three versions of Cook during his last voyage. Cadd recited these facts, gleaned from the information sheet, as if it was a crime scene.

After the powhiri there were speeches. The director opened the proceedings and warmly thanked the sponsor, a floor-wax company. An executive from the company was acknowledged but did not address the crowd. The chair-man of the Arts Council stated how important the exhibit was to our recognition of two different cultures. It was a brave new direction for the publicly funded gallery, and he was excited to see corporate sponsorship for the arts. Next, the mayor of Auckland spoke—he was meant to be first but he had been late and now most people ignored him, as they did a representative from Tahiti who claimed kinship with Omai but had a thick French accent. No one seemed to care what he said, and the Maori present ignored him.

.   .   .

Grimble wondered if he should have invited his wife to his first art-gallery opening. She would have loved to attend and mingle among "society", as she called it. But she would have declared she had nothing to wear and bought an expensive dress. Better he was on his own, as he was officially working, and there was his new associate, Alexander Newton, to deal with. The commissioner had instructed Grimble to extend every courtesy to the curator. "An extra set of eyes in case anything happens" was how he explained Alexander's position.

Grimble felt awkward standing alone, as if he was deciding who to interview next, even though no crime had been committed. Alexander came over and Grimble relaxed, unknotted his eyebrows and began to see the people around him.

"What do you think of the show?" Alexander asked his new law enforcement friend, after introducing Tsara. The inspector raised his eyebrows at her and her tight red velvet dress, and was momentarily at a loss for words. "Oh, I don't know. Not my usual beat."

"Lots of local personalities here. Artists and dealers. Business leaders. Different breed from what you are used to, I guess, but I'm sure they still have larceny in their heart." Alexander chuckled as he gazed at the scattering of older men and women, all in business attire, all scrutinizing each other. "No one sees the art at openings — though there is little art to see here, just a few carvings from the Islands, some portraits and lots of colored boards with writing and photos. What do you think, Tsara?"

Tsara forced a quick smile. "It's a little too didactic for me but they are telling a story, even if it is a little labored with all the reading and explanations. Omai's story is a compelling one, considering we are now finally realizing what different worlds the early Polynesians lived in compared to eighteenth-century Englishmen, and a lot of rough sailors. Two different worlds of men. It was definitely a man's world, regardless of where you came from."

"Well said." Grimble shook his head in appreciation, eying her tight velvet dress again. "Even now we don't understand each other. There is such a gap between cultures in our country. And not a lot of appreciation, let alone fear of the law."

Tsara smiled. "Is that where you come in? With the fear?"

"I'd settle for respect." Grimble looked around the gallery for an escape, and saw the Soviet diplomat, Raganovich. He had seen photos of the Soviet handing a mystery object to Dr. Cedric Winter. He had gone over the guest list earlier with Sergeant Cadd, and Raganovich was not on the list. Why would the villain of the famous Wellington spy case be invited? And why was his suit so shiny?

"Excuse me," he said to Alexander and Tsara. "I have to say hello to an old friend." He walked over to the Soviet and shook his hand. The Soviet burst out laughing and loudly slapped Grimble's back.

"Do they know each other?" Tsara asked. "It looks odd, doesn't it? Like it's the first time they're meeting, but they're both pretending to be friends. Why all the photos?"

"You noticed?" He adjusted his lens as if he was taking a photo of another group before he focused on Grimble and the Russian. "I'll explain later."

Tsara kept her eyes on the male couple. "I'm supposed to be a photographer. To get to the truth of a person or at least I kid myself I do, but they appear false, don't they?"

"You took the words out of my mouth." Alexander said, continuing to take photos of the encounter. "We shouldn't stare at them."

"They have no idea. They're engrossed in each other. Do you know who he is?"

"I believe he is a Soviet diplomat. From Wellington. I've seen him around. Not exactly popular with the current government, especially after the spy trial."

"Oh yes, I remember. I wonder why the inspector is being so friendly."

"Keeping your enemies closer? Probably has a photo of him in his office. If he's a Soviet diplomat, he's a spy. Although what could he be spying on here in New Zealand?"

Tsara smiled. "Perhaps it's his reward after squeezing Americans out of all their secrets. Must be a plum post here. Doesn't every spy wish to be posted to paradise? Compared to Moscow in the winter? What could possibly go wrong here?"

"Well, remember the trial? Dr. Winter walked free. The papers went crazy over the verdict. And the government, from what I hear, is mad for revenge."

"Maybe we should be more afraid of our own government?" Tsara mused.

"Much truth in jest," Alexander sighed, and changed the film in his camera. He was now on his third roll of 36 shots, with his favorite Tri-X black-and-white film.

"Are you David Hemmings in *Blow-Up*?" Tsara asked.

"So you would be, Vanessa Redgrave?"

"Jane Birkin. *Please.*"

Alexander closed his eyes. He had a flashback to the girl fight scene in *Blow-Up* with Jane Birkin wearing no panties. He had attended the last Christmas party at the Film Censors' office, contained within his government department. Only a few people were invited as the projectionist had spliced together all the censored scenes from previous years and played the loop continuously, between tequila shots. Jane Birkin's no-underwear scene featured. Alexander's drunk co-workers had taken turns to shout, "Play it again, Sam!" He could not imagine Tsara as Jane Birkin. She had never hinted at a physical relationship with him. Which was what he liked about her. He didn't have to be on his best behavior or try to impress her. He could be himself, whoever that was.

CHAPTER TWENTY-ONE

Henry Lotus and Mel Johnson had made their way into the exhibition space and were looking at the crowd. Henry had shaved and his long hair was combed back. He was dressed in his best grey slacks and blue blazer with a black polo. Mel was holding his arm and smiling, in her favorite black suit with tight pants and white shirt. She had decided to wear her Doc Marten combat boots, more for comfort than as a fashion statement. She was almost as tall as Henry.

"Oh god, check out the cop," Henry said. "He interrogated me with Mr. FBI. I hope *he* isn't here as well. That's him talking to a big guy with a crew cut and a bad suit."

Mel flicked back her long curly hair as she tried to keep a straight face. "Oh yes, I recognize him. How could I forget?"

"I want to talk to him." Henry dragged her over to where Grimble stood. The Soviet diplomat had spotted someone else to back-slap so Grimble was on his own again, surveying the crowd.

"Inspector. Henry Lotus. Nice to see you here. Are you a fan of Omai?" Henry asked. "Or Captain Cook?"

Grimble, who never forgot a face, could only stare at Mel. "Oh, how rude of me," said Henry. "Allow me to introduce my good friend Dr. Mel Johnson. I believe you met before." Henry took a friendly tone, although he wanted to say something he would regret later.

"Yes, of course. Good to see a familiar face, or faces, here. I'm not one to go to gallery openings, just a plain copper."

The three of them shook hands and Mel smiled. "Inspector. There is nothing plain about you. I was impressed how you comported yourself in the long tedious interview with the FBI."

"Well, we both thought you weren't telling us everything." Grimble said.

"I wasn't," said Henry. "Because, as I explained, of my security clearance. And it's really unfair, such scrutiny. It's harming my chances of getting a university post here."

"What do you think of the show?" Mel asked.

"Interesting. Although the word seems overused here. So saying 'interesting' doesn't say much, does it?"

"Perceptive, Inspector, but what of the show?"

"Lots of words on what? Panels? Seems geared to children, the way it's presented. Didactic. I suppose they plan a lot of school tours."

"It's the new thing in exhibits," said Henry. "Lots of curatorial direction. Guiding you how to see and think. I guess we have to read the catalog to understand what's going on." There had been a pile of catalogs at the entrance, but neither Mel nor Henry had bothered to take one.

Mel caught sight of Annie and excused herself. She made her way through the crowd to where Annie stood next to a tall young man with hair to his shoulders. He was dressed more casually than anyone else, with a brown corduroy jacket over a red-and-black plaid shirt and jeans, but he radiated confidence, as if he owned the gallery.

"Hi, Mel. Mark, Mel. Mel, Mark."

Mark beamed his famous smile at Mel. "I didn't know Annie had such amazing friends."

"You should see her boyfriend," Annie countered as she saw Henry approach.

"Mark fucking Rose! How are you, old man?" Henry's face lit up.

Mark hugged Henry and almost lifted him in the air. Henry tried to hug him back. "Where have you been?" Mark asked.

"In the States. Doing research. Mel here rescued me, and here I am in God's Own."

"Wow. It's been how long?"

"Quite a few years. I've lost count. Don't tell me you're still at uni?"

"I got a grant to do a PhD, so why not?"

Henry turned to Mel. "We were the Pipe Society at uni. Mark was the student rebel. I was the science nerd. We got on great."

"Pipe Society?" Mel asked.

"Yeah. We imported pipe tobacco, rare brands, and had long weekly meetings where we sampled new tobacco."

Mark's smile was wider now. "The most amazingly funny times ever. All with perfectly legal pipe tobacco."

"We were both in the Order of the Iron Lung," Henry recalled.

Mark laughed out loud. "It's the most exclusive order, anywhere."

"Are you based here, Mark?" Henry asked.

"Got a pad in Parnell, but I live on a commune in Hokianga."

"No way! Mel and I were just there."

"Should've dropped in and had a few drinks. We brew our own mead and other stuff." Mark beamed at Mel. "Great place. Like paradise. Trouble is, it takes a lot of work to run it and no one wants to work too hard. The trouble with socialists, they want all the glory but not the sweat." Mark laughed again. "Look, let me give you my addresses, we can keep in touch. Can't believe you're here. Our little country, but it's all good."

Mark wrote out his contact information on a scrap of paper he found in his jacket and promised he would keep in touch. He marched off to another group of people and started a loud conversation.

Mel kept talking to Annie while Henry announced he would look for drinks.

"Is he always so hyper?" Mel asked.

"Oh yes. He never lets up, at least when he's with me. Big smile, big personality. Probably bi-polar with lots of issues, but he always puts on a great show. He was a student leader. I think he still is. Hate to see him when he crashes, but maybe he won't."

In his search for wine Henry came to a crowd around an oil painting. Off to one side he saw a young man with a camera talking to a taller, younger man in a similar outfit. The navy-blue suit looked from the Thirties, the bright red pocket square like a declaration of war. They were in an animated discussion and Henry listened in.

"You can't expect me to believe this, the new way of showing art? It's not even conceptual. Just a load of trinkets and lots of writing on fancy labels. Cook is the only serious painting in the show. Rather meager, isn't it? Would be cool to have all the Captain Cook portraits ever painted in one room, in chronological order, like a deity, like he was thought of by some. It would be a Pacific temple to one of the world's greatest explorers."

"Not my show. I like the portrait, though. Painted in transit."

"Yeah. Must've been. So, you're liking Wellington, Alexander? And don't point that camera at me, makes me nervous."

"Oh, yes. Apart from the weather, the light and the wind. Are you still at uni, Nicholas?"

"Doing a PhD on Tristram Shandy." Nicholas nodded to Tsara, who stood to one side and ignored him. He was not introduced to her.

"God, it's the only book you've ever read."

"You can talk. Anyway, I've got to go, I hate these things. Only came to see you. We must catch up. You here for long?"

Alexander waved his hand. "A few days."

"See you around." Nicholas nodded again to Tsara, who did not smile back.

Alexander was saved by Henry who came up to him and asked, "What do you think of Captain Cook?"

"He's my ticket to get here. Excuse me, I am being obtuse. I'm Alexander Newton, a curator at the National. I shipped him up. And this is my friend, Tsara Burton."

Henry bowed to Tsara, clearly admiring her tight velvet dress. He went to kiss her hand but turned around instead and saw Mel had followed. She gave Henry a questioning look. Without missing a beat, he introduced her to the new couple. "Alexander here brought the Captain up to Auckland for the show. He's the curator at the National Art Gallery."

"Rough seas?" Mel asked.

"Yes, but put him on a plane, he's a great travelling companion. Apparently they were worried about him." Alexander looked at Mel properly for the first time and lost his train of thought. She was not beautiful in the traditional sense, nor handsome either, he thought, she was more than just handsome, she was gorgeous. Plain fucking gorgeous in a unique way. Her skin was white but glowed, her black hair had long curls and glistened. She had an understated but confident manner about her. Her black pant suit accentuated her sensual figure. And her eyes...He tried to discern their color. Were they golden, or amber? When she moved her head, they changed in the light, with green specks, like jade. Then her boots! No one else in the gallery wore Doc Martens. His mind started to wander, and he shuddered. He tried to get back into the conversation. Something had shifted inside him, something he could not comprehend. Women in high heels and cocktail dresses were looking at Mel instead of at the painting. The way she stood with her legs planted apart made her look in command, as if she couldn't care what other people thought of her.

"He looks okay to me," Mel said, played with locks of her hair. She glanced at Alexander then back at the Captain.

Lest he make his interest in Mel too obvious, Alexander turned to Henry. "In all his three-quarter glory, before he gets killed by the Hawaiians."

"Some say it was all his fault. Failure to understand the culture he was a guest in."

"Have you read the catalog?"

"No, I just had a really good history teacher."

"Are you a historian?"

"Theoretical physicist."

"Are you working at uni here?"

"Sore point. Was working in the States but here? No one will hire me."

"Because? Sorry. It's none of my business. We're supposed to admire the carvings." Alexander turned to Mel again but couldn't think of anything to say.

She smiled at him. "I'm not very good with the lighthearted chatter you're supposed to engage in at openings. What about you?"

"I'm just here because I'm working." He held up his camera as defense, but what he wanted to do was take photos of Mel. He tried not to stare at her and lowered his camera. He let out a deep breath and turned to his guest. "Tsara here wanted to see the show too."

Tsara just smiled and looked at Mel and Henry.

"What do you specialize in? You know, theoretically?" Alexander asked Henry.

"Energy and gravity, but if Mel hears any more of my babbling about physics, she'll launch a roundhouse kick at my head. In those boots. And she never misses."

"You do karate?" Alexander asked Mel.

"I mix it up a bit. Kung fu, some Okinawan karate and ju-jitsu. I teach at a dojo in Ponsonby."

"I should attend a class while I'm here."

"It's for women only," Mel replied. "But you're welcome to watch. In fact, we could do with a male body to practice on." She smiled. "You wouldn't get hurt. Much."

.   .   .

Most of the guests had left when Alexander saw Colin again. "I keep on hearing rumors about the party, Colin. You seem to have a reputation."

Colin shrugged. "Oh, you know what it's like. Rumors."

Tsara smiled at Colin, then asked Alexander, "Can we go now? I've seen enough."

Outside Alexander noticed two security guards were still present, but they were in the courtyard facing Kitchener Street. He had two frames left in his camera so he squeezed the shutter at waist-level.

CHAPTER TWENTY-TWO

Alexander arrived late at the gallery on Sunday afternoon. With no set hours he did not want to make a habit of arriving early. He had a hangover. Police cars and vans blocked Kitchener Street and part of Wellesley Street. He thought, "Has there been a murder?"

The entire gallery was closed. Alexander mentioned Inspector Grimble's name to the constable at the door, who radioed to someone who gave the clearance for him to step inside. Sergeant Cadd met him in the lobby and escorted him upstairs. Colin and the director gazed at the empty space on the wall where Captain Cook should have been.

"I'm sorry," Colin muttered.

"What about?" Alexander asked.

"The party last night."

"Oh. The party."

Inspector Grimble appeared around the corner and headed to where the others had assembled by the empty frame. "The powers in Wellington are upset but fully confident we can locate and restore the painting. I am to assume control of the investigation and I'd like to start interviewing everyone who was here last night in, ah, an office?"

Colin raised his hand and said the best place was the library. He would set it up now.

"Good. And I need a word, please." The inspector walked Colin towards the library. "Is it possible to get a good color reproduction of the painting and put it in the frame. I mean today? Do you have a decent negative?"

"Actually, we do. I had a large-format negative made as soon as we had it installed. I can run over to the color lab we use, and they can print it out immediately. I'll tell them you'll arrest them all if they don't cooperate!"

"You tell them. And I will." Grimble tried to smile as they marched into the library. "Come along, Cadd. I want you to compile a list and take notes."

"I already have the guest list and I added a few other names as well. Ready when you are."

"I have instructions the gallery is to open as soon as the new color photo is installed," Grimble said. "Could you tell your director?"

"He'll be pleased," said Colin, and left the policemen to it.

.   .   .

"You only saw two security guards in front?" Grimble asked Alexander again.

"Yes. Two tall Maori, with black polo necks and blazers. Tough and serious-looking."

"Were they inside or out?"

"Inside, I think. Yes, inside. Hang on. No, they were outside. Why? Were there more than two?"

"You had your camera?"

"Yes."

"And you took photos?"

"A few." Alexander thought of the photos he had shot at Colin's party. Not the sort of images you would share with a policeman. They had been on fast color film Colin had given him. "Let me develop them and I'll show you. I can use the darkroom here."

·   ·   ·

Grimble had been informed of the missing Captain Cook portrait as soon as Cadd arrived at the gallery. He called the commissioner.

"What's the situation, Grimble?"

"Well, sir, the painting's missing. Stolen."

"How could it walk out of the gallery?" The commissioner spoke slowly when he was annoyed, as if speaking to a naughty child.

"It was there when we closed a little after ten. Sergeant Cadd was in the room the entire evening."

"I see. I've stopped the papers from printing anything today. If we keep it quiet, it might force whoever did it to show their hand."

"Do you think it's political?"

"Grimble, really. Have you thought it through?"

"You know me, sir. I don't jump to conclusions. We're still collecting information."

"Quite right."

"We've put out an all-points bulletin at the ports, the airport. It could be rolled into a tube and taken out of the country. We're searching everyone. But I doubt it's been stolen to sell here. It's too well known. What private collector would want it? Which leads me to an alternate theory I don't want to explore just yet."

"Why not?"

"Because the painting might be held for ransom."

"Who would do such a thing?"

"Maori."

"What Maori?"

"Take your pick. Plenty of them want to make a name for themselves. Mana. And I don't want to mention his name, but Wiremu Wilson could be behind the kidnapping. He seems to be a leader others are talking about."

"Oh god! Captain Cook kidnapped by Wiremu Wilson? Can you imagine the political consequences? Let's keep it under wraps for now. But have a plan, Grimble. We need to act quickly to defuse the situation and seize the initiative."

"Yes, commissioner. I'll do my best." Grimble heard beeping as the commissioner cut the call. Why, he thought, did he say, "I'll do my best"? He always said phrases to his boss he regretted later. If a subordinate told him "I'll do my best" he'd yell at them.

Grimble caught Cadd in the library between interviews. "What did the young woman with the clipboard say?"

"She swore there were two extra security guards. Maori, she said. Seemed rather nice."

"Did you get her phone number?"

"I have everyone's contact information, including any phone numbers they have." Cadd replied with a straight face.

"I suppose you haven't been able to call, let alone interview, the Soviet diplomat?"

"No. I don't even have any contact information for him here in Auckland. But funny you should mention him—I saw him talking with an old student radical. Mark Rose."

"How do you know Rose?"

"I only arrested him three, four times. Student demos. Anti-Vietnam War protests. He was, is a troublemaker, a professional agitator, used to be with the Young

Communists. I swear they were funded by the Soviets, but no one would listen to me. I was in uniform, a mere constable. Too political, they said. So I shut up and just arrested him whenever I could."

"Where were they talking?"

"In the gallery, near Captain Cook. Didn't talk long, but it appeared they knew each other and were planning something, what I don't know, but didn't want it to show. You know how some things just don't look right?"

"Yes, unfortunately." Grimble nodded. "Nothing looks right here."

     .   .   .

"Yes, commissioner. We are getting the substitute portrait and we should be open tomorrow. Catelin's man here took photos during the opening. I have two photos showing four Maori security guards, which is perplexing to their security director who swears they hired just two extra guards at the entrance for the opening. I have to interview a few more people, but we saw the Soviet diplomat, Nikolai Raganovich."

"I thought he had flown back to Moscow. What was he doing there?"

"He wasn't on the invite list."

"Who let him in?"

"Probably the girl with the list. He could talk his way into anything. He was seen talking to a student activist, Mark Rose."

"Do you think it's a coincidence?"

"I don't know yet. Whoever stole the painting pushed it out of the frame and walked out with the canvas. I have no idea how that could happen. Everybody here inspected the painting and the frame after it was installed. So how this came about is a mystery to me." Grimble paused. "The security here is not very good, although it passed an international test I'd never heard of. There are four master keys. We have accounted for all four and interviewed everyone. They have a rudimentary alarm system and a night guard who seems to sleep in a closet for most of the night. We have yet to see him at the gallery. He doesn't have a phone. And there is no CCTV. Apparently, it's too expensive for the gallery's budget."

"Call me when you hear more."

Later in the afternoon Colin came back with the full-size print. Grimble oversaw it mounted in the same frame, with a note indicating the original painting was out of the exhibition for conservation work.

CHAPTER TWENTY-THREE

Wiremu and Rawiri sat in Ricky's kitchen while Moana boiled water for tea.

"What happened?" Wiremu asked. He had slept in his black security clothes. He looked a mess.

Rawiri shook his head. "Beats me."

"Can you tell me again, what you saw?" Moana asked.

"We waited till all the guests and workers had left, as planned," Wiremu began. "Then we went inside. The two other guards had gone, but it looked like they were still there, cos we were. The night watchman had checked out those two and gone upstairs. We went to see if anyone else was in the gallery. The main doors were supposed to be locked but weren't. We walked upstairs and around the main gallery until we came to the Cook painting. The frame was there but the painting was missing. Gone!"

"And?" Moana was impatient.

"We left as quickly as we could. Didn't wanna get blamed for stealing the painting. Walked across Albert Park to Princes Street, across to Grafton Road and here."

Rawiri said, "You're leaving out the bit about the Kiwi Tavern."

"Oh, yes. Once we got to Symonds Street we took a de-tour and paid a visit to the Kiwi. It was near closing time.

Our alibi. Lots of people saw us. Needed a drink or two to deal with what happened, you know?"

"What about all your great plans to win over the people and gain the initiative for land rights?" said Moana. "We were going to issue a declaration for the Monday papers."

Wiremu ran his hands through his hair and looked nervous at being interrogated by his little cousin.

"And you were security for Captain Cook, even if you were going to steal it. How could you let someone else grab it? Do you have any idea who?" Moana had the Sunday papers spread out on the kitchen table. "Nothing about the painting. That's strange."

"Maybe they don't know it's stolen yet?" Rawiri offered.

Moana threw up her arms.

"We did see everyone who went in, didn't we, Wiremu?" Rawiri said.

"Yeah. Here's the tricky part. They also saw us. So the cops will be looking for two extra Maori security guys."

"Will your friend give you up?" Moana asked.

"Nah, he's cool. He's with the cause. No way is he going to name us, or his partner. They'll deny there were two more Maori. He's solid. But we saw that Inspector Grimble. He didn't even recognize me. I turned away as soon as I saw him coming, shit, it was like a nightmare seeing him again. He doesn't know you, Rawiri?"

"Nope. I'm just another Maori."

Wiremu thought for a while. "They would have seen only two Maori security guards. We were dressed the same and we were never near them. I think we're all right."

Moana frowned and kept her mouth shut.

Wiremu stood and left the kitchen. He came back with a small package wrapped in black plastic. "I was scouting for a safe place for the painting." He started to rip the tape off and dropped three black notebooks onto the table.

"Shit! What are they?" Rawiri picked one. Moana picked another.

Wiremu leafed through the third. "Well, it's not drugs!"

"You thought it was hashish?" Moana asked.

"It did cross my mind." Wiremu stared at pages of drawings, numbers and small spidery writings. "I don't understand. Do you?"

"And you had a university education." Rawiri replied.

"In prison. No need to rub it in."

"You mentioned it."

"Where did you get them?" Moana asked.

Wiremu stood and went to boil water for more tea. "I got them from under Mel's house. They must be Henry's notebooks. He hid them for a reason. And I think I know why."

"What?" Wiremu asked to Rawiri's smile.

"If we haven't got the painting, who has? We saw everyone who went in and I think everyone who left. If the authorities don't know who stole it, why can't we go ahead with our plan anyway? We can claim we have the painting, right?" Rawiri broke into a full grin.

"I see where you're going," said Wiremu. "No one knows we don't have it, other than the people who actually stole it and they're not going to correct the police and say 'Hey! That dumb ass Maori didn't steal it, we did!'"

Moana clapped her hands. "You might just be right. We can make the call. We can exploit the situation. Yeah! Maori land rights!"

CHAPTER TWENTY-FOUR

Mark Rose sat on his sofa and admired his new acqui-
sition on the opposite wall. He would have preferred
a full-length portrait of Captain Cook, but he was happy
with three-quarters. A frame would make it more important, but the Captain with his telescope and hat surveyed
Mark's living room as if he was about to discover it for
England and lay claim to Mark's cat-piss smelly sofa. He
felt pleased as he rolled himself a cigarette. He had scored
a major coup, way beyond a student prank.

He recalled how during Graduation Week when students pulled stunts, his caused a press sensation. The
mayor had declared he had an open-door policy. Mark,
dressed in a stolen white lab coat, with a few tools from
his toolbox and a clipboard, walked into the City Council
building. When he was outside the mayor's office, he un-
screwed the door, walked to the elevator and right out the
building with the entire door. It got heavy by the time he
arrived at the Student Union building. He hung it from the
ceiling in the cafeteria. The name plate on the door read:
THE MAYOR. He resigned from the Young Communist
Party and was elected Student President. His slogan was,
"I have the open door of the Mayor."

The mayor had to laugh at the innocent stunt. What
could he have done? But not Captain Cook. The painting

embodied the power of Pakeha dominance, the brave English explorer who claimed New Zealand and brought European civilization to the natives. Mark remembered his New Zealand history and how Cook did not have any religious men on his three voyages, unlike the other European explorers. Cook was more amenable to understanding native cultures and not upsetting them, despite the behavior of his crew.

Nikolai Raganovich had proposed that Mark remove the painting and take it to his place to be collected later. He had observed the painting was not well secured into the frame. All Mark had to do was to pop the painting out of the frame from the back and walk out with it.

"There is a small gap between when the last guests and staff leave from the front entrance to when the night watchman makes his rounds through the gallery," he had whispered to him. "He goes upstairs and works his way down. You can slip out of the downstairs bathroom, grab the painting and walk out the door. Just like you took the Mayor's door. Yes?" The diplomat had overheard a man with a large Mexican mustache boast to his audience how secure his gallery was, and what his closing procedures were. "I shall reward you like I have always done. And a little more." Raganovich walked away. He knew that Mark Rose, his longest covert operative, could never resist a daring mission. And they had communicated in plain sight, right in front of a police inspector.

Mark smiled when he recalled the conversation. He could use the extra cash, but he wasn't working for money, and it was typical of Raganovich to never mention an exact sum. He imagined Annie would get a kick out of seeing the Captain in his living room, then recalled how another girlfriend had freaked when she saw a 44-gallon drum of gelignite in front of the sofa. He decided to hide it under his bed when she came over after her late shift. Having sex with her and the Captain beneath appealed to him. Captain Cook, from what he read, never had sex with any of the natives in the South Pacific. Now he could at least experience earth-mother Polynesian sex with lots of mattress creaks and nurse's shrieks.

Mark had seen Annie leave for work at the hospital and waited until all the guests had left before he hid in the downstairs toilet. He found a door inside that opened to a maintenance room where he found a large black plastic bag. He rolled the bag into his jacket. He heard the night watchman open the door to the toilets and check the stalls. Mark imagined the watchman was overweight, as he heard thighs pressing against each other, labored breathing, and slow footsteps. Mark pressed himself against the wall behind the door that the night watchman did not open. When he heard the watchman close the toilet door he opened it to see the lights go out in the corridor. He began his count to a hundred before he made his way to the floor where Captain Cook hung. The gallery was dark as he came to the painting and felt around the frame. He realized he should have worn gloves as he tried to work out how to release the canvas from the frame. Nikolai had told him what to do but it was harder than expected. He played with the gap between the frame and the wall, which was tight. He got no movement with just pressing the canvas back away from the frame, so he pressed the palm of his hand into each corner to loosen it. This didn't work either, so he slapped the canvas with his palm. That started to ease the nails securing the canvas to the frame. Each slap echoed through the gallery. He looked around but didn't hear any other sound, so he whacked the canvas again with his whole hand, being careful not to damage the paint or loosen any flakes at the corners. He saw some movement in the frame, so he kept pressing and hitting on the frame until he got one side lose. Then he worked on the other side before whacking the bottom of the frame. He stopped when he thought he heard the canvas split, but it was a noise nearby he couldn't identify. He waited a few seconds then used the back of his fist one last time to loosen the canvas and ease it out from behind. He slipped the painting into the black plastic bag without damaging the surface. He stepped back to adjust the empty frame so it was level, tucked the package under his arm and took the stairs to the next level.

He stopped when he heard loud footsteps behind him moving faster than the watchman. He slid into a dark alcove with the painting behind him. The footsteps passed him, and he waited a moment before continuing to the ground floor. He checked that no one was at the front entrance, and casually walked across the foyer and out the unlocked front door. He did not look back. From Kitchener Street he climbed the steps to Albert Park, careful to hold the painting by his side. There were a few students walking through the park who ignored him. Once he had crossed the university and was on Grafton Road, he cut through the Domain to the Ho Chi Minh Trail, across the railway track and up to his back yard off Gibraltar Crescent. He unwrapped the painting and placed it on a nail on his wall. It was a fine addition to his flat and he was sorry he wouldn't be able to keep it.

CHAPTER TWENTY-FIVE

Alexander dreaded the call to Catelin but knew he should initiate contact. Perhaps Sergeant Cadd should have slept on a cot next to the painting, if they thought it was so vulnerable to theft. He had assumed the gallery and the Inspector would have worked out all security in detail. He told himself he was not responsible, but he was, and feared he would be blamed.

"If the painting is already gone, you'd better stay and find it." Catelin's voice seemed too relaxed. Alexander imagined he was puffing away on his pipe to calm himself.

"The police are going to blame the Maori. They always do."

"Did you see anyone unusual at the opening?" Catelin asked.

"Our favorite Russian spy was there. And he knew a lot of people in the gallery."

"He's a diplomat. It's his job."

"Yes, but the person he spoke to the most was a young man, a radical, named Mark Rose. Remember the anti-Vietnam War protests? The newspaper photo of the student with a megaphone? With the long hair and raised fist? Well, I couldn't hear what they were saying but they had a kind of body language like the Russian and the doctor.

You know, old friends who are comfortable in each other's presence. It looked very odd, at least to me."

Alexander thought he could hear the pipe working. "Listen, I want you to follow him. Rent a car, no, I'll get you a small van. Call me in an hour and I'll tell you where it is. Here's his address in Auckland. It's not a consulate, but he has to register where he stays. He's with a young Russian woman called Natasha. I can't remember her last name."

Catelin read out the address. It was on Castle Drive, on the eastern slopes of Mount Eden. Oh shit, Alexander murmured.

CHAPTER TWENTY-SIX

Inspector Grimble interviewed the night watchman who had arrived at his usual time, just before the gallery closed. The man was at least sixty years old, had a short back and sides haircut, and a thick mustache that looked dyed black as his hair was turning white. He wore a silver rain jacket, and bulbous trousers that made him appear even wider. When he looked at the inspector his eyes squinted so they appeared to close. He had no idea that Captain Cook had been stolen and when questioned about the front door countered it was not unusual for the front doors to be unlocked, or at least one of them, after a party.

"You never noticed the most important painting in the exhibit was missing?" Grimble tried to keep his tone neutral.

"It's dark once I turn off all the lights. Only the night lights are on and I check all the galleries thoroughly, every hour. I didn't notice anything out of the ordinary. Frames, paintings, drawings, sculptures, all the exhibits appeared intact to me. If an artwork was missing I would have seen it. I'm not blind. I might be a slow walker, but I have eyes. I always pay attention to the Goldies. They're the most valuable."

"Do you have your own master key?"

"No. I get it from the security box and put it back in the morning. Only have it with me when I'm in the gallery. We have procedures. But it can be a little loose, you know?"

"Is it possible someone else could have locked or unlocked the front doors?"

"I suppose. Like I was saying, they need to tighten security, but they never listen to me." He explained that after the two Maori guards, whom he had signed out, had left, no other guests or staff were in the gallery. He started his rounds to check the entire gallery. He always went to the top floor taking the steps, and walked all through the galleries, floor by floor, taking his time as he turned off the lights to each room before moving to the next space. He noticed nothing odd and did not see anyone as he went through the galleries. He also checked the toilets, including the women's.

Grimble couldn't think of anything else to ask, so went out into the gallery, where he bumped into Alexander carrying a folder of black-and-white prints he had just dried. Grimble followed him into the library as the night watchman was leaving. Alexander spread out the 8" x 10" prints on the large table, leaving all the contact prints on a smaller table, including the ones with the Soviet and the inspector.

"Look." Alexander stepped away to allow Grimble to pore over the photos. "Nikolai Raganovich. Talking to the radical Mark Rose. Interesting. Almost in front of the painting. You believe it's a coincidence?"

Grimble scratched his chin and frowned. "How do you know Raganovich?"

"I work for the Department." Not getting a response Alexander added, "And I live in Wellington. We seem to thrive on political gossip and rumors."

Grimble nodded. "He's been here many times and we've kept an unofficial eye on him. SIS is supposed to follow him. But they never share or tell us anything and I think they're always losing him. They weren't at the gallery last night."

Alexander tried to keep a straight face. "Maybe all the extra security kept them out?"

Grimble leaned into the last series of photos on the table. Alexander had them in chronological order. "These the two you gave me earlier?"

"Yes. How many security guards did we have last night? I thought two, just outside the door before the girl with the clipboard. I took these before the ceremony. It's a little dark outside, but looks like two more are out there. You can hardly make them out." Alexander pointed to the last print. "At closing, there are just two, here."

"There were four? They look identical."

"Meaning?" Alexander waited for Grimble to speak, but Alexander knew the inspector wasn't going to share his thoughts with a curator he knew nothing about.

"You have the negatives?" Grimble asked.

"Of course."

"Can you blow up the last two you did? I want to see their faces."

Alexander returned to the darkroom to work on the enlarged prints. What had he missed? Tsara was right. It was like *Blow-Up*. He thought of Jane Birkin, then he thought of Mel with her long black curly hair. He shuddered as he turned on the enlarger.

·   ·   ·

The security director, Peter MacIntosh, was the last person Grimble interviewed, in MacIntosh's own office. Not the best place to question him, but Grimble didn't want to make another enemy. He sensed that MacIntosh would get upset over any criticism and exhibit the sensitive emotions of the incompetent. Grimble had had enough experience dealing with such men in the force. Cadd came with him as a witness.

"We have adhered to the most stringent security standards as stipulated by our lenders and Lloyds of London, and they approved our measures, otherwise we would not have been able to mount the exhibit." MacIntosh wiped a bead of sweat off his forehead with his handkerchief, careful not to disturb his elaborate comb-over.

Grimble broke the silence. "Go on."

"And we have a strict closing policy, so I fail to see how a painting could have been removed when you said it was. Besides, didn't you have your own man virtually attached to the painting?"

"I never said when the painting went missing. Tell me about your procedure after the party."

"We had the two extra security guards at the front, you agreed to, leave at closing time. Ten o'clock."

"There were four."

"No, two."

"No, four. Look." Grimble pulled grainy photos out of a folder showing two guards inside the doors, and outside in the courtyard the faint outlines of two similar guards.

"We only hired two extra guards. I don't understand. I don't see the other two you say are there. Maybe they brought two more we didn't know about." MacIntosh used his handkerchief again.

"They're there, in the background, same build and outline as the two by the door. Go on." Grimble watched MacIntosh stare at the photos. He had seen the same

reaction before, when a suspect was unable to comprehend the evidence presented to him.

MacIntosh coughed and ran his right hand over his
mustache. "I'll talk to the security company. There must
be an explanation."

"Already taken care of."

MacIntosh lowered his head and did not speak.

"What is your closing procedure?" Grimble asked.

"I walk the gallery and see no one's in any of the rooms
and I release all the guards, floor by floor, starting at the
top. I saw your Sergeant Cadd near the painting and told
him he could go. And he did, right?"

Cadd nodded.

"Then I go to my office, check to make sure all is secure,
and then I leave, locking the front door with my master
key. I'm the last to leave, once the night security man ar-
rives. Then he walks the gallery as well, before he has a cup
of tea. He does random walks through the gallery, hourly
and makes a note at his post. You saw the clipboard, I take
it? You and your sergeant had already left, same with the
government young man and his girlfriend."

"Correct. And the night security man, does he have a
master key?" Grimble asked.

"No. And he is here till the morning. The first to arrive
is usually me. I get his report then release him. It's all stipulated in our security procedures from our lenders. I think
he arrived later than expected last night. He had difficulty
parking as it was Saturday night. It happens. I tell him he
has to budget more time on Fridays and Saturdays."

"Is he new to your staff?"

"He's one of my regulars. Been here forever. Retired copper, like me. Very reliable. I would trust him with anything."

"How come he didn't notice the painting was missing? It was perfectly obvious, wasn't it?"

"You'll have to ask him. We will, of course, conduct our own full and thorough inquiry and I will present my findings to the director in good time. But we won't be rushed into making false conclusions."

Grimble walked out of the office before he could say something he might regret. Cadd followed.

Alexander appeared again with the two photographs enlarged and laid them out on the library table. He handed the inspector a magnifying glass. "I found larger paper and pushed the exposure just enough to show as much detail as I could pull out of the negatives. What do you think?"

Grimble leaned over the two photos and used the magnifying glass to compare the prints. He gave the glass to Cadd.

"You know them, don't you?" Alexander asked. He scanned their faces, but neither showed any sign of recognition.

"I have to make a call." Grimble took the prints with him. "Good work."

CHAPTER TWENTY-SEVEN

Alexander called Catelin to update him and receive instructions. He dialed Tsara to tell her he would be working late, and they would not eat together on Sunday night. She said that was fine, she had plans to visit her parents.

The small white government van was parked on Shortland Street. Alexander found the keys on the rear right tire and did not query how Catelin had procured a van so quickly. He scanned the area as he adjusted his mirror. No one seemed interested in him or his van. He drove around the city, working through the manual gears and selected one-way streets until he was sure no one was following. Then he headed to Epsom and Castle Drive.

He parked on Mountain Road and walked to the end of the cul-de-sac and onto the Castle property. Built in the mid-1860s, the Castle was so-named because it had a four-story concrete tower and a castellated turret. The house itself was wooden and had been turned into seven apartments. In the open carport among the other cars and empty spaces he saw Nikolai Raganovich's car. An immaculate four-door 1973 black Jaguar XJ12 with white trim tires. Easy to spot but difficult to follow, especially with the Jag's acceleration. He took a photo of the car and walked back to the van. He had not seen the car in Wellington and wondered if it was stationed here in Auckland. If so, who drove it when Raganovich was in Wellington? He looked up at the sky. Dark clouds were building over Mount Eden and it looked like rain.

At the Mountain Road intersection he had noted cars, windows and possible vantage points. He shot a few more frames. If he were SIS, he would have a static observation post, a borrowed room with a window facing the Castle to view the spy's comings and goings, with a tail car positioned nearby, out of sight, but able to spot the Jag once it exited the cul-de-sac. He would have cars positioned nearby, on Clive and Almorah Roads, switching out occasionally. The Russian would never notice. But Soviet spies were supposed to be experts in counter-surveillance and detection, Alexander had read. So Raganovich could ignore any tail he had, unless he did not want to be followed. Alexander's plan was to blend into the convoy of cars following the Russian. He could imagine the recriminations later when they had lost the Jaguar and blamed each other and suspected the small white van was another Russian ploy. Unless the SIS knew about his van and somehow they were using him.

Alexander did not imagine that possibility then. Later, he would have second thoughts.

But Alexander did have time to think why Catelin had instructed him to follow the Soviet. Did Catelin suspect the Soviet of stealing the painting? What about the two or four Maori guards who were inside and outside the gallery? Grimble seemed to hint that they were responsible for the heist. Why wasn't he following or searching for the two who were outside the gallery? He presumed he would find out soon enough. He would follow his orders and concentrate on the Soviet spy.

Of all the things he should not do, Alexander thought about knocking on the door of Natasha's apartment in the Castle. "Hi Natasha! Remember me? You tried to seduce me last year when I was here with my girlfriend. Don't worry, we've broken up, but you probably know this. Everyone else does. Thought I'd drop in and see you. How's it going?" He would claim he had been visiting someone else in the building. What would he say? 'Zdravstvuj, Natasha.' Hello in Russian. It was a stupid idea. What if she invited him inside and the Soviet spy was waiting to grill him? "Welcome, Alexander. Sit down, make yourself comfortable. Don't mind these electrodes."

He settled back in the driver's seat and made sure his rear-view and side mirrors had a clear view of the cul-de-sac. He wanted to conserve his last roll of Tri-X. He would have to get more film on Monday. If Alexander was the Soviet, he thought, he would be devious. The Soviet had left before the gallery had closed. He would have an accomplice steal it for him. He had been talking to Mark Rose.

Despite the dead-end street, Alexander speculated that Raganovich had several options. He could walk over to Glenfell Place and jump into another car, if he had an accomplice. Or he could walk around Mount Eden, take a bus on Mount Eden Road into the city, then another bus to Parnell and visit Mark Rose. That would take too long, if there were buses running, and Alexander wasn't sure about access to the summit from the back of Castle Drive.

His head ached. He had to keep Mel from interfering with his concentration. Though he did plan to visit her dojo. He tried to imagine what it would be like to be thrown by her and have her sit on him. Nothing like long boring hours of surveillance to get him fantasizing about sex.

His mind wandered to images of Deborah. He was in her apartment, across from Winter's house. He half-closed his eyes as he visualized her, like a Klimt painting, long curly red hair, soft white skin glowing in the golden dawn light seeping in through her window. The faint sound of Erik Satie's piano music came to his ears as he daydreamed, but then he spotted the black Jaguar, driven by a tall blonde woman in a headscarf. Was it Natasha? If it was, she had lost weight, although it was difficult to tell as she turned left onto Mountain Road. He thought he heard drums before he realized it was raining.

Should he follow her? Or should he wait to see if the Russian appeared by foot or in another car, a car he would not be able to identify, unless he saw the Russian clearly? He couldn't see anything without his wipers on. He started his engine and pulled out. The terrible noise against the roof of the van gave him a headache and he feared he would lose her before she reached Khyber Pass Road. He had to wait for two cars to pass him before he could follow the Jag. The downpour added to the confusion. Did a SIS spotter have eyes on his white van? Was another car about to follow the Jag? His wipers were on full speed but he couldn't see anything..

He spotted the Jag as it crossed the Khyber Pass intersection and continued on to Park Road. A dark-colored Chrysler Valiant roared past him and went through a red light, sending a cascade of water against his van. He couldn't see the driver but heard the screech of brakes. He stopped at the light to make sure no oncoming cars would hit him as he turned right onto Khyber Pass Road. He knew he would lose sight of the Jag and the Valiant before the light turned green but estimated he could intercept the Jaguar if he accelerated to Broadway and made a left onto

Parnell Road. He pressed the accelerator to the floor and willed the small white government van to go faster on the wet road.

He couldn't see the Jaguar ahead of him on Parnell Road. The rain had slowed to a light drizzle but still cut visibility. He had no idea if anyone was following him. He gambled that she would head to Mark Rose's house on Gibraltar Crescent. He didn't want to take a direct route, as that would show the van to whoever was following her. He turned off Parnell Road and went around Birdwood Crescent till he came to a place where he could park. He ran down the steps of 8A and through the garden and a line of trees before he came to a path behind the Domain next to the railway line: the Ho Chi Minh trail he remembered from when he attended the University of Auckland.

Once he was adjacent to Mark Rose's house, on the trail, he found another garden he could walk through and came up on Gibraltar Crescent. No one saw him as he strolled around the bend and spotted the black Jaguar with the white-rimmed tires parked opposite Mark's address. The street was deserted. He checked his wet shoes and brushed off grass stuck to his trousers. His denim jacket was soaked. He kept in a crouched position as he checked movement from any windows, in case anyone might be watching. He saw nothing and walked almost to Parnell Road where he had an unobstructed view to the Jaguar.

Now he was faced with the inevitable wait. He did not know if Natasha had dropped off the car and walked away, or if she was with Mark. Maybe she was trying to seduce him, just to keep her touch. Or Nikolai Raganovich could be walking into Mark Rose's house now, from below the street, out of sight. The Soviet diplomat could have used the Ho Chi Minh trail like Alexander and come in the back way.

He spotted a car like the dark-colored Valiant he had seen earlier making its way around the Crescent. Did they know about Mark Rose, or were they cruising through Parnell hoping to spot the black Jaguar? The Valiant parked between two other cars, its wipers staying on. He walked up Parnell Road to Birdwood Crescent and his van, removed his jacket and wiped his face. He drove onto Parnell Road and positioned himself further around Gibraltar Crescent, out of sight of the Valiant, but with a clear view of either exit from the Crescent. There was a turn-off to another side street that lead to a warren of other narrow streets, but they all fed into Parnell Road. It was already dark with little traffic on Sunday night. The Soviet could walk into Mark's, retrieve the painting, put it in the Jaguar and drive off. Once in a diplomatic bag with seals from the Embassy, the painting would never be recovered. It would be placed in a large crate bound for another Embassy and a circuitous route to the Kremlin. Captain Cook in Moscow. It was an idea Alexander could not grasp. Let alone the idea of the Soviet stealing the Captain. Why would he? Another counter-espionage trick to destabilize the country? Payback for the trial and accusing him of being a spy? He was still here and had not departed quickly like his other spies. Why was he still here? To steal Captain Cook out of the country?

Or maybe it was a false lead and the Maori had the painting and Alexander would hear about it in the morning. He wanted to keep an open mind. There had been four Maori guards, two real and two fake. Had the fake ones stolen the painting? He did not understand what had happened, but made himself comfortable and settled in for a long surveillance in his small white government van.

CHAPTER TWENTY-EIGHT

The dark-colored Valiant roared by at nine o'clock. No more overtime for them, Alexander thought. He waited ten minutes before he started the engine and cruised around the Crescent again. He spotted the Jaguar in the same place and found a better parking space at the apex of the Crescent where he had a good view from the rear window of Mark's entrance and the Jaguar. He craved a hot tea and a bun, but nothing was open, and his thermos had been broken by the ordinary-looking man in Wellington. If he drank tea he would have to pee, and he didn't have a milk bottle. But he did have his camera so he played with his aperture and timing and adjusted the focus, ready to shoot when needed.

As he waited, he realized how fortunate he had been with his surveillances of Winter and the shadow minister's girlfriend. His current mission might take all night. The Soviet could appear with the painting early in the morning when no one was about, and any vehicle would stand out following the Jaguar. Alexander figured that if the car left, he would lose sight of it and his only option would be to motor over to Castle Drive and confirm it had arrived at the Russian's apartment. If the Jaguar sped to another destination, he would never locate it. He adjusted his denim jacket over the passenger seat to dry.

Resigned to his new strategy, Alexander thought about Mel, and what an impression she had made on him at the gallery opening. She was unlike Deborah or any other woman he knew. He recalled his last assignment in Wellington, the photographs he had taken of Kathy and her political lover, and what fate awaited them. If he told Tsara what he had done, spying on a friend and turning the photographs over to his boss for political and monetary gain, what would she do? No one stirred on the street, just a black Labrador following a scent and a few cats guarding their territory. When he saw the dog, he thought of Deborah again. "Alexander," he muttered, "you are worse than a dog in heat."

He shook his head to clear his thoughts and realized he had not come to terms with what Deborah had told him. How other people viewed him. It wasn't because he didn't care, as he had never considered such an idea before. Did he not have a well-developed sense of self, or was he ignorant of his true nature? The whole idea of his self was perplexing. It kept him awake for the rest of the night, parked in a deserted side street in Parnell as it got colder.

Alexander had sunk in his seat and noticed at first light he had a radio underneath the console. He had put his denim jacket on and wound the window up. He half-turned the ignition to switch on the radio. The speaker blasted Bob Dylan's voice and he adjusted the volume so only he could hear the music. *John Wesley Harding*. His favorite Dylan album. He could never work out what Tom Paine had to do with the title song, but the melody was catchy and when it finished he realized he was listening to what had once been the pirate radio station Hauraki, now land-based. He turned it off. He wanted to concentrate on the house, but he kept humming the tune to himself.

He caught movement out of the corner of his eye. A large man in an overcoat was carrying a package to the Jaguar. Alexander turned to focus his camera on the figure placing the package in the car's trunk. The motor drive sounded like an automatic weapon.

CHAPTER TWENTY-NINE

"Check out the headline!" Henry dropped Monday's *Herald* on the kitchen table.

"You actually brought the paper in? What's up?"

Mel read the headline next to the photo of Captain Cook. "We saw him Saturday night."

"Yes. And look who's claiming to have kidnapped the Captain."

"Do you think it's your friend, again? He attracts trouble, doesn't he?"

"He's *your* friend. You're the one who rescued him in the bush. Oh shit!"

"What?" Mel was about to boil water for tea, but saw Henry turn pale.

"Oh no." Henry ran to the back door. Mel heard noises, groaning sounds, a large cry followed by silence. She waited for him to reappear.

Henry returned to the kitchen, pale and trailing dust. "My notebooks!"

"What about them?"

"They're gone. Gone!" He collapsed into a kitchen chair and put his hands to his head and his head into his knees. "Fuck! The FBI have stolen them. I knew it. I hid them, but I never knew he would search there. What am I going to do?"

"FBI? Who? What search?"

"I hid them under the kitchen. I thought they'd never find them if they broke in."

"You mean someone's burgled my house?"

"It's beneath the house and how would they know to look there? I mean, nothing's been touched here, right? No signs of a break-in? None of my albums have been touched. I would know."

"Shit!" Mel ran her hands through her locks. "It's my house and you're worried about your albums? You were the jaded kiwi, but you gave back the Tear. Now you're the fucked kiwi."

Henry was close to tears, his eyes darting everywhere.

Mel shrugged. "If you're talking about the States, you should go, with or without your damn notebooks."

"It's my life's work in them. Even if I'm on the wrong track, they are immensely valuable."

"Maybe Wiremu stole them. I wouldn't put it past him."

"Why would he steal them?" Henry gasped.

"He was going to visit us, and he hasn't yet, has he? You told him about them when we were in Hokianga. Remember? Maybe he came over when you weren't here."

"Makes more sense than Mr. FBI man. I doubt the FBI would look under the house first before tearing the house apart."

"If there was a break-in, I'd've sensed it."

"How would you know?"

"I just would. I have powers." Mel poured boiling water into her teapot.

"I still don't know why the FBI want the notebooks. It's not like there are valuable secrets in them."

"They don't know that. Besides, how did the FBI know about them? And what do you mean, not valuable secrets?"

"Well, it's complicated." Henry ran his hands through his hair with a pained expression.

"It always is with you."

"I need your support right now. This is horrible."

"Oh, Henry. Lighten up, will you? Look what happened. The break-in at your hotel room in New York. You know? All the fuss and violence? Someone knew about them, didn't they? And back then it wasn't the FBI who knew about the notebooks first." Mel put both her hands on her hips as she faced Henry. "Think about it. I have. It's always bothered me."

"What do you mean?"

"Well, the Soviets knew first, and dispatched their goons. Ask yourself, how did they know about the notebooks? They didn't know what was in them, but thought they were valuable. So valuable they would torture you, maybe kill you." She poured tea into his favorite mug that read "Don't be negative — think like a proton."

"So how did they know about them? I sure as hell didn't tell them." Henry ran his hands through his hair again.

"But someone did. Maybe they worked at your lab in Long Island. And that someone was a spy for the Soviets. How else would they have known?"

"Shit. And they probably thought I was a spy as well."

"I don't think so. You're here, aren't you? They let you leave the country. "

"How about the Soviets stealing my notebooks here?"

Mel shrugged. "Take your pick, Henry. The Soviets? The cops? The FBI or Wiremu? You have quite a list!"

CHAPTER THIRTY

Moana walked out of the dairy on Park Road with the Monday morning paper and milk for their tea. The *Herald* had bought the story, and included a photo of Captain Cook, but not the correct painting. Down Grafton Road she scanned the neighbors' houses and cars for anything odd, anyone spying on them. Adjacent to the scarred landscape of Grafton Gully there were still older two-story wooden houses at the bottom of the road on each side. Ricky had taken the Holden to his family farm in Pukekohe. It was good to have him out of the way. The house, which stood against urban progress in its scruffy Edwardian glory, could only fit so many egos.

"Read it to me again, brother. You have such a fine voice." Rawiri relaxed on the sofa in the living room, surrounded by boxes of martial arts equipment.

"If you make me another cuppa and a slice of bread with honey."

"Oh, just read it, will you."

"A new Maori rights group calling themselves 'Land Rights for Maori Justice' claims to have stolen the recently installed Captain Cook portrait by John Webber at the opening of the 'Two Worlds of Omai' exhibition at the Auckland City Art Gallery on Saturday night. A source at the gallery confirmed the painting is missing and has been replaced with a color reproduction. Next to the label is a small sign declaring it is being repaired.

"The director of the Art Gallery stated the painting was not present in the gallery but refused to acknowledge it had been stolen. Calls to the police for confirmation went unanswered.

"A Maori group is claiming they are about to release a list of demands for the return of ancient tribal lands stolen since the Treaty of Waitangi and that once their demands have been met the painting will be returned. Calls to Maori leaders and Land Rights activists revealed the possibility of a new activist group, but none of their leaders were known.

"An art historian from the University of Auckland, Professor Anthony Browne, called the painting one of the most famous in New Zealand and a priceless icon of the discovery of New Zealand by Europeans in the 18th century."

"Shit. What? How valuable is priceless?" Wiremu asked.

"A Maori name for the group would be better," Moana said. "I didn't like it in the first place, and now seeing it in print, well, it's daft."

"Yes, would be good, Moana, but little Wiremu here can't speak much Maori and is afraid he'll get it wrong."

"Hey! I know a waiata, a few sayings. I'm still learning. It's a journey we all have to make."

"Do we have the list of lands we want back?" Rawiri asked.

CHAPTER THIRTY-ONE

Alexander tucked the van out of sight on a small road off Grafton Road and walked to Tsara's house with his camera bag on his shoulder. "You'll never guess where I've been all night," he gushed when she opened the front door. "But first I need to pee!"

Later: "Well, as you read in the *Herald*." Alexander sipped his tea and took a bite of Tsara's cake. "It was stolen sometime after we left for the party. The usual Maori are suspects, and I've been told to keep an eye on the Soviet diplomat we saw Saturday night. I've been hanging out where he's staying in Epsom. But here the plot thickens."

Tsara held her hands up. "No more cake. You have to finish the story."

"He used a decoy to drive his car to where the painting was stashed. I think. I gambled and followed the car and parked where I could see both the car and the house. I thought she had gone too."

"She? The decoy?"

"Yes. A young Russian woman I lost sight of. I didn't want to be seen following her and by the time I figured out where she was, she was gone."

Alexander did not know what to make of the face Tsara made.

"I've seen her before, but she disappeared. I stayed all night waiting for the car to move. At about six the Soviet showed, put a package in the boot and sped off. It was the size of the painting, but it was dark. I lost him when he turned off Parnell Road onto one of the side streets. I couldn't follow because I sensed he was going to crisscross all over Parnell until he knew he didn't have a tail. I gambled and headed to where he was staying in Epsom, hid the van on a side street and went for a little walk. Sure enough, a few minutes later the Jag cruised to his dead-end street and backed into a space where I couldn't see him."

"My favorite spy."

"What, him?"

"No, you, silly. You made pretty big decisions and won. Or did you?"

"I called it in just now from a payphone, told everyone where the painting is. Well, where I think the painting might be. Anyway, it's out of my hands." He lowered his voice. "I think I deserve a present now."

Tsara went into the kitchen for another slice of her fruit cake. "You've turned into quite a ladies' man haven't you?"

"What?"

"First, it's that doctor. 'Oh, I do want to see your dojo,' and now it's a mysterious Russian woman."

The phone rang. Alexander leapt up. "I have a bad feeling."

Tsara blinked.

"Hello?"

"Newton, where are you? It's almost nine o'clock. Report to the gallery right away. Leave the van parked on Kitchener and come to the library. Bring your camera and any film you have."

Alexander looked at the phone, at his cake, and back at Tsara. He grabbed the slice.

"Who was that?" Tsara asked.

"The cop you don't like. I have to go." He was annoyed that Grimble knew where he was and had ordered him to work. And he had to develop the photos from last night. "We'll talk about what you just said later. What if I'm coming out of my shell? Can't be a shy young man all my life. And the gallery job helped. I have skills. Love your cake. See you."

.   .   .

District Commander Superintendent Thomas Jarvis had read the *Herald* first thing in the morning. He thought he was under siege from a new Maori group who held hostage "the most famous painting in New Zealand", as the *Herald* called it. They demanded the return of ancestral lands stolen by the Pakeha. He summoned Inspector Bernie Grimble to his office and demanded answers. Inspector Grimble summoned Alexander Newton to the gallery and demanded answers. Permanent Under-Secretary Richard Catelin had been summoned by his minister to account for what had just happened. The minister had been summoned by the Prime Minister who wanted to know why the most valuable painting in New Zealand, guarded by half the army and police force had been stolen. The Prime Minister had been assured the painting was perfectly safe in Auckland. The Prime Minister was furious. Catelin was on the first flight to Auckland. His minister did not trust the police there to find the painting. Which led to the question, who had the painting? The new Maori group, the Soviet diplomat, or someone else?

The editor of the *Herald* had slept in and a junior editor, unaware of the agreement with the commissioner not to publish anything about the painting, decided to go with the headline "Maori Land Rights group kidnaps Captain Cook'" for the early edition, the one delivered to homes. When the editor arrived, he changed the headline for the late edition to "Painting missing from gallery" and moved it off the front page. But the story was out and had been picked up by radio and TV news. The editor was embarrassed; the commissioner was furious.

CHAPTER THIRTY-TWO

Alexander was concerned he would be towed as he parked next to the gallery on Kitchener Street. Sergeant Cadd, who had been waiting for him, drove the van onto the pavement and told him not to worry, Grimble would be coming soon. Alexander went to develop the photos in the gallery's darkroom and thought nothing of Cadd's cavalier attitude about illegally parking an unmarked van.

By eleven Alexander had spread the prints on a table in the library. He could make out the outline of Natasha. She wore a headscarf: part of her disguise, he thought. The Jag had stayed in the same place for hours until dawn. It had a number plate with the letters DC, a diplomatic plate. The silver letters were just visible in the grainy photo.

A tall man, in an overcoat like the one Alexander had seen in Wellington, emerged from a pathway on the far side of the Crescent. He carried a large package wrapped in plastic. Alexander had shot one frame of the package being slid into the trunk and another of the Russian driving away. The last photo on his roll had been the Jaguar turning into a side street. He did not have any film to document the car parked in Castle Drive about twenty minutes later.

Grimble, once briefed by Alexander, drove Sergeant Cadd and the photos to police headquarters. Alexander had another set of prints in the darkroom, where he returned to see if he had missed anything.

.   .   .

"Do you have any photos you shot at my party?" Colin asked when Alexander appeared outside the darkroom.

"Oh, yeah. I have the film in my bag."

"What did you think?"

"What? Of Cook missing?"

"No, the party. Was it radical or what?"

"Colin, I respect your professionalism in the gallery, and I've been thinking hard what to say here. But to be blunt, you were dressed as a Nazi, as were a bunch of your friends. One had an SS uniform. You had a Wehrmacht uniform!"

"Yeah. Weren't they cool?"

"No, Colin, they weren't. Let me explain. Nazis did terrible things to other humans. Correction. They weren't human. They were monsters! They organized the Holocaust. They killed millions of people. Millions. Gays, Jews, gypsies, retards, anyone they didn't like. It's not cool to dress like a Nazi, ever. I can speak for quite a few people who were upset by your uniform."

"We were having fun. It's innocent. The Nazis lost and good riddance to them."

"You don't get it, do you? Here's the film. You develop it. I'll see you tomorrow."

CHAPTER THIRTY-THREE

"What makes you think he would be so stupid as to hide Captain Cook where he lives?" Alexander was aware his voice was higher and louder than normal.

"I've been told to tell you to not follow him anymore. They think you've been made, and the Soviet is aware of you."

"They? You mean Grimble? How would he know that? I never told him."

"There are parts of this investigation you are not aware of and will not be briefed on. Your job was to keep an eye on him. And now you don't have to."

"It was Grimble."

"As I said, there are many parts to this investigation, and you are only one piece. All you have to do is follow orders. Is that clear?"

"No. It isn't." Alexander realized he was now shouting. He had to calm down. He couldn't risk being dismissed by Catelin. He had been fired from the *Listener* over one word in a thousand-word article about Nicolas Poussin when he described the Queen's curator Anthony Blunt as a "spy" and the editor had objected. He'd lost his temper over *one word*. Now he was doing it over Captain Cook and one Soviet.

"This is the last shot?" Catelin asked as he surveyed the prints.

"Yes. He turned off Parnell Road in his Jag. And a few minutes before he had placed the painting, or what looked to be a package that had the same dimensions as the painting, into his trunk. As you can see here." Alexander pointed to a blurred photograph he had taken a long time to develop and produce a good as print as he could conjure up from the poor negative he had captured. He expected Catelin to take out his pipe and start stuffing it with tobacco. But Catelin stayed still, moving his eyes across the fresh set of prints Alexander had laid out on the library table. The permanent Under-Secretary had flown from Wellington to oversee the return of Captain Cook and represent the government in any police action.

"He would have dropped it off somewhere. Somewhere where we wouldn't find it."

"Newton!" Catelin took a deep breath. "I stuck my neck out for you, to have you escort this unique painting of Captain Cook to Auckland. You had one job. To make sure it was safe. And it's been stolen. I don't want to be lectured by you on what the Soviets can or can't do. Is that clear?"

"I suppose the cops told you I lost the Russian deliberately, and if I had followed the Jag I would have seen where the painting was hidden?" Alexander did not mean his words to sound so sarcastic. "And I suppose the SIS know all about this, because I didn't see any cars go whizzing by in pursuit. You know they pulled out from their position opposite Mark Rose's place on Gibraltar Crescent at exactly nine o'clock last night? As if they couldn't work on overtime."

Catelin patted his pockets.

"The Soviet knows he is under surveillance by the SIS. If he spotted me he would have thought I was part of them. And if Grimble is going to raid where Natasha lives, they aren't going to find anything, are they?"

Catelin stopped looking in his suit pockets and stared at Alexander. "You think he would drop the painting off somewhere between where you lost him and his flat at the Castle?"

"I read the book you lent me. The KGB are experts in counter-surveillance. Natasha might have been waiting at another destination for him and spirited the painting to a safe space."

"You think Natasha is involved in this?"

"She drove the car, didn't she? She's staying at the Castle."

"Don't do anything until we tell you," said Catelin. "Go back to your place and rest."

"Yes, sir." Alexander drove back to Tsara's, thinking about Natasha and how he could engineer an encounter with her or at least follow her, to see if she would lead him to the hiding place for the painting.

CHAPTER THIRTY-FOUR

The first thing Alexander did on his way to Mel's dojo was stop at a second-hand furniture store called Steptoe & Son to buy a used single mattress. The owner helped him carry the mattress into the van and had made a comment about how Alexander could use it. Alexander thought the comment inappropriate. He had spent little of the money Catelin had given him for operational expenses, and he wanted to be comfortable if he had to endure more nights in the small white government van. He positioned the mattress to act as a sofa where he could relax in comfort while looking at his mirrors. It also fitted flat, if he had to sleep in the van.

Why was he going to see Mel at her dojo and not stay next to the phone at Tsara's, where he could be contacted? Training, he rationalized. If he was going to be a spy, he would need martial-arts expertise. How hard could it be?

He found the dojo above a boutique on Ponsonby Road. The street had changed since his student days and was now lined with small shops, clothing boutiques and other small businesses. Up the wooden stairs the room had rubber mats spread across the floorboards. There was a line of women's shoes along the wall next to the door. He took off his shoes and hung his denim jacket on a hook. There were students in a wide circle. Inside the circle was

Mel. He spotted an outline of a male with long hair on the other side of the room leaning against the window.

"See how I'm standing? Balance is key. I want to keep my balance but make my attacker lose his. It's difficult to think of balance when someone is trying to harm you, but with practice it comes naturally. So, what we're going to do first are small moves. They are small. Nothing dramatic. Here, Annie, come at me with both hands aimed at my throat. The attack could be anywhere on my body but let's keep it here for the time being."

Annie threw both hands at Mel's neck.

"Remember, we are doing everything slowly first. We want to get comfortable moving our bodies. Because you're just moving your body. She has me by the throat, but I don't use force against force. How many of you are strong enough to fight off a large male attacker? Okay, I have the wrong group here."

Three of the larger women laughed.

"Notice I do not tense up. You can't move if you're tense. How do you stay relaxed when you're being attacked?"

The three larger women laughed again.

"What I do is I move my right leg back a little and move my hips to the right like so, and keep my shoulders aligned. I windmill my arms clockwise, to the left and down to the right. Nothing too forceful. Small movements. See? I'm not punching or pulling or grabbing. But Annie is off-balance and I step at an angle, keeping in the same direction I'm going."

Mel moved her right foot and, with her arms moving clockwise, Annie lost her footing. "We haven't rehearsed. I keep my balance, she loses hers. There."

Annie fell forward and rolled over to avoid falling on her face. "See how she recovers by rolling? Comes naturally after more training. You can catch yourself before falling. We are going half-speed here, at the most. And she's relaxed. She can't hurt herself. We'll work on relaxing you. Just worry about the small movements for now."

Mel looked around the room and saw Alexander by the door. "Oh. we have a new training partner. Girls, meet Alexander. Alexander, come into the circle. Oh, good you have your shoes off. Stand here. Now come at me with both hands."

Alexander tried to grab her neck. He had not heard her talk, and was faster than the female attacker, but she matched his speed. She stepped back, moved her hips and grabbed his right hand, sliding her grip to his right wrist. Her left hand pressed on his right triceps and she moved slightly, bending her knees to force Alexander to the floor, still in her grip, her left hand pressing on his upper right arm. He grimaced as his face hit the mat. He managed to break his fall with his free hand, but the others gasped at the sound.

"You okay?" Mel asked. "Remember, we always say pain is your ego leaving your body."

The women laughed.

"I forgot to say, tap out if you feel pain."

Alexander kept a straight face. He was pleased to have such physical attention applied by Mel.

.   .   .

Alexander sat cross-legged on the mat, relieved his first martial arts encounter was over. He had learned to tap out after the wrist locks, arm bars and other techniques tried on him. He had been redirected to the floor countless times, but he couldn't complain.

Mark, who had kept in the corner, came over and Mel introduced him to Alexander. "Didn't I see you at the opening?" Alexander asked as he got up. His shoulders and knees were going to hurt the next day. He knew his face was red from all the contact with the rubber mats.

"Yeah," said Mark. "Now I recognize you. You were with Tsara, the photographer."

"You know her?"

"Been around a long time. She always used to come to the demos. Stop the war. Stop this, stop that, save the whales." Mark smiled; he sounded sincere, not ironic. "You didn't bring her? She'd love the dojo."

"Maybe seeing me thrown around, but it's not her cup of tea." Auckland was as small a place as Wellington, Alexander realized. Everyone knew everyone else or at least someone connected to someone else.

Mark clapped his hands together. "Why don't we go out to that new restaurant just around the corner?"

"You mean the Firehouse?" Mel replied.

"Yeah. But I don't think we can all fit in my truck."

"Not to worry. I'll take my car. Is it open? It's Monday night."

Mark smiled.. "It's open, and I've taken care of the reservation."

"Can I hitch a ride?" Alexander asked Mel. He didn't want Mark to know he had a van.

Walking to her BMW Mel kept her leather jacket open as she was still flushed from the workout. "How did you find your first time?" she asked once she turned the ignition. Alexander adjusted his seat and ran his hands down his outstretched legs. "Not as bad as I thought but better than I expected."

"What do you mean?"

Alexander tried to shrug and pulled a face. His shoulders hurt. "If you want to know, I was floored."

Mel laughed and the curls around her face shook.

"And didn't you say pain was my ego leaving my body?"

"What? The pain?"

"No. Losing my ego. If I even have one. I've been wondering."

She glanced at him as she turned into a parking space across from the Firehouse, a historic brick building wedged into the corner of Williamson Avenue and Rose Road that had once housed the Ponsonby Fire Brigade, but was now an expensive restaurant. Mel parted her lips and leaned forward before adjusting her hair. She looked around the street then turned to Alexander. "What do you do at the gallery?"

"Which gallery?"

"How many are there? Auckland, I suppose."

"Oh, I'm just here to look after the Captain Cook painting."

"How's it working out for you?" She scrutinized his face.

He kept still.

"Sorry, I didn't mean to be rude." She smiled.

"No. You can never be rude. Not after you threw me around like I was a dish rag. Good question, though, since it's missing. Which reminds me. Got to make a phone call. Do you mind?" He pointed across the street to the bright red call box. "I'll be right in."

Tsara answered on the first ring.

"Where are you?" She sounded annoyed, which was unusual for Tsara, Alexander thought, but he had not seen her for a long time.

"Out in my van, I'm afraid. Work. Any calls for me?"

"No. Are you coming back?"

"Not sure. Got work to do. I'll tell you later, I promise, but don't wait up for me. Gotta go."

When Mel and Alexander found their table in the back, Mark had already ordered a local Cabernet Sauvignon and was tasting it. He nodded and the sommelier poured the wine for Annie, Mel then Alexander before replenishing Mark's empty glass. "How are you feeling, Alexander?" Mark asked. "A little sore?"

"Oh, not bad. Enjoyed it, actually."

"Now you know why I tried to be invisible. Didn't want to be picked."

"Good move."

Mark raised his full glass. "Let's drink a toast to Alexander and his brave audition." They clicked glasses. "Speech! Speech!"

"Well, here's to Captain Cook!" Alexander proposed.

Mark almost spat out a mouthful of wine. He put his napkin to his mouth. "You do know it's stolen?"

"Oh yes. But without the Captain I would never have met you all." Alexander emptied his glass and insisted on refilling everyone's.

Mark dominated the conversation: his commune where no one wanted to work, his own brand of marijuana versus the wild plants he had found growing around his property, the current government and how repressive it was—the usual issues, Alexander assumed. He was content to listen and gaze at Mel without, he hoped, the others noticing.

Mark ordered more wine from the attentive somme-lier, making three bottles, and they had consumed three courses. Alexander could not remember when he had eaten so well and found it odd that a student revolution-ary could be such an epicure. The French onion soup had a hard layer of molten cheese on top. When he broke through he pulled out long strings of cheese he tried to eat without cutting them. He first used his teeth, before he tried his soup spoon and then his fingers, while Mel tried not to laugh. Mark glanced at Alexander's performance with the cheese strands, and how Mel looked at Alexander. Annie was engrossed in retrieving a large slice of onion at the bottom of her earthenware bowl.

Next time, Alexander decided, he would not order the Cornish hen. He hadn't realized how small it was. He had no idea what was in the stuffing: the menu had been taken away, and he couldn't recall what it said. The apple pie à la mode was more filling even though he had no idea what à la mode meant and didn't want to ask. Mel gave him her vanilla ice cream; she kept glancing at him, Alexander thought.

The waiter brought small glasses of port for the table. Later he placed the check in the middle of the table and Mark grabbed it. Taking out a large roll of notes, he counted out the dollars and left, Alexander noted, a generous tip. "For the workers," Mark smiled.

CHAPTER THIRTY-FIVE

Alexander walked with Mel to where she had parked. Mark had left with Annie in his red truck. The fresh air went to Alexander's head and he swayed.

"Are you okay?" Mel asked.

"Yes. I had such a good time tonight. I don't want it to end. Do you want to come to the top of Mount Eden?" He moved closer to her. "The stars are out. It's a special place, and I haven't been there in ages."

Mel unlocked her door and turned to face him. She had a flashback of Henry taking her to the summit the last night he was in Auckland before he flew to America, to his new position at a lab in Long Island, New York. She had thought she would never see him again. Henry claimed he had seduced her in the darkness of the parking lot, but Mel had been in control. She shuddered. She didn't know if it was a good memory or a bad one. Now she was struck by the look on Alexander's face, his vulnerability, and how close he was standing to her.

Mel and Henry had had a verbal fight before she left for the dojo today, and she was still upset. If Henry left her again, it would be final. Why would he return? Hadn't she rescued him in New York from American mobsters and Albanian thugs? Had she wasted the last six months of her life trying to make something out of Henry, only to see him fly off again and leave her? With or without his damn notebooks. She didn't want to go home and face him.

Alexander kept his eyes on Mel's face, waiting for her response. He could tell she was thinking. He hoped it was of him but could not be sure. Alexander the irresistible spy, the dashing curator, the mysterious government agent from Wellington. He had his mouth open but couldn't think of anything witty to say.

She sighed. "Why not? I need to get out more."

"Can you drive me to my van? I left it near your dojo."

"Oh, you are sneaky! Didn't want Mark to know? The incognito curator?"

"Are you able to drive? We did drink rather a lot. Or shall I follow you?" Alexander took deep breaths to clear his head.

"Let's do it. I know a short cut. Follow me."

.   .   .

Had Alexander paid more attention, he would have seen Mark in his red truck on Ponsonby Road waiting for his small white government van to appear. Despite reading and theorizing about counter-surveillance in his book about the KGB, he was not used to practicing such security procedures, especially after three glasses of wine and thoughts of Mel in her BMW just ahead of him. The red pickup followed his van to the entrance to the summit.

Several cars were parked with their lights off in the parking lot. Most faced the city rather than the Manukau harbor. Alexander pulled in next to her, away from the other cars and furthest from the trig point at the top of the parking lot. It was dark, and impossible to see if any of the cars were occupied, but one was rocking side to side.

Mel got out of her car and climbed into Alexander's van. She smiled. "Nice and cozy. Yours?"

"No, borrowed. From the government."

"Oh, and you have a mattress. Got plans?"

"Now you're making me blush."

"You've turned red. My goodness. I made you blush, Alexander. You of all people."

"What do you mean? Just cos you threw me around tonight doesn't mean I don't have feelings."

"Oh, you're too sensitive. Can't you tell when I'm teasing you? And those dimples," Mel sighed. "Blushing and dimples."

Alexander leaned back and turned off the motor. "Dimples?" He screwed up his face.

"Why the look?" Mel asked.

"I'm sorry. I can't help myself. It's just I've never met anyone like you before, and I don't know how to act. I'm thrown. First physically, and now, well, I don't know." He wanted to shrug but his shoulders were sore. Everything ached. If he knew the effect his dimples had, they would probably ache as well.

Mel looked at him again in a way Alexander couldn't decipher. To break the tension he said, "Let's walk around the crater and count the stars." He opened his door and Mel followed, shivering as she zipped up her leather jacket.

Alexander marched to the trig point so he could see over Epsom and across towards the Manukau. He walked further along the trail on the south side of the extinct volcano until he came to the split in the path around the main crater. He tried to see flashing blue lights, a visible sign of a police presence, on Castle Drive, but saw nothing. All he heard was the dull hum of a city that refused to sleep.

"It's a little dark, isn't it?" He stated the obvious as Mel bumped into him. Low clouds obscured the stars and the moon. He looked down at her boots. "You don't wear bell-bottoms, do you?"

"Not one pair."

"Don't like them myself. I'm just not fashionable."

Mel sighed, almost touching him, but she didn't move away. He leaned forward and held her waist to draw her nearer. She did not resist and pressed her hips against his. It felt different from when she was in contact with him in the dojo.

Alexander could smell the wine on her breath, sweet and close. He brushed his lips against hers. She pressed herself closer to him and kissed him tenderly. She placed her hands on his shoulders. They spent a long time just touching each other's lips in slow little kisses. They could hear each other's heavy breathing. Alexander pressed against her. She moved her hands to clasp his neck and she whispered into his ear, "Let's go to your van."

Alexander unlocked the double doors and Mel climbed in first. He almost fell on top of her.

"Have you locked it?" she asked.

He draped one leg over her. "We're safer than Captain Cook."

"That's not exactly reassuring," she murmured into his ear.

He was intoxicated with the wine, her presence, the smell of her hair, the soft seductive feel of her breath on his lips. The rest of the night was a blur .

Alexander reran the events in his mind the next morning, and questioned if they were real, or if he had imagined them. He hoped it had lasted for an eternity. But he had the impression it was quicker than he had wished.

.   .   .

He woke up cold, alone, with his trousers off, and the glass misted up. He looked out of the driver's window and saw Mel's car had gone. The man at Steptoe & Sons had been right. He dressed and walked to where he could see the Castle and flashing blue lights. So they were raiding the Russian's apartment, trying to find a connection to the missing painting. No wonder they never called him. But he knew they would find nothing. The Russian was too clever. He decided to drive over to Gibraltar Crescent, but first he had to witness the sun rising over the Waitemata harbor. There were no clouds.

The sky took its time to change from a dark purple to a deep blue. Light was launched across the distant water, like rays shooting out at great speed, and a giant white orb rose from the water, as if it was the birth of the universe, and Alexander felt overawed by what he saw and what had happened to him with Mel. He glowed as the sun hit his face and he lifted his square chin to the brightening sky. He wished he was holding Mel now and they were witnessing the start of the day together. Life coming into the world again after darkness. Rangitoto, always a serene presence in the harbor, gradually became more distinct and changed from black to an intense, unfathomable green. He loved the light in Auckland. Everything seemed brighter, more intense, than in Wellington.

On Parnell Road, he saw the Crescent had been cordoned off by police cars. They were raiding Mark's place as well. He thought all they would find would be a few bags of marijuana. Would they press charges against him? He could hear Grimble's voice: "The law is the law." It was too early to hear the inspector's voice. He bought the morning paper, parked in his usual place and walked across to Tsara's. He was getting used to the van. And the mattress had been a touch of genius.

CHAPTER THIRTY-SIX

If Alexander had been a few minutes later, he would have seen Moana walk into the dairy to buy her *Herald* and a bottle of milk for her boys' tea.

Moana saw Ricky's Holden parked outside his house. She rushed inside and leapt into his arms and smothered his neck in kisses, her hair falling over his face. "When did you get in?" she asked.

"Just now. God, you smell so good. I missed you, Moana." Ricky Wong looked bigger than his average height with his barrel chest and thick arms. He had grown his straight black hair to his collar and almost over his eyes. He shook his head to stare into her deep brown eyes.

"Same here. Have you met Rawiri?"

"Yeah, we were just talking. Catching up. What are you doing?"

"Well, it's messy. Should I rush you upstairs or do you want a cuppa? No. Better we go into the kitchen."

"There's another story here."

Moana showed the paper to Wiremu and Rawiri who sat at the kitchen table, drinking tea. "We need a Maori name for our group and a list of lands we want back. But if the cops are searching for Captain Cook and a Soviet spy, it doesn't look good for us." Moana started to shake. Sweat came out on her forehead, her cheeks were wet as if she had been crying. She sobbed and gripped her hands together to stop them shaking.

Ricky went to hold her, but she moved away. She tried to raise her hands and took several deep breaths. She held her forehead as she kept her balance. Her face went pale and her eyes were dilated. Ricky guided her to a chair. She sat, as if in a trance, then jolted upright, her eyes shut tight.

The three men stared at her. Her eyes opened, red and out of focus. She started to talk in a language they could not understand.

When Moana had finished she stood still. She closed her mouth. She had nothing left in her. She gazed into the distance. She wiped her wet face with both hands and let out a series of fast deep breaths, to try and gain back her sanity. "Sorry. I, I, don't know. Oh, Ricky. Please forgive me Ricky, I love you, I'm sorry. You went through so much more. I'm sorry. I'm sorry." Tears rolled down her checks. Moana collapsed.

"Think I better take her upstairs."

"Yeah, mate. Need a hand?" Wiremu offered.

"No, I can manage." Ricky bent his knees and placed his right hand under her knees and his left around her back. He slowly rose and pulled her closer to his chest. Her arms flopped down, and he balanced her head against his chest. Her hair spread over his face and he blew away a few strands so he could see. He went through the kitchen door sideways, careful not to hit her head or her arms.

CHAPTER THIRTY-SEVEN

"You found Mark Rose's personal stash? A couple of plastic bags of what you hope is marijuana, and you let him go? Let me get this straight. Two highly organized and coordinated police raids at dawn, involving reams of paperwork and signatures for two search warrants from two different magistrates, who you contacted last night, who both called me in the morning, rather displeased, and you created two different search warrants because you didn't think one magistrate would sign both, because you were searching for the same painting in two different places. You requisitioned dozens of officers, all of whom are pulling overtime, because it was night or rather early Tuesday morning. And you find out it was in neither place? And you let Mark Rose go? And you haven't found Captain Cook?"

Grimble had held his breath throughout the commissioner's tirade. He now let out all his tension and frustration with one sentence. "We thought we had reliable information from two different sources." He took a deep breath. "We were obviously too late."

"And all we have is a couple of bags of weed. Really, Grimble? Under-Secretary Catelin is on his way to your headquarters now. Give him a full report and I will communicate with him. I must report to the minister. And why didn't Superintendent Jarvis brief me? We'll talk later, in person. Stand by for my call."

"I'm just following orders, commissioner," Grimble shot out as he heard the click again. He hated being made to look a fool. "At least no one died," he wanted to say.

CHAPTER THIRTY-EIGHT

Ricky came downstairs an hour later. Wiremu and Rawiri were still at the kitchen table, the *Herald* spread out in front of them. "How is she?" Rawiri asked.

"Asleep. Never seen her like that before."

"Well, she's a strong girl. But no one should have to go through what she went through. Pretty radical." Wiremu said.

"She's Ngapuhi. Built strong and tough."

Ricky wasn't going to argue with two of the hardest Maori he had ever seen.

"Tell me, Ricky, do you know the Russian in the papers, Nikolai Raganovich?"

"Oh, him," Ricky grinned. "It's a small world, isn't it?"

"Is it?" Wiremu asked.

"Yeah. If he's Russian, he's bought every martial arts weapon we have here. You've seen our store room in the front, right? Let me check our records."

Ricky came back with a card. "Here he is. Raganovich care of Natasha Windsor, 11 Castle Drive, Epsom. It's an apartment house, sort of. They call it the Castle, right? Pretty cool building. Top apartment, in the rear. Can't miss it."

Rawiri turned to Wiremu. "The joker they let in the gallery?"

"The same. He was a regular, I hear, and he can talk his way into anything."

"By the way, Ricky, did you bring any weed? You're still growing it? The super-genetic stuff?"

"Funny you should ask." Ricky pulled out a large plastic bag from his inside jacket pocket. "I think we all need therapy. I saw a whole stack of these at uni. I was just checking on the lab. Here, big protest tomorrow at noon. You might want to check it out."

Wiremu and Rawiri grabbed a poster each and whistled. Wiremu tapped the poster on the table. "We should go. See what's going on. Moana needs to go too. Meanwhile, you mentioned something about therapy?"

Ricky pushed his long hair from his eyes and opened the plastic bag full of buds as he watched the two Maori and their intense reaction before he produced Zig-Zag papers.

CHAPTER THIRTY-NINE

Alexander did not know how Tsara would react when he arrived early in the morning with the newspaper, a bottle of milk and pastries he had bought in Grafton. He wasn't her boyfriend, but he felt he was abusing his guest privileges.

She opened the front door, grabbed the milk and walked to the kitchen without looking at him, which to Alexander was a good sign. He used the bathroom first, washed as much as he could and joined Tsara at her kitchen table.

"What happened to you last night?"

"You haven't read the paper? We raided, I mean the cops raided the Soviet diplomat and Mark Rose's place as well. It was a big deal."

"Shit. Mark? Our Mark?"

"Yes, the same. Apparently, they think they are linked. I was there, I saw it all. But guess what?

"What?"

"They didn't find anything. No painting, nothing."

"All this for Captain Cook?"

"Yes. Some people seem to think he's important."

"Doesn't a Maori group claim they have Cook?"

"Well, it gets complicated. We don't know who has him. But I think the Russian or the Soviet, whatever you want to call him, does. And here it gets sticky."

"Sticky?"

"Yes. It's a technical spy term." Alexander kept a straight face.

"Oh, you. I can never tell when you're joking."

"I'm perfectly serious. If we don't get the painting back, my job is toast."

"Whatever happened to the shy old Alexander? The long-haired hippie with a beard and sandals? Save the whales, stop the war, up the government. You remember those sandals you wore all year, made of tires?"

"Oh yes. I do love shoes. Ruined a new pair of Italian loafers the other day but that's another story. And you are correct. Now I work for the government."

"So, what happened to you, Alexander?"

"I don't know." He lowered his head and looked at his old friend. "I grew up and wanted more. But I didn't know the price."

CHAPTER FORTY

"You came home late last night." Henry was about to plunge the French press for his morning coffee when he saw Mel come out of the shower. She had a towel wrapped around her hair and another around her body.

"Are you going to do anything about your notebooks?" she replied.

"And have the police tell me I should have given them to the Americans for safe keeping? No. I am not saying a word to anyone. Besides, if word leaks out about my notebooks, there go my job prospects anywhere."

"What are you going to do?" Mel stood still, dripping wet.

"I might be the jilted Kiwi, not the jaded Kiwi, but I made copies after my last interview with the FBI. Couldn't trust them."

"My god! You went all drama queen on me, and you had a backup copy?"

"Well, I'm supposed to be smart. Rejected in more ways than one, but still smarter than the average bear, or scientist."

Mel tightened the towel around her body. "What are your plans?"

"Go to Dunedin for a few days. See an old buddy. Work out what to do next. What about you?"

"Off to work. The same old thing." Mel sighed as she thought about her escapade in the small white government van. It was such a contrast to the time she had been with Henry at the top of Mount Eden.

"I'm flying out today," said Henry. "In the afternoon."

Mel went to the bedroom to dress. She could not reconcile how she felt, both excited and empty.

CHAPTER FORTY-ONE

"Thank you for meeting me here."

"Not at all commissioner. It's a little tense upstairs."

"Thought you wouldn't want another round of golf."

"Thank you." Grimble could never find the right words to say to the commissioner.

"And I'm not sure who's bugging who now. Your car is as good as it gets."

"I don't understand."

"Well, it's all gone to shit. The Prime Minister is furious. The minister is angry. I'm supposed to be mad, but I'm retiring at the end of the year, so bugger it. And the Security Services? I wouldn't put it past them to try to blame me to cover their asses. They're useless. Couldn't follow a bitch in heat. I hope you're treating our young man from Wellington well. He's been helpful. Catelin just briefed me on what he's doing."

"You mean Alexander Newton?"

"Yes. Don't sound surprised. He's got quite a future."

"Yes, he captured some good photographs otherwise we'd be nowhere."

The commissioner laughed. "You are somewhere?"

"What about those Maori and the demands we just received? Clever of them to contact a journalist at the

Auckland Star and use a code phrase for future communications. Means no one else can get in on their, what? Act? Extortion? Plans? It's what the IRA do all the time in England. Not original, but shows they are looking overseas for models, how to act. So they might be professional and well organized. What if they have the painting and not the Russian?"

"Oh, we'll placate them, patronize them, give them a little and they'll think they're winning. Then we'll ignore them, again. We've been doing it for years. We're pretty good at it."

"You're not going to give them any land?" Grimble asked.

"Truthfully? What they really want is for us to go away. Get on a boat and never come back. And you know what would happen? They'd start killing each other and wiping out whole tribes. Just like in the Musket Wars before we began to civilize them and teach them not to eat each other. So, you see, it's cyclical. We can't win, but we can't lose either. But they can lose. They can lose big time."

Grimble had never heard the commissioner talk in such a manner before. He swallowed. "What are we going to do about the Soviet? We can't touch him. Diplomatic immunity."

"You just raided where he was staying. It's not his safe house. It's not a consulate. I'm sure we're going to hear complaints from the Kremlin soon enough."

"But we have an in."

"An in?"

"Yes. Alexander Newton."

CHAPTER FORTY-TWO

With no wind and a blue sky, Albert Park was a perfect setting for a picnic lunch or a spontaneous demonstration in the middle of a mild winter. Students and office workers ate lunch on the grass and ignored the crowd gathering at the band rotunda. Students armed with identical posters stapled on long wooden sticks chanted in unison; "What do we want? We want our land back!" The black-and-white posters of Captain Cook had orange vertical stripes to make him look captive. Pamphlets being handed out and littering the park showed the same portrait and the name of the organizers, the Free Maori Land Movement.

Policemen in uniform had been hastily assembled for the illegal protest near the Wellesley Street entrance to the park, but were far outnumbered by the growing and noisy crowd. Mark Rose planted himself on a tea chest and held a megaphone to address the students who became more agitated and energetic with their placards.

Wiremu and Rawiri stood at the edge of the crowd near a clump of trees on the path to the fountain. Wiremu thought the statue of Queen Victoria would have been more historically appropriate. The sound from the megaphone was too distorted to hear distinctly but they heard the words "Maori" and "land" and "march". A group of young Maori next to Mark did not look happy.

"I like the placards with Cook on them," Rawiri shouted to Wiremu. The noise was getting louder.

"Isn't that a copy of the three-quarter portrait?" Wiremu asked.

"I don't know. We never got to steal it."

Wiremu nodded and saw a few officers further away near the path to the Auckland City Art Gallery. "Look at the higher ups. Doesn't look good."

"Yeah. Shouldn't Moana be here by now?"

"Let's wait here. Look." At the opposite end of the park there were two lines of uniformed police marching towards the crowd from the other direction. Mark was still speaking, punching out his fist and holding the megaphone high. A few photographers were now in the crowd. "Do you think those Maori want to punch the joker with the megaphone?"

Rawiri nodded. "I would."

One of the police officers held up a larger megaphone and started to give orders to the crowd.

"Shit. Have you seen these?" Moana appeared holding a larger poster of the Captain Cook portrait with GIVE MAORI LANDS BACK NOW stenciled across it. "They're all over the uni and the city." She looked over at the demonstration. "Doesn't look good, does it?"

"Nah. We're staying here. They look like they're getting ready to break it up."

"Don't think they have a permit, so they can. Oh, I made the call down by the wharf. Went well, I think. Stuck to the script."

Wiremu nodded and continued observing.

"Aren't you going to speak or do something?" Moana asked.

"Nah. We have plans." Wiremu looked at Rawiri who kept a straight face.

"And we don't want to be linked with these guys, whoever they are. Or that Pakeha clown. Do you know them?" Rawiri asked.

"Students. A group I never heard of, like in the pamphlet. Neat though, right?"

"Yeah, Moana. You caused this. Without the publicity they would never have protested. Good job."

Wiremu scanned the faces of the protesters. "Mostly Pakehas here."

"Maori, Pacific Islanders — doesn't matter," said Moana. "As long as they're on our side."

"Look." Wiremu nodded to another group of policemen in formation nearby. "Going to be the Battle of Waterloo before they finish. Let's head over there." He pointed towards the floral clock. "They're going to charge and force them into the university quad."

An officer stepped forward and grabbed a Captain Cook placard from the nearest student, who appeared to be the leader of the demonstration. The student, who was bigger than the officer, turned and hit the officer's helmet with his stick. It scraped the officer's face who sprang forward with a punch, knocking the student to the ground. Several other students with placards began to hit officers with their placards and sticks. The police near Wellesley Street drew their batons and formed a line to advance into the crowd. The officer with the megaphone yelled at the crowd to leave immediately, but his voice was lost in the uproar as the young men fought back. The officers surrounded them and dragged away the first attacker, who screamed and struggled. Other students, seeing one of their own being arrested, aggressively used their wooden sticks like swords to strike policemen on the arms and legs.

Mark lowered his megaphone when he saw the first attacker dragged away. He got off his box and walked into the crowd, raising his fist and egging on the students, chanting, "What do we want? We want our land back!" Heading towards the fountain he saw a larger column of policemen marching up from the Kitchener Street path, so he cut across the lawn, ducked between trees and headed to Princes Street. Before he got there two officers sprinted after him and managed to tackle him on the grass.

Just then the officer with the bleeding face pulled out his baton, turned to his uniformed men and ordered a charge into the angry protesters who were at the band rotunda. From the other side of the park the column of policemen advanced, batons drawn.

"Time to leave," said Wiremu. "We've seen enough." By the floral clock they saw a photographer being chased by two policemen. He fell over and one of the uniforms started to beat him with his baton. "I'm a journalist!" he pleaded. "I work for the *Star*."

The policeman stopped, turned to his partner and saw Wiremu and Rawiri looking at them.

"What are you looking at, boy?" He pointed his baton at Wiremu. "Get going." The other policeman strode up to Wiremu with his baton drawn as if to hit him.

Wiremu stared at him but remained, his feet spread. Moana grabbed his arm and pulled him away before he could do anything. Rawiri held his other arm and they turned their backs on the policemen. Two more uniforms came running up and one shouted, "Get them!"

Moana turned to see four policemen charging them and, out of the corner of her eye, the journalist kneeling on the pavement adjusting his camera.

"Fuck this!" Wiremu broke free of Rawiri's and Moana's grip and sidestepped the first uniform swinging his baton at his head. He grabbed the policeman's arm and twisted it around his back before propelling him into the uniform behind him. Rawiri had already started to charge the other two policemen who, seeing their fellow officers sprawl onto the ground helpless, hesitated then retreated as fast as they could. Moana ran into Princes Street waving her arms, and cars braked and honked their horns at her. Rawiri and Wiremu walked to where they could see Moana on Alfred Street. She was holding up a poster and chanting, "What do we want? We want our land back!"

Wiremu and Rawiri kept walking. They had a rendezvous to plan.

.   .   .

Grimble heard about the demonstration from Police Superintendent Thomas Jarvis's secretary when he returned to his office after his confidential talk with Commissioner Thompson. Jarvis had rushed to the park to take control. Grimble was concerned as he remembered Jarvis's lack of tact in the anti-Vietnam War demonstrations he broke up. Grimble grabbed Sergeant Cadd and they drove to Wellesley Street in his Honda. Two black police vans pulled up next to Grimble and more police jumped out. Several ambulances were parked nearby.

By the time they reached the band rotunda Grimble could see a full-scale riot in progress. Policemen with batons were hitting or chasing students who were fighting back with long sticks torn from the posters they had been brandishing a few moments ago.

"Isn't that a copy of the stolen portrait?" Cadd asked.

"You're the expert, Cadd."

They stared at a poster on the ground. Groups of students were fighting police nearby. Screams, shouts and the sound of batons hitting flesh filled the air.

"Looks exactly like it. Wonder where they got the print from?" Cadd held a poster in his hands, then dropped it to the ground and looked around. "Do we get stuck in?"

Grimble sighed. "The idea is to clear up the mess. Get the arrested into the vans. I'll see where Jarvis is and make sure…" He stopped, not wanting to finish his sentence.

Jarvis was receiving medical care from a St. John's ambulance volunteer as he sat against a large oak tree. He had blood on his tunic and a large bandage on his left cheek.

"Reporting for orders, sir!" Grimble shouted as he neared his commanding officer, who did not look happy to see the inspector standing over him.

CHAPTER FORTY-THREE

Rawiri and Wiremu sat on the side of Mount Eden with grass terraces and faced the Castle.

"Well, that got my heart racing. Haven't had such fun since I blew out the windows in the Three Lanterns pub and scared a bunch of cops out of their helmets."

"Yeah, I heard about the shotgun and the search for you. Why were they chasing us? We weren't even in the demo."

"We're Maori. We are a target."

"Shit. Wouldn't've looked good to my probie." Rawiri looked up at the small clouds racing across the blue sky. "Don't think they are going to file any reports."

Wiremu smiled. "Two Maori scared them away? Don't think so."

"It doesn't change, does it?"

"Nah. We're Maori, fair game for arrest, a beating, anything. Not good."

Rawiri nodded

They were quiet, absorbing the calm atmosphere, the clouds, the tall grass moving in the breeze. A thrush was singing in a tree nearby.

Wiremu gazed in the direction of the building, as if he could see through the trees to where he thought the Russian sat, in a chair in his apartment. "Are you sure you want to go alone?" Rawiri asked. "What if he has a gun? You know Russians can be tricky."

"He's probably really pissed off about being raided by the police. Ruined his breakfast." Wiremu said, not taking his eyes off the Castle.

"How do you know he has breakfast?"

"Of course he has breakfast. He's a diplomat. Diplomats always have breakfast. Maybe he has oatmeal."

"Russians don't eat oatmeal. They drink vodka."

"You can't stereotype Russians. See how we've been stereotyped. It's not right."

They looked in the direction of the Castle for a long time.

"Wonder if he has the painting. Maybe we could swap it for the notebooks," Rawiri suggested.

"Not a bad idea, brother. But he would never admit he has the painting. And if we did get the painting, what would we do with it? It's better to make a lot of noise about land rights and get the publicity rather than have the painting and organize an exchange."

"A lot of noise?" Rawiri frowned. "You're chickening out now?"

"Well, think it through. It's good we're getting all the publicity over the theft of our land, and it's raising the public's consciousness about our rights, but getting land for the painting? It's never gonna happen. They would never go through with it. Why would they? And we would be cast as the bad guys, which we don't want. Victims of injustice is good, but not the people who killed Captain Cook all over again. Bad publicity."

"Did you see the journalist take photos of us?"

"No. Let's hope not. All we need, a connection to Cook."

"And won't other Maori, once they get wind of who we are, disown us, or out us or something? All for their own political advantage."

"A wise observation. Cynical, Rawiri, but realistic. We haven't thought this through."

"Wouldn't selling the notebooks be betraying Henry? He's a friend, isn't he? And he gave you back the Tear, right?"

"Older brother, you're getting soft in your old age. He's going back to the States. He can make more notes. And the Yanks would steal the notebooks if they could. And we need the money. Besides, I have the Tear, which means I have the mana now." Wiremu put his hand to his chest and pulled out the pendant for Rawiri to see. He rose up, looked around and headed to the Castle.

.   .   .

Wiremu walked through a gate at the rear of the garden and onto the Castle property. The back door was unlocked. He found the stairs to the second floor and walked to the door at the end of another corridor. "N. Windsor" was printed under the buzzer. He pushed it and after a minute and another buzz the door opened. A large man with short red hair and beefy complexion, dressed in a sports jacket with a cravat tucked into his white shirt, peered at Wiremu. "Yes?" he said.

"Mr. Raganovich, sir. I need to talk to you about a business proposition. I have the notebooks you are interested in." Wiremu held them in his left hand.

The Russian looked at Wiremu's left hand, his face, and back at the notebooks. He put his right index finger to his lips and motioned for Wiremu to enter. He was ushered into a large sitting room where the Russian pointed to a sofa with lots of pillows. The Russian had tuned the radio to classical music. He turned up the volume and sat next to Wiremu as trumpets blared out the start of Mussorgsky's *Pictures at An Exhibition.*

"We can talk now," he said. "Did you see anyone when you came in?"

"Not a soul. I came in through the back," Wiremu whispered. "My name is Wiremu Wilson. We know you are interested in the notebooks. They contain extremely valuable formulas and calculations for a new weapon system. It's all top secret and the FBI, the Americans, have been trying to get them ever since Henry Lotus came back here from the States. I understand you or associates of yours know of him from New York. Right? So we are offering them to you. For sale. You should get first refusal, of course."

"Mr. Wilson, can I see them?"

"Of course." Wiremu handed him the first one.

Raganovich leafed through the pages. He stopped to go over a formula, read a note, admire a sketch. Wiremu did not take his eyes off the Russian.

"And the other two?"

Wiremu motioned for the return of the notebook before handing him the next one. He continued to the third one.

Raganovich spent a long time going over the pages of the third, then lifted his head. "Mr. Wilson, can I keep them? I need to show them to our experts. I have no idea what they contain. Nor do I know their true value. All can be sorted out, if I have them for a few days."

"No, Mr. Raganovich." Wiremu shook his head. "You can talk to your people, but you already know the value of the notebooks. You've been told to retrieve them, haven't you?" Wiremu could have sworn the Russian squinted for a second.

"What do you want, Mr. Wilson?" He sounded annoyed.

"We know you tried to steal them in New York. Now I am offering them to you. Three notebooks for $10,000 each. Which is a bargain, considering all the time and energy and research you will be saving. Comes to a nice round figure of $30,000 total for all three. It's not negotiable and if you can't afford them, the Americans want them and will, I know, pay more. But it's not about the money, Mr. Raganovich. It's about our land. It will go towards liberating our land for our people. Maori collective ownership of land. You must understand, as a Marxist, right?"

The Russian returned the third notebook and rose from the sofa. He looked at the notebooks, at Wiremu and back at the notebooks while the music blared. Wiremu watched him calculate his next move. He's used to playing chess and being five moves ahead, Wiremu thought, always with a backup plan. But now he has been taken by surprise. First, an embarrassing police raid, most undiplomatic, and now a Maori offers him intelligence treasure, totally unexpected. If he could go back to Moscow with the notebooks, he would be a hero and well rewarded. His mana intact. Did Russians have mana?

"How can I reach you?" Raganovich asked.

Wiremu could sense another person through a half-opened door across from where he now stood. "Don't worry, we'll contact you. Now if you don't mind, Mr. Raganovich, I'll be on my way." Wiremu placed the three notebooks inside his jacket and waited for the Russian to lead him to the front door.

"We have a deal, I hope," Raganovich smiled. "Give me a few days to make arrangements, Mr. Wilson. Thank you."

"No, thank you, Mr. Raganovich. We are running out of time. I will contact you tomorrow." Wiremu caught sight of a woman's eyes through a slit in a door as he turned to exit.

The hairs on the back of his neck were still rigid as he descended the back exit. He could hear the Mussorgsky from the radio, it was a piece Hone liked to play on his sound system, just as loud. He shuddered. Pictures at an exhibition indeed.

Rawiri was at the top of the crater. "No sign of any activity. Didn't see any cars."

"Amazing."

"What?"

"Just walking in there and offering him the books."

"Did he take the bait?"

"Oh yeah. All three for thirty K."

"Shit. Our dollars, right? Not their funny rubles."

"What do you know about their funny money?"

"About as much as you know about what they have for breakfast, brother."

They walked to the other side of the crater and once they were sure no one was watching them they sat down facing Rangitoto. Wiremu laid in the grass and gazed at the few clouds chasing each other, light and fluffy, changing shape as they travelled across the sky. He felt he could reach out and touch them. "He's a scary fellow," he said.

"How so?"

"I looked into his eyes and knew he's a killer. He's done a lot of bad stuff. I can tell. You know? Like when we were inside. Some of the guys we saw."

"Yeah," Rawiri let out. "So, what about his eyes?"

"I don't trust him. It's just a holiday for him. What he's done in other countries makes being in New Zealand appear easy, dealing with little Kiwis, Pakeha, you know?"

"What can we do with him?" Rawiri asked. "Of course, we could rob him of the money, and give the notebooks to Henry. The paper hinted at him being expelled today after the spy trial and now the police raid."

"There was a woman hiding in the apartment, watching me all the time. It was spooky."

"Spooky?"

"Yes. Unnerving."

"Little brother, you're getting soft."

CHAPTER FORTY-FOUR

When Alexander walked into the library for his late-afternoon meeting with Richard Catelin, the inspector had already talked about the demonstration, Superintendent Jarvis's intervention and injury, the resulting chaos, and the students' arrests. Grimble expected bad publicity from the papers, and many of the protesters' parents would be calling the Commissioner or their local Member of Parliament to demand an official inquiry into police brutality. "I've got people at the courthouse combing through property files, others looking at the Council records," he said. "We've drawn up a list of every possible side street in Parnell before the Russian returned to the Castle. Cadd is leading the search for any connection, any lead."

Catelin scrutinized the photos spread out on the table. He pointed with his pipe to the blown-up photographs of the two Maori outside. "How do you know they didn't steal the painting? If the Russian doesn't have it, why not suspect them?"

"Interesting, sir." Grimble replied. "The commissioner, when we first spoke of Captain Cook, alluded to the fact he had information a Maori group planned to kidnap the painting. The reason security was so tight. However, we haven't heard anything else. The commissioner, we assume, would have informed us if there were any more leads."

"You mean the police or SIS were bugging someone? The security company?" Catelin asked.

Grimble sat back in his chair. "I would never hear from SIS, of course. A domestic intelligence warrant is sealed. And Jarvis hasn't informed me of any such operation. We can do it, but I've heard of no recent warrants. So it must be SIS keeping tabs on some Maori. Which is more than interesting. Nothing came of interviewing the two security guards, which is revealing in itself. I don't think my superiors want to raid any Maori homes now after the morning's…" He struggled for the appropriate word. "Fiasco sums it up, I suppose."

"An accurate assessment of where we are at, inspector," said Catelin. "Now we need to determine what we can do next. Over at headquarters they don't seem to have any ideas other than to ignore the demands of a Maori group no one has heard of. Add the new Maori group on the posters who organized the demo and they are even more confused." He turned to Alexander, hovering in the background.

"I know what I saw. He has it stashed away." Alexander stopped and made sure he had their full attention. "If Sergeant Cadd can find a connection, great. But time is running out. If he's still in Auckland, we must ask ourselves why? He should've flown back or driven to Wellington to hide out in his Embassy where he would be safe and protected. I would guess if or when you deport him, he will already have Captain Cook mounted on a wall in the Kremlin. A trophy they can drink vodka toasts to."

Catelin shook his head. "I don't see why he would steal the painting. Doesn't make sense."

"We have to ask ourselves why is he still here," said Alexander. "I mean, the others involved in the spying case left, didn't they?"

Catelin nodded.

"And we don't want to declare him persona non grata, do we, at least for now. Better the devil we know and all that. You said the P.M. wants to sell beef and butter to the Soviets, and we have the new Ambassador in Moscow to think of. It's a delicate balance, as you explained. So we have to ask ourselves why did he steal the painting? From a counterespionage point of view it's what, stupid? What has he got to gain?" Alexander walked around the table. "Was this approved by Moscow? Or is he doing this alone? Again, we have to ask ourselves why? Is it a distraction? Are there loose ends he is tying up we don't know about? New contacts to make after the Dr. Winter trial, or Winter's new agents to prepare before he leaves? We don't know what else he was up to — the SIS never found out any of his dead-letter drops, if he had any. Or who his other sources were. Or should I say *are*? There's a lot we don't know about him." Alexander took a deep breath and tried to read Catelin and Grimble.

"There is the photo you took." All three looked at the last photo again.

"The one lead we haven't explored is Natasha," Alexander stated in the silence.

"Of course!" Grimble clapped his right hand to his forehead. "The name on the buzzer at the Castle. 'N. Windsor'. We never saw her. Why didn't I make the connection?" Grimble grabbed the phone next to the desk. He dialed a number and barked a series of orders to whoever answered. He waited for what seemed like ages, before he started to write on a pad next to the phone. When he hung up, he turned to Catelin.

"She's not a diplomat but came over five years ago from the States as a student on a visa she keeps renewing somehow. She doesn't have any income and is studying Russian and Germanic languages at the university. She's either Raganovich's lover or his daughter. She drives a red Mini. We need to find it. Have you seen it, Alexander?"

"No. As I said, the only active car was the dark-colored Chrysler Valiant I spotted a couple of times Sunday night, following the Jag and cruising around Mark Rose's place."

"And you know Natasha?" Catelin asked.

"Yes. I just need to think of a way to approach her."

Catelin grinned for the first time. "She's the Russian girl you were talking about? She's not American?"

"No, she's Russian."

"Well, we haven't much time." Catelin stood. Grimble was already at the door clutching his piece of paper when Alexander ran to him and whispered in his ear.

"She's not in the phone book?"

"No. She's a doctor."

"Yes, I know. Call me in half an hour and I'll tell you." Grimble left and Alexander turned to Catelin. "Work-related." He shrugged. "I need help to get to Natasha."

CHAPTER FORTY-FIVE

Annie had parked illegally on Albert Street, opposite the District Court. She watched as Mark appeared to dance down the steps, recognized her older black Holden and walked across the small parking lot towards her. "So, you're free?"

Mark leaned over and kissed her. "Yeah! Again. Thank you for the ride."

"You even made the morning paper."

"Shit! The raid or the demo?"

"The raid on your house. Oh, you were at the demo as well? We had a whole bunch of students walking in wounded. What happened?"

"Free Maori lands movement, inspired by the stolen painting. I had to talk. I was invited." He thought for a second. "The *Herald* goes to bed early and I wasn't raided till 5.30. Fuck! I was set up. What a day. Those cells are just as nasty." He kept his eyes on her. "I'm getting too old for this shit."

"You were invited to talk at the demo? About Maori land? Who by?"

"Oh, you know. Connections. Besides, I had my megaphone. Shit."

"You and your megaphone! Heard you on the radio at the hospital. Probably going to be on TV tonight. I'm sure you're going to get a lot of calls." Annie headed towards her house in Greenlane. "But they haven't mentioned you in the demo yet. Have to wait for the *Star*. How come you didn't get arrested during the raid but got nabbed in the park?"

"You're asking me how cops think? I'm going to go into hiding and don't want anything to do with anyone but you. I need a bath and a massage, at least."

"You're pushing it."

"Baby, you have no idea." Mark gave her his million-kilowatt smile, all he had. His attorney had worked out an agreement with the Crown not to prosecute, in return for Mark's silence. If he talked to the media the deal was off.

"So do tell, why did they let you out? Aren't they pissed off?"

"Justice is its own reward." Mark lost his smile as he estimated that all the money Nikolai Raganovich had given him would go to Alan Crispfeldt, his expensive but effective counsel. He sighed. "They vandalized everything and won't pay for any of the damage. The reason I wasn't arrested was they were searching for the lost painting, the Captain Cook we saw on Saturday night. Nothing about drugs in the warrant, so they couldn't charge me. They made an illegal search, but heaven forbid they return my stash! Of course, it's disappeared. It's highway robbery! I got tackled walking across the park for no reason, and my megaphone stolen. I got released on condition I don't talk. To anyone. I'm muzzled."

Annie smiled. "Perhaps I can unmuzzle you tonight. After you've showered."

Mark sank back into his seat and thought about the raid on his house and who had ratted on him. He kept coming back to the image of the small white government van and its driver, Alexander Newton.

CHAPTER FORTY-SIX

Grimble had a copy of the *Auckland Star* on his desk when Cadd returned to his office with lists of garages and warehouses where Raganovich could have stored the missing painting. Cadd was about to admit he could not find a direct link to the Russian.

"Seen this?" Grimble pointed to the headline COPS BEAT JOURNALIST IN LUNCHTIME RIOT IN ALBERT PARK. "I can't begin to imagine what the commissioner is going to say. Lucky for us we weren't present until the end. And look at the photo—recognize anyone?"

"Christ! Is that Wiremu Wilson? He was there? And the other guy from the photos?"

"Yes." Grimble had read the article twice and was still digesting the information.

"At least I got to arrest Mark Rose again. Well, I put him in the van," Cadd smiled. "Seemed like old times."

"Did he appreciate it?"

"Not in the least."

"If we had arrested him earlier on our raid perhaps the whole riot wouldn't have happened?" Grimble pulled a face. "We've got work to do."

Cadd nodded.

Grimble picked up printouts from the Wanganui computer. Natasha was the Russian's daughter and rented the apartment at the Castle in her own name. "Here's the plate number. All you have to do is find it nearby. It'll be in Parnell, give or take a few side streets between where Mark Rose lives and the Castle. Oh, and one other thing. She's enrolled at Auckland University as a what? Masters student by now? In the Russian language department? Do they have one? Chat up the secretary, chat up everyone and find out where she is, where she studies, what courses she's enrolled in, anything you can—but I don't think we should contact her yet. We should work out our approach. And there's Alexander Newton. I've yet to work him out. Is he just a curator, or a plant? Is he related to Catelin and his department? Is he SIS as well and they're not telling us?"

"He seemed at ease in the gallery and at the opening," said Cadd. "I think he's in it for the girls and the glory."

"We were all young once. Well, I was. Once. Let's go for a drive."

"All the garages will be closed but we can check parking areas and, anything we can see from the street."

"Yes. Nothing else to do. Haven't you got somewhere to go? It's just gone seven."

"No, I'm single. And I need to find Captain Cook if I want my career to advance."

"No girlfriend? What happened to whatshername, Donna? You haven't talked about her in ages."

"Thanks for asking, but after Titirangi she left. Couldn't stand the stress, she said."

"Oh, I'm sorry. I didn't know. We get too engrossed in our work, or at least I do. We forget about the real world. Makes you wonder why we do our job. I should be taking my daughter to violin practice tonight, but the wife understands. I think. Before I forget, Jarvis approved you getting out of uniform and working for me, but the other bureaucrats haven't signed off on you yet. It must be frustrating."

"It's why I want to find the painting. I feel like I should have had it handcuffed to me the whole night."

Grimble drove his red Honda through the side streets of Parnell and Cadd crossed off each block they cruised past.

"Do you still think of what happened in Titirangi, Cadd?"

"Not any more. I was annoyed when Donna left, but I think I told her too much. What did you say?"

"Don't bring your work home. It will stay and poison any real relationships you have."

"Do you tell your wife anything?"

"No. She knows not to ask. Besides, she isn't interested in police work. She has her own job to think of." Grimble glanced at Cadd as he turned back into Parnell Road. "She's a teacher, head of her English department. Very busy and hasn't time to bother me, thank goodness."

"Do you think about what happened to you?" Cadd asked, after a silence. "It's been six months but feels longer, doesn't it?" They were now driving through deserted industrial streets.

"Well, I still get headaches, but not as much."

"You get headaches? From when you were knocked out?" Cadd sounded surprised.

"Yes, Cadd. Remember the head bandage? They called me the sheikh at HQ for weeks."

"I thought it was the Sikh."

Grimble turned into another side street and stopped outside what appeared to be an auto repair shop. "You should come back here tomorrow and see what's inside. We could break in now, but, after what happened, I don't have the stomach for a little B and E anymore."

Cadd looked at his boss, puzzled.

"Let me explain, Cadd. We used to believe anything was okay, as long as we got the collar. We would bend the rules. Hell, there weren't any rules but the ones we wrote. So, anything would stand up in court. We didn't have to lie as leave out certain details. What magistrate would rule against a cop? The house fire really threw me, and you too, I think."

"You mean Hone Wilson?"

"Yes." Grimble drove on as Cadd made marks on the map.

"I don't want to be that cop anymore, and I don't want you to turn into that type of cop either Cadd. You have a bright future ahead of you. If we can find the bloody painting."

CHAPTER FORTY-SEVEN

Mel checked the bedroom. Henry's clothes had gone. His books were no longer by his side of the bed. She was in no mood to change out of her work clothes, a simple black trouser suit and a plain white shirt. She kicked her shoes into a corner and checked the bathroom. Shaving kit, toothbrush, all gone. She walked into the living room. The huge speakers and turntable were intact, but a few of the LPs were missing. She opened the refrigerator and poured herself a full glass of a white wine she had saved for cooking.

She felt abandoned. All her work on trying to reform Henry over the last six months was in vain. Why had he returned the jade piece, the Tear of Tane, to Wiremu? To save Wiremu or undermine himself? Mel saw it as an act of self-destruction. She sensed again he was going to return to America, and she would never see him again.

She should have been thinking of her amazing night with Alexander, she knew. She could find no sensible answer for her new infatuation. She didn't feel guilty about the tryst on a bare mattress. She, a respectable doctor, having great sex in the back of a van, on top of Mount Eden, at her age? With a man at least ten years her junior, she calculated?

Then an extraordinary thing happened. The doorbell rang. Mel ran to answer, hoping it was Henry back from the airport to confess he had made a big mistake and he was going to live with her forever, marry her and they were going to have a lot of kids, well, two would be nice. But as she flung open the door, she saw Alexander, with his dimples. He held a dozen red roses, a bottle of wine, and a bottle of Southern Comfort. "Oh god! It's you!" she gasped.

"Were you expecting someone else?" Alexander asked. He saw Mel's body melt. What had he done? She'd thrown him around, seduced him in his small white government van and now he was standing before her smiling, bearing gifts and wondering how she would respond.

"I'm sorry, you caught me off-guard. Come in. I was drinking crappy wine but…" She opened the paper bag. ""Penfold's Cab Sav. Private Bin. Looks expensive. But you kept the price tag on. So it's not."

"Did I?" Alexander gasped. "You can't take me anywhere!"

"How did you know where I lived?"

"Simple. I'm a spy, remember?"

"You. Don't stand there. Come in. And didn't you tell me you were a curator?"

He followed her into the kitchen where she arranged the roses into a vase. Alexander thought she kept looking at him as if to figure out what to do with him. He had ideas as well but did not want to over play his hand. He was still unsure about what had happened the night before and doubted events could happen so quickly again. But he kept hoping.

He felt giddy to be in her presence as they drank the good red wine in her living room. Her boyfriend, whom Alexander had met at the gallery opening, wasn't in the house, and she seemed excited to see him. We'll always have Mount Eden, he thought, but dared not say it aloud. She squatted over the albums, went past the new Rolling Stones album and placed *Mental Notes* by Split Enz, on the turntable. She turned to show him the painting of the group on the cover and caught Alexander looking at her rear.

She did have a great bottom, he was thinking, not too big or too small. Perfect, like everything else about her. He was sitting in her living room, a glass of wine in his hands, about to listen to an expensive sound system and with a kickboxer doctor, all to himself.

"I hope you don't mind me dropping in," he said. "But I was drawn here."

"I can't remember the last time someone bought me roses," Mel murmured. "They're beautiful."

"After last night, I thought I should. I, I'm not good at these sorts of situations. I guess I have no experience and I had to see you again. It's not like I've thought of anything else. God. What am I saying?"

Mel scrutinized him over the rim of her wine glass.

"I just, I just wanted to see if what I felt was real. After last night, I mean, I was swept off my feet and, well, you know. Who's playing? I've never heard them before."

"Split Enz. You like it?"

"I'm sitting next to you sipping wine, listening to music. What's not to like? I still don't think it's real. This is stranger than fiction. Hit me."

Mel did.

"Oh. That hurt."

"You told me to hit you."

"I should have said pinch me."

Mel pinched him on the same arm.

"Ouch! That hurt too! Now I know it's real. Wow." Alexander finished off his wine. "Can we change the album? It's the first time I'm hearing it, and I need to concentrate. I can't with you sitting next to me."

Mel finished her wine and got to her feet to select another album. She flicked through Patti Smith's *Horses*, Joni Mitchell's *The Hissing of Summer Lawns* then came to Supertramp's *Crime of the Century*. She bent over to put the needle on the opening track, turned to face Alexander and caught him staring at her again. He did not seem to be leering; he looked to be in awe. "I'm going to change," she said. "Can you pour me more wine? And don't move."

Alexander refilled both their glasses and sat back. He emptied his glass and poured another. He had lost track of time. Then the lights went off and before him was the outline of Mel's body and her curly hair looking wilder. She dropped the needle and turned up the volume. She switched on a floor lamp near the door.

When Alexander adjusted his eyes, he needed to be hit or pinched again.

Mel stood across from him in black high heels, a garter belt and black nylon stockings. She swayed to the music. Her hair swept across her face and her shoulders. Her breasts bounced from side to side. Her skin was a luminescent white. She did not take her eyes off him. He didn't know where to look. He just soaked in the music and Mel dancing in front of him.

When the piano solo kicked in with swirling chords, the rhythms overwhelmed him. He got to his feet and held her by the hips. He could feel the garter belt. She responded by holding his waist and gazing into his steel grey eyes. They began to move in a clockwise direction, slowly, gaining momentum as the music became more intense. The room spun. Mel took small steps in her high heels, but Alexander was shuffling his feet in wider arcs, as he tried to keep his balance while holding her gaze. When the song ended, he lost his balance and she fell on top of him. The carpet broke his fall and he wrapped his arms around her and with her hips and breasts pressing into him began one breathless deep kiss that lasted for the rest of the album.

"I shouldn't do this." He kissed her on her other breast. "And I shouldn't do that."

"Don't stop," Mel moaned. He thought they were the two greatest words in the English language.

Alexander woke in the middle of the night. He had no idea of the time. He was not alone. He was naked below the waist, like last night. Mel had a duvet covering them. She had taken off her lingerie and they shared a pillow. He could feel the heat of her body and her slow breathing. He wanted to wake her again and make love to her, but he moved his legs and felt how sore his knees were, as they rubbed against the duvet. He closed his eyes and remembered he had not called Tsara. Mel put her arm around him, and he moved closer to her. He fell into a deep sleep.

CHAPTER FORTY-EIGHT

"Damn! The Mini isn't in Parnell or anywhere. We've cruised around every single street, right?"

"Yes, sir. I've marked them on the map. Nothing."

"There's a pie cart on Queen Street and Shortland. Care for a pie?" Grimble asked.

"You're driving," Cadd replied.

They headed to Shortland Street and parked opposite the long white cart, really a converted bus made into a kitchen with stools for customers, a serving area with a canopy and a few drunks nearby, eating pies or drinking sodas. "Haven't been here in years," Grimble said. "Only things changed are the girls' skirts are shorter and the guys' hair is longer."

The two plainclothes policemen stood by the counter and ate their meat pies. Other men with long hair kept their distance.

"Cadd, there's something I've been meaning to talk to you about," Grimble said between mouthfuls. He hadn't realized how hungry he was.

Cadd stopped chewing. He lifted his right arm and smelled his armpit.

Grimble almost smiled. "Not that."

"About your boss? Jarvis? And the riot?"

"No. We're going to enjoy that fiasco later."

"You mean the explosion on the Southern Motorway?"

"How did you know?"

"You trained me. And it's unlike you to take the official line. The explosion just happened and the two biggest crooks in Auckland just happened to get wiped out? Got to be more to it. Maybe they were planning the crime of the century and blew themselves up by mistake. I don't know and, like you taught me, I don't want to jump to conclusions." The sergeant took another bite of his pie. "And I just didn't want to ask."

"I see what you mean. Once Cook is found, we need to rethink the whole trail of events through. You're right, it does seem too neat. I don't think the commissioner is buying the official line either. He just doesn't want to say anything officially."

"Or unofficially?"

"Yes, Cadd. You're beginning to understand cop politics."

"What can we do? Unofficially, of course. We have to bring solid evidence to the table to get it reopened. You know Terry Turner's wife Barbara is one or two steps ahead of us in her investigation."

"A scary thought. We need to go over all the traffic accidents around the explosion. I do believe no one ever looked at them, tried to find any links, names, anything related to the truck. I don't think it blew up on its own. A high explosive, probably C-4, according to our expert's report."

"Probably?" Cadd raised his eyebrows. "You would never let me use that word."

"The expert said it, not me. We need to talk to this expert. They don't always put everything into written reports for a number of reasons."

"You want me to get *all* the accident reports?"

"Yes. The truck was heading to Auckland when it exploded. Where had it come from? What was it carrying? Did they know they had explosives on board, or were they set up? Which begs the question, who was following them? Hard to imagine Turner was fooled."

"It happened at the same time as the shootout. Didn't you always say there is no such thing as a coincidence?"

"Yes, Cadd. We need to pull every phone call logged, every accident, any record we have, including further south. The two events are connected somehow." He rubbed his eyes. "Let's call it a night. We have an early start tomorrow."

Cadd glanced at his watch. "It's already tomorrow."

CHAPTER FORTY-NINE

"Is there a reason why we slept on the floor? My back is killing me. And my knees. What did we do last night?"

"Everything." Mel leaned over and kissed him again. Her breasts pressed into his body and he felt he could stay in this position all day, feeling the warmth of her body, even if his back was sore.

"You put on quite a show. Supertramp, right? I think it'll always be my song, I mean our song. And what you wore. My god. It was like, no, it *was* a fantasy come true. I'm spoilt for life!"

"It was meant for someone else but —"

"Oh. But I was the lucky recipient."

Alexander didn't want to mention Henry's name. He should have felt guilty, but he had no reason to be. If Henry had run out on Mel, he must be a fool. "Tread softly because you tread on my fantasies," he said, struggling with all the emotions racing around inside him. "What have I done to deserve such an amazing time with you?"

Mel stroked his cheeks, ran her finger along his nose. He kissed her finger and leaned over to kiss her on the lips. "Hey," she said, "I have to go to work soon."

"I am thankful Captain Cook was stolen, otherwise I would never have met you."

"You met me at the gallery opening."

"Yes, but you were, um. I was, what's the right word? Besotted? Gob-smacked? Thunderstruck? I tried to keep myself under control, but you inhabited my daydreams, my night dreams. And all the spaces in between."

"Are you an incurable romantic or a jaded spy?"

"Me jaded? Not sure I'm there yet. Incurable romantic? Are you the antidote?" Alexander watched Mel, naked, rise up and stretch. "I know I'm the curator who lost the explorer who discovered New Zealand."

"I didn't want to say anything, but what are you doing about the situation?"

"The situation? Well, it's completely fucked! I've been reporting to the gallery and summoned by all sorts of people. Inspector Grimble, for instance."

Mel saw his white shirt on the sofa and put it on. "Oh, him. Yes, I am familiar with the inspector." She used one button to secure the shirt.

Alexander was mesmerized. "Really? What have you done?" He went to undo the button, but she held his arms. He had a flashback to an old James Bond movie — was it *Dr. No?* — and the woman who wore a man's shirt when Bond returned to his apartment. Or was it a pajama top?

Mel looked into his eyes. "Wouldn't you like to know?"

He shook his head. "Seriously, what's the connection?" Her thumbs and fingers were still gripping his wrists. "And you look amazing in my shirt. My only shirt."

"I'll tell you another time. You were saying about the stolen painting?"

He kissed her again. He could get used to being with Mel naked under his shirt. He followed her into the kitchen where she made coffee. "There is my real boss from the Department of Internal Affairs and a few others I have to deal with. I came across a young woman called Natasha

Windsor who, we discover through the wonders of the Wanganui computer, has an apartment in the Castle, and of course it was raided yesterday. She's connected to the Soviet spy, Nikolai Raganovich. You know, from the Dr. Winter spy trial a couple of months ago."

Mel nodded as she put the percolator on the stove.

"They want me to make contact with her and find the damn painting, I suppose."

"Oh, you're going to seduce her?"

"God, no! I met her a couple of years ago, and she tried to seduce me in her apartment. Freaked me out. Not exactly beautiful, and a little, how can I put it? Plump?"

"You are funny."

"First, I'm romantic, then I'm funny? Funny nice or funny ha-ha?"

"I need to take a shower. Want to scrub my back?" Mel checked the coffee was percolating.

"I am your official scrubber."

·   ·   ·

Alexander drank black coffee in Mel's kitchen. He was dressed in his wrinkled shirt and he loved the fact that Mel had been wearing it. Her hair was wet and brushed back. With no makeup, in her own white shirt and black pants, she looked stunning. He couldn't keep his eyes off her. She was wearing her black Doc Martens. Joni Mitchell's *Blue* was playing on the sound system.

"I never took you for a Joni Mitchell fan," he said.

"What did you take me for?"

"I haven't thought about it. Well, a Supertramp fan? I want to explore that album again."

"Not now, I have to go." Mel leaned with her back to the sink, eyeing him.

"And this." He picked up the *Horses* album with Patti Smith on the cover in a white shirt, black pants and hair to her shoulders. "You know you look like her."

"Come on, my hair is longer and curly. I don't have her nose or chin. I could go on."

"Well, it's more a feeling that you're in command and you transmit this smoking sexiness."

"Smoking is bad for you."

"You know what I mean."

"No, I don't."

"Were you a tomboy growing up?"

"Are you saying I'm androgynous?" She shifted her weight off the sink and positioned her left foot forwards.

Alexander looked down and pulled a face. "After what happened last night? No way. Anyway, I couldn't spell it. Changing the subject, there is something I want to ask you."

"What?"

"Is your first name just Mel or is it short for Melanie?"

"Do you know how many people assume that?"

"It's not, is it?"

"No."

Alexander noticed her mood change. "So it must be, er, Melanie? Like the singer." He scrutinized her face then shook his head. "No, it's Melody. Just like the song on the new Stones album?" He smacked his hand on the table. "It is! Wow."

"And it's spelled with an ie not y."

"Different. Your parents?"

"I don't want to talk about it."

"Why not? It's part of your identity, isn't it?"

"Promise not to tell?"

"I am the keeper of secrets."

"I bet you are." Mel looked at him in such a way that he knew he could not ask any more questions about her name.

"Talking of which, when I mentioned the Russian, Natasha, you made a funny face."

"I did?"

"Just for a second."

Mel put her coffee cup in the sink, avoiding his eyes.

"You must know her or have come across her? Yes? You have. She came to you for a, consultation? Health check? No. She wanted to—"

Mel waved her hands. "I'm not saying anything. I can't talk about my patients."

"True, you can't. Ever. But we do know she is a patient of yours and came in with, whatever, and you can't tell me. It must be pretty bad. Recently?"

Mel folded her arms. "I'm not playing your game."

"I'm not playing games. I just need a way to reach her without knocking on her door and saying, 'Hey remember me? You tried to seduce me with my girlfriend in the other room a while back, and now I'm in town and free, what about it?' I don't think so."

"Well, maybe you could bump into her where she works. Maybe she works in Parnell, in an office, say, off Parnell Road, on maybe Garfield. You could see her if she goes to lunch nearby."

"Mel, you are amazing. Are you doing anything tonight?"

She wrote out her home phone number on her business card. "You might be busy yourself tonight."

"I have no idea what's happening. Every day is different. But I'll call you later, even if it's to say I miss you and want to see you, see you immediately, without being too over-bearing or whatever it is we men are not supposed to be when courting."

"Are you courting now?"

"Have you got a better name for it?"

They had one last kiss and the passion and longevity of the kiss belied any doubts about not wanting to see each other soon.

CHAPTER FIFTY

"We have to issue another communique with the *Star*, with our demands, specifically."

Rawiri raised his eyebrows. "Specifically?"

"Hey! I can use big words," said Moana. "I'm a grown woman."

"I think they know who we are anyway." Wiremu pointed to the front page of yesterday's *Star* with a photo of them. The caption stated: "Two unidentified Maori were assaulted by police in Albert Park after the illegal demonstration on Maori Land Rights was broken up." He snorted. "I wasn't assaulted. I threw a cop to the ground and the others ran away. Scared buggers."

"Lucky they didn't get your names." Moana squinted. "The photo's not so clear. In fact, doesn't look like you at all."

"I can see it," Ricky said.

Moana sighed and pointed to the other paper on the table, the front page of that morning's *Herald*. The police raids on Raganovich's apartment and Mark Rose's house in Parnell were covered in detail. The article continued inside with a side panel featuring Nikolai Raganovich and his role in the Dr. Winter spy trial. Another panel covered Mark Rose with his history of student activism, and his famous Vietnam War protest photo holding a megaphone and looking like Che Guevara. It looked identical to the one in the *Star* on page three where he stood on a box by the band rotunda, holding a megaphone.

"You've got people talking about land rights," said Ricky. "A whole news segment last night talked about what lands would be considered. Every Maori activist is getting air time or being quoted in the papers. Heck, you caused a riot with lots of people arrested, including this joker Mark Rose. And you showed up to the demo and didn't get arrested. So you've achieved your aims. I'd say it was impressive. Don't take it the wrong way, but it's just you three. You haven't broken any laws, I figure, just pissed off quite a few people." He massaged Moana's tight shoulders as he kept talking. "And if the authorities do recover the painting, even if they don't get it from you, which I'm sure they won't, right?, you'll be seen as responsible for its safe return. Either way you win. There's no downside."

Moana said, "I agree with Ricky. One day at a time. While the painting is still missing, we should come out with a list of lands we want returned."

"Yes. Call it in. Give them a list, the more the merrier. Start with Bastion Point and Raglan golf course. Include Pakaitore and the Wanganui river, and all our fishing rights along the coast. The foreshore and seabeds do not belong to the Crown but to all Maori people. Mention Parihaka, all those lands seized after the arrest of Te Whiti. And put in the words 'spiritual sustenance' and 'tribal dignity'. Confuse the heck out of them."

"And don't forget Paremoremo," Rawiri smiled, "the Pakeha prison for Maori, built on Maori land. I heard inside an iwi used to own the land. Te Kawerau something. That'll piss them off. Giving back all the land!"

"Yeah, but we want to keep our demands spread out," said Wiremu. "Make sure no one can say, it's the buggers from the renegade whanau of Ngapuhi who are up to no good. We want to remain anonymous. It's our strength, right?"

"Yes. Anonymous like in our photos on the front page of the *Star*." Rawiri stood up. "Aren't the pubs open? Let's go." The brothers had agreed not to tell Moana what they intended to do with the notebooks. She knew they had them. And Ricky would be left in the dark. For his own protection, they rationalized.

·   ·   ·

"Shit. Fuck. Do you see this?" The petite blonde jumped from her chair and stabbed her finger at the front page of the *Auckland Star*. She had been Miss Hamilton 1956 but now, in a floral housecoat with no makeup and her hair tied back in a ponytail, she looked like a tired housewife. She squinted at the two Maori men in the photograph, making her frown lines even deeper. She turned to her younger brother. "Do you know who that is. Michael?"

He shook his head and continued to sip his coffee. With short hair, a tight shave and impeccably dressed in his navy blazer and khaki pants with brown brogues he looked like a financial consultant, but for his cauliflower ears, broken nose and cold blue eyes.

"It's that damn Wiremu Wilson. The one Terry told me about. They were in prison together and he supplied us with their pot from up north. Terry was setting him up to be ambushed by the Drug Squad but somehow Wiremu wasn't there and his gang was wiped out."

"I remember. They called it Hei Hei's last stand. The girls at the Flamingo talked about it. Quite a shootout. What's that got to do with us? And where are my pancakes? You promised me pancakes. That's why I came over so early. Missed my run to get here on time."

Barbara Turner sat down again and pointed at the photograph. "Look at them. That's his brother, who must be out of prison now. He's a mean bastard. What are they doing here in Auckland?" She screwed her eyes up. "And fuck your pancakes. I want to know what they're up to. Shit. I'm gonna change and we'll look at that Wong house again."

"What? We've been there, how many times? And seen nothing."

"Timing. Timing is everything. It's what Terry used to say."

"Yes, I've heard it before. As in comedy and getting pregnant. And in making my fucking pancakes."

CHAPTER FIFTY-ONE

Alexander drove to Tsara's, smelling of lavender soap. He didn't want to tell her about last night's adventure. "Oh, you remember the good-looking doctor we were introduced to at the opening?" The honest approach wouldn't work. They had always been open about their relationships but with Mel, he felt different. He thought it better if he slept elsewhere. He didn't want to camp out on Tsara's sofa and listen to more melancholy music with disturbing album covers.

He couldn't count on Mel to invite him to sleep over. He was unsure of her relationship with Henry. They hadn't broken up and he didn't want to get in their way. Henry's presence was still felt in her house and he hadn't left the country. Alexander had figured out why she didn't want to use her bed: Henry had slept there the night before and she hadn't changed the sheets.

Was laundry detergent the perfect way to protect yourself? Wash away the smell of your previous man? He didn't know what to make of his relationship with Mel. It had happened so fast. What of his affair with Deborah? He had gone from no women in his life, to two. What sort of trouble would he fall into with two romances in two different cities? If they were in separate cities, did it still amount to cheating? Was it a romance in Wellington? Or was it pure necessity? Or was it lust and professional spying? He had more than enough romance here in Auckland. He was in a moral quandary. Can spies have quandaries? he wondered. Their work could be ethically questionable. Would he dare to admit his dirty deeds to his best friend in Auckland, Tsara? He doubted she would accept his explanation and he would need more than laundry detergent to wash himself clean.

He parked the van and walked across to Tsara's front door. He rang the buzzer, knocked on the door then, with no answer, leaned over to rap on her side window. It was after nine, so maybe she would be at Elam. He had brought the morning paper and pastries she liked. He used the key she had given him, opened her door, and called her name.

After changing into a clean pair of jeans and a white shirt he made a cup of tea and ate all the pastries. Her bed did not look slept in. He couldn't rationalize his feelings because they had never slept together and she was free to pursue her own romantic agenda. If it was romantic.

He saw a note with a phone number and his name. He recognized her handwriting. He put it in his pocket and wrote her a note to leave on the table.

Dear Tsara

I am sorry I did not call you last night. I had another all-nighter. I seem to spend more time in my van than with you! I am under incredible pressure with the lost painting. Lost! It's not lost, it's stolen and I must recover it or I am finished. I will call you tonight when you get back. I have a lot to tell you. Got my suitcase as I am not sure what will happen tonight.

Best
Alexander

He read his note again. It wasn't too brief, not too long, just the right tone, he thought.

He packed all his belongings, took his shaving kit and toothbrush from her bathroom and locked the door. He would keep his suitcase hidden beneath the mattress in his van.

.   .   .

If Alexander had been more aware of his surroundings, or conducted a counter-surveillance drill, he would have seen a red four-door Mercedes 280 SE parked further up Grafton Road with a man and a woman inside.

"Who's he?" Barbara Turner now had her hair in a bun and thick blue eye makeup inspired by Elizabeth Taylor in *Cleopatra*. "Came out a couple of doors down. Tall guy."

"Fancy him, do you?"

"Oh, come on. That's not even funny."

Michael looked at her then at his dashboard. He enjoyed the new Mercedes. As co-owner of their car showroom in Ellerslie he could drive any car he wanted. He would return it, reset the odometer and select another car. It was better than picking another girl from their massage parlor, the Flamingo Paradise. The cars never talked back. "What do we hope to prove here?"

"Don't know till we see it. We know Ricky Wong lives there. We'll just have to wait. Give me an hour or two. It'll be worth it."

Michael looked at his gold Presidential Rolex. "I've got some trades to make and—" He stopped as he looked down the street. "I can't believe it!"

"Holy shit! It's them. What are they doing in the Wong house?"

"Are you making a joke? My little sister making a joke?"

"What the fuck are you talking about? Don't stare at them. That's how you attract attention. Let them walk by. Shit. What the fuck are they doing?"

"One way to find out." Michael started the engine when the two brothers were further up the hill, slowly turned around and parked further up the road to see where they were heading.

CHAPTER FIFTY-TWO

"Are you serious about going to the pub?" Wiremu asked as he and Rawiri walked up Grafton Road to Khyber Pass Road.

"No way, little brother. What could I say in front of Moana? 'Let's plan how we're going to exchange the notebooks for cash with the Russian'? We need to think it all through and we might as well be in sight of his apartment. I want to watch the Castle."

They headed to Nugent Street, unaware the red Mercedes had started to follow them as they turned onto Normanby Road. They came to a track on the side of Mount Eden and walked around the lower crater to a point where they could sit and watch a slice of Castle Drive and part of its four-story Gothic tower. The gardens surrounding the area were full of large trees and native plants, obscuring most of the paths and driveways.

"Should've brought a picnic," Rawiri said.

"Moana would have planned one if we'd included her."

"Yeah, she is quite a woman now. The communique she wrote is a work of art. I hope she calls it in from another payphone. Can't be too careful." Rawiri stopped. "I'm sorry. I didn't mean to conjure up, you know, sorry."

Wiremu ignored the reference to their dead brother.

"Moana is real switched on. Doesn't miss a trick. Bet she suspects we are on to something. " "Wouldn't put it past her. Shit, she's smart. Talking of smart, how are we going to handle the exchange?" Rawiri looked at Wiremu, concerned.

"Hey, it's just a business transaction. He gives me the money, I count it, see it's all there and not fake, and I give him the notebooks."

"Wiremu, younger brother. You know how many lads I talked to inside who said the same thing to me? And do you know where they finished up?"

"Talking to you? In prison?"

"You can't trust the Russian. His place might be bugged now and he'll be watched. Can you see anything from here?"

"No."

"Exactly. Because they don't want you to know they're there. Never underestimate your enemy. We have to plan it out in detail. If it goes wrong we need a backup plan, just in case. Too much money at stake here for us to be so casual."

"Okay, older brother. Let me hear what you think we should do."

CHAPTER FIFTY-THREE

Barbara Turner wanted to call off the tail once Wiremu and Rawiri crossed Khyber Pass Road. Michael insisted they wait. "They're walking somewhere. Let's see where they're going."

"At least we now know the Chinese are working with them," Barbara said. "Shit. That changes everything. What if the Chinese have protection? We can't move against them with Wiremu."

"Let's not jump to conclusions. We can catch them again. It's not like they're difficult to follow." Michael found a place to park among the other cars and trucks in the industrial area.

Wiremu and Rawiri turned into the park next to Clive Road. "They're not going for a picnic, are they?" Barbara spat out. "Shit. Now I'm fucking curious. Let's go up to the top. I want to know what they're doing."

· · ·

Wiremu woke from a nap. Rawiri sat next to him and watched the Castle, or rather the top of the tower. He had no idea what was going on around the Castle or the Drive or the track that lead up to where they were in the grass. He was happy to be outside, to listen to the trees, watch the clouds. He had been free for only a few days and was still getting used to the idea of open spaces he could wander in with no restrictions, no one telling him what to do. A thrush chirped nearby but he couldn't see it.

Wiremu raised his head and breathed in the fresh wind from the Waitemata harbor. The trees below him swayed. "Did I fall asleep for long?"

"Not long enough for the ants to eat you."

Wiremu jumped up and brushed off the ants. He stretched and selected another spot to sit.

"Do you know tohunga used to sit on the side of the pa and communicate with the other world, maybe with other tohunga on other volcanoes? They had special spots where they could draw energy from the earth and used it to communicate with each other. It's how they got their power out of the land. One of the reasons our land is important to us."

"Are you sitting on a power spot or an ant hill?"

"Oh fuck! More ants. How come they like me not you?"

.   .   .

After parking at the summit, Barbara and Michael walked around the large crater. When they had crossed to the lower crater and looked further south to a clump of trees, they saw Wiremu and Rawiri sitting in the grass.

"What the fuck?" Barbara asked. "Is this the teddy bears' picnic?"

"Must be looking at a house. But what can they see with all the trees? Looking for someone? Maybe they're setting up a robbery." Michael shivered. He was dressed in his navy blazer and the wind was cold.

They kept walking so as not to draw attention to themselves. Barbara looked back before they lost sight of the brothers. "Those two don't do breaking and entering. Too small. They must be planning something else. Let's go. We've found out enough."

On the short trip to the Turner house in Epsom, Barbara kept conjecturing. "They were casing a place. For what, we don't know. What we do know is they're here in Auckland. Up to no good, and in league with the Chinese. That's enough to go on for now. We just have to keep an eye on that lot down south, make sure they're planning another harvest."

"Yeah, why wouldn't they? They lost everything last time," Michael smirked.

CHAPTER FIFTY-FOUR

Alexander started his search where he had last seen the black Jaguar turn on Ruskin Street. He crisscrossed the side streets until he came to St George's Bay Road and doubled back to Parnell Road. He did not spot a 1968 red Mini. He saw a blue Mini and a green Mini, but no red one. Once he had ventured through all the side streets he parked on Heather Street, opposite Garfield Street, and across from Parnell Road. He had a good view of the main street. It was close to eleven o'clock. He decided to walk around the neighborhood, see what coffee shops or lunch places would be open and get a feel for the area. As he walked, he felt the raw skin on his knees and was reminded of their ferocious lovemaking last night. Which led him to remember a piece of paper in his jeans. He found a payphone and called the number Tsara had left for him.

"Newton? Where have you been?" Grimble barked once Alexander was patched through. "I've been waiting for your report."

"I'm following up on what we talked about. I'm in Parnell. If he did drop the painting off and if his daughter is involved, I have a feeling as to where she would be. She's working close by."

"A feeling?" Grimble took a deep breath. "Okay. Cadd is in the area as well, looking for the red Mini. When you see her, call me here."

There was a click followed by the dial tone. At least Grimble had told him about Cadd. Sharing information? Perhaps I am part of the team, Alexander thought.

He walked up and down Parnell Road and around the side streets connected to Heather Street before he came to the coffee shop on the corner. He peeked inside and saw a tall blonde at the counter. Alexander slipped in beside her. "Can I get a turkey sandwich as well, please? And a Fanta?" he asked the counter man.

The blonde let out a smile as she turned to face him. "Alexander? It's you?" In her high heels they were almost the same height.

"Oh, my god! Natasha! What are you doing here?" He wanted to say how fabulous she looked in her tight blood-red dress cut to the knees and how she must have lost a lot of weight but thought that might not be appreciated.

"I was about to ask the same thing."

"I'm here for the Omai exhibit. At the Auckland City Art Gallery. I escorted the Captain Cook painting from the National Gallery—but it's gone missing."

"What, the gallery?"

"No. The painting."

"Oh? I don't read newspapers. Too depressing. If you're at the gallery, what brings you to Parnell?"

"I'm meeting a friend later, and thought I'd get an early lunch. Can we eat together?"

Natasha pushed a strand of hair behind her ear. "I'd love to."

Alexander followed her over to a corner table. "You said a painting is missing?" Natasha asked as she draped her shoulder bag over her chair and adjusted her hair again.

"Yes. Seems like I am out of a job. But let's not talk about me — what about you? Are you still living in, what do you call it, the Castle?"

"Yes. It's an amazing place. You remember the night you were there, with your girlfriend?"

"How could I forget? We split up a long time ago. I live on my own now."

"Oh, I'm sorry." Natasha took a bite out of her sandwich and stared at Alexander as he examined his own sandwich, a thin slice of processed turkey on two slices of white bread cut in half. "Damn, no mustard."

Natasha held his gaze with her blue eyes. "Why did you say, 'How could I forget?'"

Alexander let out a sigh. The turkey sandwich was a disappointment, but Natasha was a surprise. "It's just how you acted, I suppose. You seemed to know, er, what you wanted."

"It's a good thing, no? Like feminists act?"

"Was it an act?" Alexander returned her look. Her eyes appeared deeper and more vivid than he remembered. "I was taken aback by you. You seemed like you wanted to be in control. And my girlfriend was in the next room."

Natasha finished her sandwich. "Well, she isn't now, is she?"

"What are you doing now? I thought you were studying, what was it? German?"

"Oh yes. I got a Masters in German and political science. Now I'm doing a Ph.D. in Soviet history and working nearby while I complete my thesis. God, it's tedious. Lots of writing. I have no idea how it will turn out."

"Well, you seem to be good at anything you turn your mind to." Alexander sipped his soft drink.

Natasha glanced at her watch. "I have to get back to work. But what are you doing later?"

"After my meeting I'm just hanging out at the gallery, I think. Want to have a drink later?"

"Why not? Say six at…?" Natasha thought for a while and shrugged. "Don't go out much. Any ideas?"

"Auckland's changed since I lived here. Why not start at the Kiwi Tavern? It's near the gallery. Do you have a car?"

"Yes but it's in the garage. British engineering. Not so reliable."

"Sounds like my first car. A Morris Minor. Whoever designed it should've been shot."

"Mine's an Austin Mini. Do you have wheels?"

"Not on my government expenses. I do a lot of walking. Seems to keep me fit."

"Okay. I'll see you at six." Natasha stood and kissed Alexander on both checks. He managed to return her kiss on one cheek, feeling awkward about her quick intimacy.

He watched her as she crossed Parnell Road. She turned on Garfield Street and looked back in his direction. Alexander had his head down, so he hoped she did not spot him staring at her. When she was out of sight he rushed out of the café and ran across the road to catch sight of her as she turned left onto Bath Street and stepped into the first door on the right. He waited a few minutes to get his breath and walked past the door, taking a note of the company name on the side of the building, and the street number. He kept walking along Bath Street until he could turn left again and arrive at Parnell Rise. He looked for a payphone where he could call Grimble. He was on hold for a long time. When he was finally connected, Grimble was abrupt. Alexander got the sense that Grimble was angry he had located Natasha and his own man, Sergeant Cadd, had not.

Alexander had enough coins left to call Catelin, his real boss. He found him on his second call. "I just found Natasha, the Russian girl," he reported. "She works at an engineering firm, with a loading dock." He gave Catelin the exact address and a description of the office front. "It has enough space for a Jaguar to back into," he said. "I'm going to run out of coins soon, can I have your local number? I'll call collect."

Catelin gave him a new phone number in Auckland and as Alexander had predicted the beeps started: he was cut off. He called the operator, gave her the new number and asked if it was on High Street. After a short wait she informed him it was on Shortland Street and gave him the street number. He waited to be connected.

"I have a collect call from a Mr. Alexander. Will you accept?"

Catelin said yes.

Once Alexander had briefed his boss on what had transpired since he last talked to him, he confessed. "I didn't tell Grimble, but I'm meeting Natasha tonight at six at the Kiwi. I figure we'll have a few drinks, she'll take me to her place, and I'll see what I can find out."

"Yes, you will," Catelin said sharply.

"What do you mean? Do you realize what a situation I am in now because of a fucking stolen painting? When all's said and done, it isn't my fault the bloody thing was nicked!" Alexander looked around to see if anyone had heard him. He hung up, annoyed at Catelin's response. Was his boss hearing rumors about him as well? He walked to his van. Driving would calm him down.

Alexander took a slow circuitous route around the university before parking in his spot across from Tsara's house. He killed the motor and sat in silence to think. He had never met a woman like Mel. Confident and forthright, she personified for him the perfect woman, the perfect lover. But he felt the relationship was unreal. What had happened between them was a fantasy—and a reaction to breaking up with her boyfriend, Henry. He couldn't imagine his relationship with Mel would last, or the intensity could be sustained.

He had to come clean with Tsara and tell her what he had been doing with his spy work in Wellington. At university they had always confessed their adventures to each other, however bad they might have sounded. What he had done for the government would not be so awful, he reasoned. Just a few photos, a little spying. He had done good, he had confirmed Dr. Winter was a Soviet spy and exposed his sauna friend's affair with the shadow minister. Infidelity in high places. Perhaps he should be afraid of the government. He had started a series of events he did not know how to stop. If he could talk it through with Tsara, there might be a way out for him. If Tsara would listen and understand. By confessing to his best friend, he would be betraying his promise to Catelin. But he felt he had to.

Alexander stepped out of the van. He looked up and down the road and saw nothing out of the ordinary, no men sitting in Chrysler Valiants or Ford Escorts. He brought his camera bag. At Tsara's front door he hesitated for a few moments before knocking twice.

She opened the door, turned and walked towards the living room. She had her arms folded, and when she looked at him, it made Alexander even more nervous than he already was. She did not look serene — she looked upset.

"Tsara, I'm in so deep, I don't know where I am, or who my friends are. I've been keeping away, because it's about to get real hairy. It's all rather complicated. The Soviets, the local spies, the police, Maori land activists, the student activist we met at the opening and the doctor? What's her name? Doctor Mel and her boyfriend. It's all a big mess, and if I don't find the fucking painting of Captain Cook, my job is over, and I won't have much of a future here. I'll be known as the curator who lost Cook."

Tsara took a deep breath. "Where were you the last two nights?" she spat.

Alexander hesitated for a second. How could she know? "I was in my van doing surveillance on the Soviet."

She kept her lips closed.

"Two nights ago, I went to the Doctor's dojo and I met Mark and his girlfriend Annie. We went out to dinner. Mark is linked to Captain Cook, but I can't tell you much more."

"Where did you go after?"

Alexander wondered if he was under surveillance. "I couldn't use the van because I didn't want Mark to know I had it, so I was with the doctor. You've never been jealous. What's with you?"

"I know about Wellington."

"Wellington?" Alexander was puzzled. What could Tsara possibly have found out? "You mean the librarian? I told you about her. We've never hidden anything from each other."

"No. I know about your spying on Kathy. The photos. The scandal it's caused."

"What?" Alexander thought for a moment, then his jaw dropped, and he collapsed on the sofa. He tried to compose himself. A feeling of dread swept over him. The moment he had feared—and he hadn't had the opportunity to explain himself.

"I know Kathy from when she was at uni here. We did English together. She told me everything, and she's heartbroken about her best friend's father and mother. You know they're getting divorced? And it's because of you and your damn photos." She clenched her fists and stomped her right foot. Alexander had never seen her so angry. He buried his face in his hands, as if to save himself. He didn't know what to say or do.

"Just leave. I see you've taken your stuff anyway, so just go."

Alexander realized he could not talk his way out of this. He saw her eyes fill with tears. "I, I," was all he could utter.

"I don't want to hear your lies. I don't know who you are any more. Just leave. Now!" Tsara turned away and went to the kitchen.

Alexander wanted to follow her, plead with her, tell her she was someone special he had known for years as a true friend, and he would never dream of hurting her. But instead he froze with his mouth open.

Tsara stood in the kitchen door and stared at him. "Get out!"

Alexander grabbed his camera bag, walked to the front door and ran across the road to his van. Once inside, he gripped the steering wheel. He could not cry. He sat in the van unable to move for some time before he turned the ignition and, with the engine running, started to recover a measure of his usual composure.

He drove to Mount Eden and parked at the summit. Perhaps he would spend the night in the van, on his mattress. He walked around the crater in a clockwise direction and headed to the lower crater. From where he stood most of the Gothic-inspired building was obscured by pohutukawa trees and nikau palms. He felt the wind in his face as he looked at Rangitoto across the harbor. He took deep breaths and tried to get his mind into his job: find Captain Cook. He had to keep his mind occupied and away from Tsara's complete rejection of their friendship.

When he came to a crest in the track at the lower crater, he noticed two large Maori men sitting in the grass. He recognized them and stepped back, to keep out of their line of sight.

CHAPTER FIFTY-FIVE

"You know we could just swap the notebooks for Captain Cook. We would have the painting and negotiate with the government for its return in exchange for our land."

Rawiri had not moved from his cross-legged position. "Good point," he said. "A bit late now, isn't it? Who knows if he has the painting? It might be somewhere he has no control over it, or he might not have it at all. The money makes sense. If he pays us."

"You think he'll pull something?"

"We'd be naïve to think otherwise. And what would we do with the painting? It creates more problems. They'd never forget we stole it or had it. Even if we recovered it and gave it back, we would still be prosecuted. Correct?"

"Even without the damn painting, we're creating a lot of discussion," said Wiremu. "And we don't have to worry about Captain Cook. I mean, he is proving useful to us even now."

"When are you going to slip the envelope to him?" Rawiri asked.

"Just as soon as I am convinced no one is watching the building. I'll sneak in like last time."

.   .   .

Alexander walked to where he could watch the two Maori. He was far enough away, he was just another hiker. What were they doing above the Castle where Natasha lived, with Raganovich? He walked around the lower crater again as he kept the two in sight until one disappeared and the other kept his back to Alexander. It didn't look right.

He had his upcoming rendezvous with Natasha at the Kiwi to plan. He decided to keep the van at the summit where he could retrieve it later. Maybe after his visit to the Kiwi? Or after meeting Natasha? He knew he was not thinking clearly because of Tsara.

He assumed Grimble and Cadd would pay a visit to Natasha's workplace and he would hear what happened when he met her later. Would she tell him? She had not batted an eyelid when he mentioned the stolen painting, yet her apartment had been searched by the police. If she had the painting, why would she hide it in her own apartment? He couldn't understand Grimble's strategy. They weren't dealing with common Kiwi criminals. Russians were more cunning and devious. Natasha was working off the books for a company in Parnell, which would explain why her employment had not been in the Wanganui computer Grimble seemed to rely on. So would they raid where she worked after she had left for the day? Or keep it and her under surveillance? Alexander discounted the police keeping watch on her, as he had seen how easily the government lost their targets. And Cadd hadn't been able to find her Mini.

He saw both Maori walk across the lower crater. They were easy to follow with big strides and, unlike the Soviet, they did no counter-surveillance drills. Alexander kept them in sight, from a distance, and figured they were going somewhere in the city. He could use the long walk to clear his head. Across Grafton Bridge they turned right on Symonds Street until they came to the Kiwi Tavern and went inside. Alexander crossed Wellesley Street to get a decent view of the pub from the opposite side of the street. He would be able to see Natasha approach on foot from Parnell, and he could keep an eye out for any surveillance.

He spotted her on Symonds Street. She wore a red wool coat with large lapels, left open to show her matching blood red dress. Her blonde hair trailed behind her as she drifted across the street. Alexander ran against traffic and bumped into her by the entrance to the pub.

"Hey, you look great," he managed to say. "Love the coat." He had taken his denim jacket off and his white shirt felt damp. It was cool outside, but he had been walking fast to keep up with the two Maori.

"My car is still not fixed. It's so annoying."

"What's the problem?"

"One part they have to import. What a country. Everything is imported."

"Well, the beer's local." Alexander smiled and waved his hand at the pub. "Do you want to go inside or get something to eat? There's Charcuterie on High Street. Decent food, I hear."

"Let's have a beer first. I've never been in here."

"Years of studying German and never been here? Used to drink the place dry when I was at uni."

They went into the public bar, ordered beers and stood next to a window. The pub smelled of stale beer and cigarette smoke. A group of Maori were opposite them. Alexander recognized the two guards who had been inside the gallery at the opening, and the two he had followed. They had been outside the gallery according to the photos he had blown up for the inspector. He turned to Natasha and made a small hand gesture only she could see towards the Maori. "Do you recognize them?"

"No. Should I?"

Alexander noted she had not turned to where he had pointed. Didn't everyone immediately look, even if you told them not to? Maybe she had already seen them. Maybe it was part of her training as a Soviet spy, to scan a room as soon as she entered.

"Two of them were at the gallery for opening night."

She kept her eyes on him. "Well, I wasn't invited."

"I didn't know you were here. I mean, I haven't been to Auckland in what, two years?"

Natasha sipped her beer and moved closer to him. "Are you going to hold it against me?" she asked.

Alexander smiled.

"Your dimples." She touched his face. "I remember those dimples. Big trouble."

He shrugged. "I hope not."

"Where are you staying?"

"An interesting question." He finished his beer.

"And you are not telling me? It's a national secret?"

"Are you hungry? We can go eat. I haven't eaten all day. No, come to think of it, I had a marvelous lunch with a mysterious old friend I had not seen for a long time."

"Mysterious?"

"Oh yes. Well, you are, aren't you?"

"Are you teasing me?"

"I wish." Alexander's easy manner belied his wariness towards her.

"Why don't we go to my place? I can cook."

"Sounds good. Can we walk?"

"It's a little far. You don't have a car?"

Alexander shook his head and wondered if she knew more than she was letting on. If she knew about his van, so did her father. She was so cool, nonchalant and scary. Was he walking into a trap? "We can take a taxi," he said.

They walked to the cab stand on Wellesley Street. Natasha gave her address. In the back of the cab Alexander sat with his legs touching Natasha's. "Ah yes, the Castle," he said. "Quite a place. And you live alone?"

"Yes. But my father is staying with me."

"He's a Kiwi?"

"Don't be silly. Russian. He's a diplomat in Wellington. He's here visiting, but I am not expecting him home tonight." She leaned her head on his shoulder. "We will not be disturbed."

At the Castle, Alexander followed Natasha as she waltzed into the front vestibule. The space where the black Jaguar should have been was empty. He tried to remember everything he saw: the front entrance, the mailboxes, her name over her box, 'N. Windsor'. He could make out the rear entrance as he followed her up two flights of stairs and the long corridor, trying not to look at her long legs and the way she swayed her hips.

When Natasha opened the door, she saw an envelope on the floor and kicked it under a chair. She turned to Alexander and smiled as she flung her coat on the chair, hiding the envelope. "I've had enough beer to last me a lifetime. What is it with Kiwis and beer? I have a very nice burgundy. French. Yes?"

"I am in your hands. So, you were born in Russia?"

"No, thank goodness. My father married an American and I was born in Washington. I am an American citizen. They are divorced, and I haven't seen my mother in years."

"I'm sorry. Must be hard. Was your mother's name Windsor?"

"Yes. Like the Queen. And I see my father a lot. He is very attentive."

"And being a diplomat, you get immunity as well?"

"I wish. No more speeding tickets."

·   ·   ·

At the Kiwi Tavern, if Alexander had moved a little closer, he would have heard a conversation between the four Maori. The owner of the security company explained to Wiremu and Rawiri how the inspector had questioned him about the opening night. He had stuck to the script they had agreed to. He thought neither the inspector nor his sergeant had been able to identify the two other Maori who had been outside. He said his men had not let anyone in who was not on the approved guest list except for the mayor, who had been a late addition, and a Soviet diplomat from Wellington whose name no one could pronounce. The security company owner knew better than to ask about the stolen painting.

CHAPTER FIFTY-SIX

Mark Rose walked the Ho Chi Minh trail behind his apartment, across the Domain, to a small road near the Wintergarden pavilion. He came to a blue Datsun parked nearby. The garden and the museum were closed. In the early dusk, few runners were in the park. No one paid him any attention, the reason why it was his emergency meeting point. Mark had phoned the Castle twice. He hung up on the first ring, and then on the second ring. As his Soviet handler has said years ago, always keep it simple.

Mark peered into the car to make sure he recognized the driver before getting into the Datsun. "They're onto you, you know," he said. Mark looked at the Soviet who was dressed in a dark blue track suit. Mark wore a red and black lumberjack checkered shirt and jeans with his work boots. His standard student revolutionary outfit. "But I guess you know that, as you switched cars."

"Yes." Nikolai Nikolaevich Raganovich smiled. It was not a pleasant smile. Only his lips moved. His eyes were blank. "But *how* do they know?"

"That's what I wanted to talk to you about." Mark gritted his teeth. "It's the damn curator from Wellington. He knows we took Captain Cook. He drives a small white van."

"Ah. The white van. Not a vehicle the SIS uses. Is he SIS too?"

"No. He's just a curator. Caused the raid on my house. And I spent a lot of money on him at a restaurant the other day."

"You know what Sun Tzu said? Keep your friends close and your enemies closer."

"Very funny. What are we going to do with him?"

"I thank you for the information and you are not to worry anymore. Understand?"

"Yes." Mark resisted the effort to shiver. The Soviet gave his bear smile, as if he was dinner. Mark looked ahead, into the twilight, chills running down his spine.

"I will be leaving soon. I want you to know how much I have enjoyed working with you and how much I appreciate and respect all your efforts. You should be proud of what you have accomplished. The right people know of you and will stand by you if ever the time comes. I want you to know there is a medal waiting for you if you can ever visit us in Moscow. The Order of Lenin is being held for you, in your name. You understand?"

Mark nodded and could not say anything.

"At a future date you will receive a postcard from Spain. Later, you will be contacted our usual way."

"Like we met before? Seems a long time ago."

"Yes, my friend. We have had a good relationship. Here. For you." The Soviet nodded to a small envelope beside the gear stick.

Mark did not look at the Soviet again as he stuffed the envelope in his jeans pocket and slipped out of the car. He looked around to see if he could spot anyone suspicious before heading back towards the Ho Chi Minh trail.

.   .   .

Raganovich drove up and down the side streets of Parnell and then across to Mount Eden, checking for any surveillance. He eventually arrived at Mountain Road then turned into the cul-de-sac, Glenfell Place, and parked at the end near Government House. He took off his jacket and made for a track up to the smaller crater. He couldn't run as the track was too steep for him. But when he got to the top he broke into a light jog and looked like an aging rugby player trying to keep in shape in his track pants, T-shirt and running shoes. At the summit he stopped to admire the view and noted all the people around him, as well as passengers getting back onto a tour bus. Nothing looked out of the ordinary. Not for the first time he wondered why the New Zealand security services were not following him. Was it because he was due to be deported and they had given up? Or was the curator involved? He did not want to speculate. He had a job to do.

The small white government van was parked facing the Waitemata harbor. He checked the plates in the approaching darkness. He was thankful for the network of helpers who had told him where it was parked. He had first heard of the van when a neighbor had called him a few days ago when it was parked on Castle Drive. A young man had walked around with a camera, taking photos and had returned to the van to follow Raganovich's Jaguar. The next morning he had spotted the van in his rear-view mirror when he sped down Parnell Road. No other car had been behind him.

He looked through the windows. A mattress was rolled up in a bundle. He walked to the other side, checked the doors and knelt near the front tire on the passenger side. Taking a small folding knife out of his pocket he eased underneath the van and reached up until he located the brake fluid hose. He severed the line with his knife and then stabbed the inside of the tire a few times. He stood up, rubbed his hands and brushed the dirt from his T-shirt and track pants. No one had noticed him, and he continued his jog around the large crater and down to where he had parked the Datsun. He drove to Castle Drive and parked where he could see the corner window of the apartment.

CHAPTER FIFTY-SEVEN

"Are you going to give me the grand tour?" Alexander asked as Natasha began to take containers out of the refrigerator. They had finished off an open bottle of burgundy.

"You want to get into my bedroom now? And not eat?"

On the noticeboard opposite the refrigerator were a series of papers, recipes, a class schedule and one small business card. It had a car printed on it. It was from a garage. Natasha turned her back as she bent down to get another bottle of wine from the refrigerator. Alexander twisted around and read the exact address on the card. Before she could stand, he grabbed her by the waist. Natasha giggled. "You are in a hurry, aren't you? Perhaps we can eat later. Follow me."

Natasha held his hand and led him into her bedroom. There was lacy material over two lamps and a Gustav Klimt poster on the wall. Another, *Danaë*, was above her bed. It all reminded him of Deborah. But he was shocked when Natasha pushed him onto the bed and leapt on top, pinning his hands and legs. He hadn't realized how strong she was. She looked into his eyes and he couldn't tell if she wanted to devour him or kill him. He was afraid but tried not to show it. Her blonde hair covered his face and he couldn't breathe. She moved her head to one side and brushed her lips with his, then flicked her hair away and leapt to her feet. "Don't move," she commanded She grabbed her large shoulder bag and retreated into the bathroom.

When he heard the bathroom door shut, he looked up to see a set of handcuffs secured on each side of the bedposts. He rolled off the bed onto the floor. He peered under the bed and saw something. He touched a hard rubber object. He pulled it out. It was a giant strap-on dildo. He put it back and crawled as fast as he could out of the bedroom, then crept into the kitchen to look at the notice-board again. He memorized the address on the business card and made for the front door. As he tiptoed out he heard the floor creak but dared not look back. He twisted the lock, eased the door shut with both hands, slipped into the corridor and ran to the staircase. He took two stairs at a time and made it down both flights before turning around. He could see no one. At the front door he slowed down and debated for a second which way to go, then ran back to the rear entrance and cut across another right-of-way. He did not to go into the street.

Using his hands to keep his balance, he climbed up the grass-covered terraces until he arrived at the narrow one-way road. He looked down at the castellated tower and tried to catch his breath. In the dark he could not make out any movement around him with the low cloud and no moonlight. He continued walking up the hill till he came to the parking lot, unlocked his van and grabbed his camera bag from underneath the mattress. Nothing seemed out of place so he locked the van again and walked to the edge of the summit.

At the first terrace and out of sight of any cars he stopped to regulate his breathing and think. What had he got himself into? What sort of game was this? Because it was no longer a game, it was deadly. What would Natasha have done to him? The thought of that giant strap-on made him shiver and reminded him how cold he was in his shirt and denim jacket. He decided to double back to the safety of the trees below the summit and hide in the dark. He took out his camera and waited, not knowing what he was waiting for but alert to anything odd that could happen. Several cars came up to the summit and parked, but no one got out. He could just make out his van in the distance. No vehicles were near the van. Some time passed before he realized he couldn't see further past the trig point or from where he had escaped from. He thought he should stay where he was: his camera loaded with Tri-X film gave him some comfort. He knew something bad was going to happen and relying on his instincts he kept very still. He would be safer for now hidden in the dark.

Despite the quiet, Alexander could not get over his sense of unease. Some time passed before he rose from his hiding place and began to move carefully in the dark. He kept sliding down the overgrown grass terraces in between trees, until he came across a track that lead to Batger Road. He turned left on Mount Eden Road and walked briskly to warm himself. He could see no cars on the road, but he had a distinct feeling someone was after him.

·   ·   ·

"It's not too late, is it? I just escaped from the Russian woman's place." Alexander scanned his surroundings. He was in a phone box off Mount Eden Road, hidden from passing cars.

"And?" The voice sounded neutral and for a moment Alexander thought he had called Grimble instead of Catelin. He must have woken him. It was an apartment he had called, not an office.

"For a start, I've had a terrifying night. I won't go into details, but it was not good."

"Grimble raided where she worked tonight. But no sign of the painting. We still don't know where her car is."

"Because it's in a garage. And I bet anything the painting is in the car. He must have slipped it in when I was following him." Alexander gave the address he remembered from Natasha's noticeboard. "And I didn't see his Jag parked at the Castle either. He must be hiding out. He wasn't in the apartment."

"Anything else?"

"Yes. At the Kiwi pub tonight I saw the four Maori who I took photos of at the opening. They were in deep conversation. They knew each other and from their body language they must've been close. They have a history. There really were four, as my photos showed. Can you get in touch with the inspector? I can't reach him."

"Get some sleep. You did a good night's work. Brief me in detail later. Call in the morning."

"Wait, don't hang up. I was at the top of Mount Eden at about four, and I spotted the two Maori who were outside the gallery. They were sitting in the grass overlooking the Castle, the place I was tonight. I thought it odd."

"Good. I'll call Grimble." Alexander heard a click.

He walked to another red payphone with a door, nearer the shopping center. He dreaded the next call, but he had to make it. He closed the door, took a deep breath and dialed Tsara's number from memory. The phone rang forever. When she heard his voice, all she said was: "Don't ever call here again." She hung up before he could reply.

Alexander stepped out of the phone booth and stamped his feet. He looked around and decided to go back inside. He called the operator and asked for a person-to-person call to Deborah, collect, at her home. If he didn't call her now, he never would, and he needed to hear a friendly voice after what had just happened to him.

He heard the operator connect him and a muffled voice.

"Hello, Deborah? It's Alexander. Sorry it's so late but I had to call you."

"Alexander? It's you?" She sounded as if she had woken from a deep sleep.

"I miss your voice and being with you. Should I call later?"

"Mmmm. No, it's fine."

"You heard about the painting? Captain Cook has been stolen, and I'm working night and day to get it back. Bit of a nightmare."

"Yes. Lots of rumors. How are you coping?"

"Could do with a cuddle from you to make me feel better."

Deborah moaned and Alexander didn't know if she was yawning or thinking of him.

"What rumors?" he asked in the silence after the moan. "And I'm serious about a cuddle. Lots of cuddles."

"Oh, you know, it's a Maori gang who have no intention of swapping it for land. They want to keep it for themselves. My favorite is Muldoon has set the whole thing up himself."

"Oh god. Really? Still, I miss you, and I'm sorry I haven't been able to call you. I don't even have a hotel room. Last night I slept in a van I borrowed."

"On your own?"

"Yes. And I was freezing cold."

"Good. When are you coming to see me?"

"Don't know. Once Captain Cook is found, I hope. I'm working on a lead now. I can't wait to tell you all about it. I want to see you. Badly."

He thought he heard her moan again, then all he could hear was heavy breathing. "Deborah? Deborah?"

"Mmmm?"

"Miss you. I'll call you when I'm flying in. Sleep tight."

He waited for a response but only heard her breathing. He hung up, dug out Mel's card with her home phone number and dialed.

"I was wondering when you were going to call or if you were just going to show up unannounced."

"I was just checking in to see how you were. I've been busy, and I just had to hear your voice before I crashed tonight."

"I was asleep, Alexander."

"My sense of time is screwed, sorry. I should talk to you tomorrow. I'll let you go back to sleep."

"No, wait. Now I'm awake, you might as well talk to me. Where are you?"

"In a phone box nearby."

"Why don't you come over? I'll make a cup of tea."

"Best offer I've had all day."

CHAPTER FIFTY-EIGHT

When Natasha switched the reading light on and off three times, her father knew something had gone wrong. He ran up to her apartment. She was at the front door and, mindful of any bugging devices still in her home, whispered, "He ran away. I don't know why. I think he got scared."

"Don't worry. You have the bag?"

"Yes."

"Stay here. I'll see if I can catch him."

Raganovich worked his way up the hill along the track he had taken so often. When he could see the parking lot at the summit, he saw the white van. He jogged across to make sure no one was inside. He couldn't see any leaks. It was hopeless to pursue the curator on foot. Too much time had elapsed. He ran to where he had parked his Datsun on Castle Drive and started to drive around Mount Eden. He would drive in concentric circles covering every road in the hope of spying a tall young man on foot with a denim jacket and white shirt. He could have taken any number of roads to escape and left his van at the summit for a reason, Raganovich surmised, to speed his exit and not be seen in the van at night.

CHAPTER FIFTY-NINE

Inspector Grimble called Cadd as soon as he had finished Under-Secretary Richard Catelin's phone call. Cadd was at headquarters finishing the paperwork from their earlier unsuccessful raid on Natasha's work. He instructed Cadd to use the same search warrant and insert the address for the garage Catelin had spelled out for him. "Use the same affidavit of facts, make sure you specify the Mini as well. No good searching the garage and not being able to search the car. In fact, include all vehicles in the garage. Get it signed by the officer in charge—Jarvis should still be there—then go to our favorite magistrate, wake him and get him to sign the warrant. He can't complain, he knows he's on call, and it's of national importance. Tell him. Radio me as soon as you have it signed."

Cadd acknowledged the order.

"And I don't have to say don't come back until you've got it. Hurry. I'll have the command post nearby on the corner of Fox and York."

CHAPTER SIXTY

"I spent half my life being woken at odd hours or not sleeping on endless shifts, but having a strange man ring my doorbell? What can be going on?"

Mel had kissed Alexander on the lips when she opened the door. She wore a red satin dressing gown. He looked behind him and quickly shut the door, saying, "It's not that late." He dropped his camera bag in the hall and followed her into the kitchen where she had brewed tea. He wondered what she was wearing underneath.

"You take it black, no sugar, right?"

"Thank you."

'Why are you so jumpy? You're usually so cool."

"I am? Cool?"

"God. You are so—"

"Jumpy?"

"Why are you on edge? Was it the Russian?"

"Well, yes. Glad I escaped her. But I'm with you and I think…I think I'm a mess with you. It's as if I want everything to be perfect but I feel foolish and insecure. Then there's this other feeling I got that I'm being followed. It's very odd. Does this make sense?"

Mel nodded and kept still.

Alexander drank his hot tea and looked at Mel in the kitchen light. Without makeup, she was even more sexy to him. In other circumstances, he wouldn't be able to restrain himself, but he felt off-balance.

"Natasha Windsor is the daughter of the Russian diplomat cum spy Nikolai Raganovich. He wasn't at the Castle tonight, thank goodness. But she was a handful."

"Handful as in?" Mel cupped her hands in front of her chest.

"No, we didn't get that far, thank god. She was rather direct. She took me into the bedroom and pushed me onto the bed. Pounced on me. She promised, well, I never found out what. When she went to the bathroom to do whatever, she took her shoulder bag with her. What woman takes a great big shoulder bag into her own bathroom? It's as if she didn't want me to search it."

"Which you would have."

"Oh yes. Anyway, I looked up and saw handcuffs bolted to the bedposts. Bloody handcuffs. Ready for me."

Mel laughed and checked his wrists.

"Always the doctor. I have never run so fast in my life. I left my van at the summit. Seemed like a good place to hide it, in plain sight."

"You are a spy. My, I am impressed. What now?"

"Now? I feel safe again, with you. I have a terrible feeling though. I can't put it into words, but someone is out there searching for me. I had chills down the back of my neck."

"Oh dear. You do need protecting."

"Yes, I do."

She walked over to him, stroked his hair, and kissed his forehead. He lifted his head and they kissed. A long sweet tender kiss.

.   .   .

When Natasha closed the front door to her father, she went to the bathroom and opened her bag. The thick envelope was inside along with her Polaroid camera and the Makarov pistol. At her front door she bent by the chair where her coat lay. She found the white envelope and opened it. She read the handwritten note and smiled. It was just as her father had said it would happen. She set her alarm for six o'clock.

Raganovich had spent over two hours cruising around looking for his suspect spy. He decided to head back to Parnell. When he eased his Datsun around the corner of Fox and York Street he saw what looked like a police van without any markings and a red Honda next to it. He kept driving and zigzagged back to Parnell Road. He had one last task to arrange.

.   .   .

Alexander woke to feel Mel under the sheets. He thought he was dreaming until he felt her teeth. He was thankful he was not handcuffed to a bed in the Castle.

After she had finished, she snuggled into his neck. "I've been thinking about that since yesterday," she murmured.

"I must return the favor sometime."

"I'm sure you will."

"Mel, I'm still in shock over you. I mean us. And that, well, that was amazing." He breathed out. He held her for some time before he spoke again. "You know I'm not impressed with myself. I feel like I barely get through each day. Half the time I have no idea what I'm doing and the other half…"

"Well, I think the other half is functioning very well. You're not a little boy any more, despite your vulnerability,. You just don't know you project confidence and what's the word? Virility."

"I do. Really?"

"Yes. I'm jumping in the shower. Join me?"

CHAPTER SIXTY-ONE

Natasha took a little-used track to climb to the top of the lower crater. She was dressed in a black parka, black pants and boots. Her hair was tied in a bun underneath a black watch cap and she had a black shoulder bag at her waist. When she arrived at the main crater she had an excellent view of the trig point, the designated rendezvous, as well as all possible approaches from the winding road to the parking lot and the other walking tracks. She waited for half an hour crouching next to a tree, obscured from view. Her father had told her a long time ago, "Arrive early and kill everyone." At first she thought he was joking, but he never joked, so she got the point.

Natasha watched the Waitemata harbor become visible. The dark water glistened like molten silver. She heard a tour bus come to the top of the parking lot. The brakes squealed, and doors cranked open. A stream of tourists with cameras came walking around the trig point and down the track to where she was. She heard an older man's voice directing a group of tourists to her tree and realized it was her father. He wore a tweed jacket and a trilby hat and looked more like an English squire than a Soviet diplomat.

She was surprised when a large Maori loomed over her from out of the crowd of middle-aged tourists and asked if she was the girl from the Kiwi last night. And did she have a package for him?

"Do you have the notebooks?" she asked. Among all the people with cameras was another large Maori at the edge of the lower crater facing in her direction. Tourists were walking around the summit, but Wiremu ignored them. Natasha scanned her immediate surroundings for any other possible threats.

Wiremu put his hand inside his leather jacket and pulled out three medium-sized, black, worn notebooks for Natasha to see. "The money?" he asked.

She reached into her black shoulder bag and he moved a step closer to her. She adjusted her hips and showed him the fat envelope. Her blue eyes bored into him.

"It's all there?" he asked.

"See for yourself. I presume he's your lookout?"

"One of them." Wiremu grabbed the envelope with his left hand, staring at her without blinking. "It's what you can't see that you should be afraid of."

Natasha looked at the crowd and frowned.

Wiremu peeked inside the envelope and thumbed through the three thick bundles. They were not New Zealand dollars. He glared at her, annoyed.

"American dollars," she said. "We couldn't get the Kiwi dollars. Besides, no one wants them. Much better for you, $25,000 U.S. currency. All hundred-dollar bills. Count them. And a better rate than you would get. Now, the notebooks?"

Wiremu handed her the three books and counted with both hands one stack of hundreds. He estimated what the other two contained.

Natasha flipped through the notebooks. They went into her leather bag and she kept her right hand inside. "Now walk away," she said, " and I never want to see you again."

.   .   .

Wiremu retreated behind a group of photographers and watched her walk away. When she reached the first grass terrace she raised both hands in the air as if stretching. Wiremu looked around to try to see who she was signaling to and saw Raganovich standing right by the trig point. Wiremu turned to Rawiri and waved the all-clear. Rawiri repeated the sign to two other Maori who were out of sight of Wiremu and the Soviet.

"I think our next stop is to our Mr. Crispfeldt. We have an investment to make." Wiremu showed Rawiri the open envelope of U.S. $100 notes and slid it inside his leather jacket as they made their way to Mount Eden Road. "It's going to burn a hole in my pocket."

CHAPTER SIXTY-TWO

"I'm not sure what's going to happen today. Can I see you again tonight?" Alexander was eating marmalade on toast and drinking coffee Mel had prepared.

"Yes, of course. I talked to Henry last night. He called me from Dunedin. I think he's returning today but I'm not sure. He said he's going to the States. If he stays here he can sleep in the spare room until he leaves. He's not sharing my bed again."

"Ouch! Harsh. I'd never leave the country if I was with you. Correction. I hope to be with you. I have no idea what is going on between us. All I know is I love being with you. And if I did anything to piss you off, I'd work damn hard to make things right again." Alexander ran his hands through his hair. "I don't know how to say what I want to say."

"I have to go. We'll talk tonight. I'll see you at the dojo at seven?"

"Wouldn't miss it for the world."

Alexander hiked to the summit parking lot. It was easier in daylight as he could see the track he had plunged down the night before. He checked the van's doors and windows before slipping into the driver's seat. For a moment he panicked, until he remembered he had left his camera bag at Mel's.

The van wouldn't start. The engine was cold. He tried the choke but thought he had flooded the carburetor. On his fifth try he managed to get the motor to turn over, and on the seventh it started. He let go of the hand brake and reversed out of the space. He kept the van in second as he descended the narrow one-way road. The engine whined as he shifted into third. He was dying to know if the painting had been recovered from the address he had given Catelin last night.

He picked up speed as he headed down the summit road and came to the roundabout. He began to brake but the van didn't slow. The brake pedal hit the floor. He pumped the pedal but could feel no pressure, so he tried to jam the gear down to second. The cogs made a loud grating sound. Alexander remembered to double declutch to ease into second. He had enough time to look both ways on Mount Eden Road and saw no immediate oncoming traffic as he cut across. He accelerated, forgetting about his brakes and weaved between slower cars in the morning rush hour.

The van felt odd, pulling to the left. He kept having to steer to the right. He was lucky to make it through a series of green lights until he came to the Karangahape and Grafton Road intersection. In the middle lane he tried pumping the brakes and the van slowed, but not enough as he edged closer to the car in front of him. He yanked the hand brake and tried an emergency stop. The van skidded and almost side-swiped the car in front. He looked down and saw he was a couple of inches from the car's bumper. Other drivers were honking their horns. He ignored them. When the light turned green he straightened out the van and continued, careful to keep in second gear.

Alexander did not want to pull over, he was so close to the gallery. He continued down to the Wellesley Street turn-off and eased into third gear. The engine was revving high, and a thumping noise was coming from his front tire. The traffic light turned red and he was going too fast to stop. He saw no cars directly in front of him in his turn lane, so he accelerated as he veered left. Oncoming cars screeched to a halt or swerved to avoid the white van as it came around the corner on three wheels, one of which was losing its grip. He could see the Auckland City Art Gallery coming up on his right at the corner of Kitchener Street as he tried to pump the foot brake and wrestle with the stiff steering wheel.

He rammed the gear stick into first even though he double declutched as the van screamed down the hill, unable to stop. He eased the hand brake up one notch at a time as he steered towards the other side of the wide, four-lane road. He weaved between cars heading up the street, narrowly missing a larger van until he thought he had enough space to glide into Kitchener Street and stop. The left tire burst, and the hand brake failed. He ripped it upwards until it came apart in his left hand. He braced both hands on the steering wheel as he crashed into a parked car, a red Honda Accord. The Accord crumpled with the impact; Alexander twisted his body and hit the windshield. The glass cracked but he bounced back into his seat, dazed, still gripping the wheel. His forearms were stiff. He looked around and saw no one else was hurt. Traffic had stopped and he tried to exit from his side but was blocked by the squashed Honda. He managed to get himself out of his seat and slide over to the passenger side. The door was stuck.

A young man ripped open the door and helped him out. "Are you all right?" he asked breathlessly.

Alexander shook his head. He ignored the startled onlookers and drivers and walked like a drunk to the gallery entrance on Kitchener Street and through the double doors. The guard at the entrance recognized him and informed him he was expected upstairs. He patted his shirt and heard pieces of glass fall to the floor. He ran his hands through his hair to shake out more glass and checked his hands for blood. Pausing at the entrance to the Omai exhibit he saw a group of men crowded around a painting. For a moment, he thought it was the color reproduction — then he saw the look on Colin McMillan's face. He walked towards them. Colin hugged him. Alexander grimaced. He had pain all over his body.

Inspector Grimble and Sergeant Cadd started to clap, followed by the director, Thomas Jones, Peter MacIntosh, the director of security and the other curators.

"What? What's going on?" Alexander asked, running his hands through his hair again.

"It's back! It was where you said it would be. In the red Mini in the garage. We got it last night. It's in perfect condition. Colin just checked it. Well done." Grimble shook Alexander's hand, followed by everyone else. Alexander had never seen the inspector smile before. He had a sickening feeling about the red Honda.

CHAPTER SIXTY-THREE

By the time Rawiri and Wiremu returned to Moana and Rickey's place in the afternoon, they were a little drunk. Wiremu had been upset at the exchange rate and thought they had been ripped off by the Russians, but Rawiri consoled him. They were richer than they had been earlier in the morning. They had cashed a few American bills for expenses and embarked on a pub crawl from Vulcan Lane to High Street, finishing at the Kiwi Tavern where they met members of the security company they had drunk with the previous night and who had provided additional oversight to the exchange earlier.

Wiremu had used the payphone at the Queen's Ferry, the oldest pub in Auckland. He dialed Central and asked to speak to Inspector Grimble. "Listen, inspector. You know my voice but I'm not telling you my name. Three important small black notebooks are in the possession of one Soviet spy named Natasha, at the Castle in Epsom. I believe you know the place well, and if you go now, you'll find them. You owe me one, inspector. Let's hope I never have to collect."

Wiremu ended the call before Grimble could ask any questions and was at his beer mug before Rawiri came out of the bathroom.

Grimble did recognize the voice. He dialed a number. He had one more raid to organize.

CHAPTER SIXTY-FOUR

Moana waved the new editions of the *Auckland Star* and *NZ Truth* in their faces. "Look! All for nothing! Read that!" she spat.

"CAPTAIN SAFE, NOT COOKED. MAORI LAND RIGHTS HOAX," Rawiri read out loud. "What a paper. I'd hate to read what's inside."

"It gets worse," Moana sighed.

Rawiri turned to page three. "SOVIET SPY LOVE NEST SEARCHED. CAPTAIN COOK SAILED. Wow. They don't mess around, do they? It goes on: 'Police and Security sources stated the love nest of Soviet diplomat Nikolai Raganovich, who was linked to Dr. Cedric Winter in the sensational spy case, was raided by police earlier today in a desperate search for the missing Captain Cook painting stolen from Auckland City Art Gallery last Saturday night. *Truth* has found out the painting was not recovered, but the police are satisfied they are closing the net on the conspirators who stole the only three-quarter portrait of Captain Cook in the world. 'It's just a matter of time before we catch the thieves,' a police source stated.'

"Well, page three isn't talking to page one. Anyway, I thought they had naked girls on page three? What is the world coming to?"

Wiremu sat at the kitchen table and started to read the *Star* front page. "It's almost the same headline. I thought the *Star* was classier," he said.

Moana snatched the paper from him. and read the beginning of the article aloud. "CAPTAIN COOK RE-TURNS. KIDNAP WAS A HOAX. The painting was being restored after its trip from Wellington, a government spokesman who preferred to remain anonymous, stated. There were never any Maori land hostage negotiations which the spokesman claimed was a hoax. Captain Cook is back in the Auckland City Art Gallery special exhibit 'The Two Worlds of Omai', under strict security, the spokesman assured the *Star*, and will be on display until it returns to the National Art Gallery in Wellington."

"Well, it's over," Wiremu sighed.

"Guess so," said Rawiri.

"What about all our plans? The land? The cause?" Moana was angry.

"No one got arrested," said Wiremu. "We put Maori land rights in the media again. It got everyone talking. It's all good, right?"

Rawiri shook his head. "Yeah, it's good. Don't want to go back inside."

"Toi te kapa, toi te mana, toi te whenua."

"When did you start speaking Maori, Wiremu?" Moana had her hands on her hips.

"Since I've been taking lessons. And the proverb en-compasses what we hope to do. Rawiri and I have a plan."

"Since when?"

"Since we came from Mangawhau."

"What?"

"Mount Eden. We did a lot of thinking up there and we're going home tomorrow. We're got new classes in Rawene and in Kaitaia. Maori language and Maoritanga. We've elders we're going to hire as well as new teachers. And we'll be talking to Northland Education Board or whatever it's called, getting more Maori language into their lessons. All good, eh, Rawiri?"

Rawiri burped and smiled. "Yes, all good!"

Moana looked from one pair of bloodshot eyes to the other. She did not seem convinced.

•   •   •

Inspector Grimble called the commissioner to inform him of the anonymous phone call and ask, again, if he could raid the Castle apartment.

"What do you mean she has the notebooks?"

Grimble had known the commissioner would be angry but he hadn't expected to be blasted out of his chair. "Commissioner, I called you first because I think it's connected to what the FBI wants from that scientist, Henry Lotus. I was at his last interview. I think he lied about the notebooks and the Americans are after them. We know now the Russian has them."

"I understand. It's just I thought the whole episode was over. Talk to Jarvis and I'll call the magistrate you used to make sure he's still sober. You'd better make it snappy."

CHAPTER SIXTY-FIVE

Alexander walked into Mel's dojo at seven o'clock. The women recognized him from his previous appearance. Mel came out of the dressing room in a track suit and lined up her students. They started with breathing exercises and stretching.

"We're not going to be practicing on Alexander tonight," she said. " He's had a rather rough day." She didn't elaborate.

The women laughed; Alexander kept a straight face.

After the class, Alexander waited outside on Ponsonby Road. Mel appeared dressed in a black polo and tight black pants, her leather jacket open. She kissed him and took his hand. "What's the matter?" she asked.

"Oh, it's just my arms."

"You're fine. I checked you out. The pain in your tendons will go away in a few days."

"Thank you. Better than the telling off I got from that cop."

"Well, it's not very diplomatic to crash into a cop's car."

"At least nothing is going to get reported. Too embarrassing for everyone. Now answer my question I asked earlier. What did you do?"

"You mean the fingers in the throat? There's a little hole above your sternum, just here."

"Okay, I got it. Does that always work?"

"You collapsed, didn't you?"

"Every time."

"Well, you've learned a new technique. Remember, pain is your friend."

"I thought pain was my ego leaving my body." He twisted his neck left and right. "I think all my ego left my body today."

"Not to change the subject, but what do you want to do on your last night here?"

"I was thinking we could drive to the top of Mount Eden again. Are you game?"

"You mean in the car?" Mel put a finger to her lips. "Well, maybe."

They walked around the corner to where she had parked. As she drove, she kept glancing at Alexander. "You look sad," she said.

"Our last night, and I'm getting to know you, as much as I can know you. Yes, I'm sad."

"When are you returning?"

"I hope when the exhibit ends I can escort the Captain safely back to the National Gallery. Do you want to see me again?"

She smiled. "Of course."

Alexander felt relieved. "It's unexpected, what happened to us, or at least to me. I still can't believe it's true. But it is. Isn't it?"

Mel smiled again. "What do you mean?"

"You know I operate on instinct, and I could be wrong, but I feel a deep connection between us. Right from the moment I met you in the gallery. And ever since, we've just clicked."

Mel made the turn on Mount Eden Road. "Can we talk about this when I'm not driving?"

"Of course. Are you okay?"

"Of course. I'm with you." Mel kept her eyes on the dark narrow road to the summit.

Alexander smiled as he watched her.

"What?" she asked.

"You. I love being with you."

Mel drove in silence. She stopped in the same place Alexander had parked. She got out of the car before Alexander got any ideas and walked to the rim of the big crater. "Now I know why you wanted to come here," she sighed.

Alexander saw a giant round hole in the sky. It let in all the light from the universe. The moon illuminated Rangitoto, the symmetrical volcanic cone floating in the Waitemata harbor where the water glistened as if millions of silver fishes were on the flat surface.

There was no wind. They held hands and walked to the other side of the crater, along a narrow path. A few stars in the Southern sky competed for attention. Mel leaned against Alexander and kissed his cheek. Their foreheads touched.

She held him in her arms, and he felt safe.

EPILOGUE

The ordinary-looking man in a grey suit was sitting opposite Richard Catelin when Mavis informed her boss by intercom that Alexander Newton was waiting outside. Catelin told Mavis to keep him there.

The ordinary-looking man swirled the last of his Scotch with the melted ice cube. "The librarian proved her worth, didn't she?"

"Yes." Catelin smiled. "Though I think she got more than she bargained for." They both chuckled.

The ordinary-looking man put his empty glass on the table. Catelin made no offer to refill it.

"Absolutely discreet! Well, she is a librarian." The ordinary-looking man rose from his seat and adjusted his trousers. "Did you ever think Newton would turn out to be this good?"

"I like to think we provided him with solid on-the-job training."

"Yes. A nice way of describing it. And the current project?"

"He'll deliver."

"By the way, the Brigadier wants you to know how pleased he is with how this all worked out. He hopes we can continue." He adjusted his cuffs and looked down at his empty glass again. "Didn't know you had such good Scotch."

Catelin stood and they shook hands. He motioned to a door hidden by a curtain and waited for the ordinary-looking man to disappear before he called Mavis on the intercom.

Alexander strode into Catelin's large office with a big smile. He wore his dark blue suit, an indigo silk tie, a blue paisley waistcoat and a white shirt that looked as if it had a spotlight shining on it. He held the red-covered book in his left hand. It was the same color as his pocket square.

The Permanent Under-Secretary of the Department of Internal Affairs stepped forward to shake Alexander's hand. "Well done, Alexander." He smiled. "Here, sit."

Catelin made himself comfortable in his favorite arm-chair; Alexander chose the sofa. He looked around the office lined with paintings and sculptures, then at the table with its piles of books and magazines. He placed the KGB book Catelin had lent him on it. "I read it. I think I lived it," he said.

"Yes. Quite an education."

"Are you going to deport our favorite KGB agent?"

"Raganovich is leaving of his own accord by next week. In return, we are not prosecuting his daughter."

"You're not going to deport him, after what he did? He tried to kill me."

"Yes, but he didn't succeed. It's smoother our way. Besides, we think he was acting on his own. The Soviets are touchy about their own history and got nervous about the painting once they found out about it. We think it was a rogue operation, revenge for the trial. But his daughter gets to stay and complete her doctorate on Soviet relations."

"Irony or what?"

"Yes, it is rather delicious. But we'll keep an eye on her, now we know who she is."

"You don't think stealing the Captain was a ploy for something else? Like settling old scores or preparing his agents? Or maybe the notebooks he acquired from Henry Lotus?"

"That we don't know, and this is the problem with espionage, Alexander. It can be all rather vague and ambiguous. It's not like a novel or film where everything is tied up neat in a bow at the end. Real spying is messy, and you never know the full story." He studied Alexander, who appeared lost in thought. "Would you like a drink? I think we deserve a Scotch."

Alexander raised his eyebrows in agreement and occupied his time with adjusting the crease on his trousers and admiring his new Oxfords. Two empty glasses were on the table in front of him and he wondered why he had not bumped into anyone leaving the office. A lingering smell of Old Spice cut through the pipe smoke in the room.

Catelin pushed a button. Mavis entered and asked, "Ice?"

"Yes, thank you Mavis, the usual. And you, Alexander?"

"I'll have what you're having."

Mavis took ice cubes from the ice bucket and poured two scotches into fresh glasses from the cocktail cabinet. Once she had left and each had savored his drink, Catelin said to Alexander, "You heard about the notebooks?"

"Yes, I did. Henry was ecstatic. He's flown to the States. Funny how the police found them at Natasha's apartment. I don't believe she originally had them."

"We'll never know. She's not talking."

"But you made copies of them anyway and gave them to the FBI man who was searching for them?"

"You're a quick study, Alexander. But, I hear from Inspector Grimble, not a very good driver."

"I've been called worse things."

Catelin selected a pipe and found his leather tobacco pouch. "That accident went away. Price of doing business. Grimble is a little annoyed. Wouldn't want to run into him."

He started the ritual of preparing his pipe. "On the table, the envelope." Catelin pointed with his extinguished match. "I had to fight to stop them deducting expenses for the van."

Alexander noticed a large brown envelope with the government crest on it in front of him.

He opened the clasp and saw a bundle of $100 notes. He was tempted to take them out and count them. Instead he looked at Catelin, who was puffing on his pipe and staring at him. He had a distinct feeling he was being played but he was too committed to his new role as a spy to think about stopping. He tucked the envelope into his inside jacket pocket then took a sip of his drink and rolled it around his mouth. He was beginning to understand he had been used, and the strange aftertaste was not from the Scotch.

"The minister wants to extend his thanks to you and all your efforts. And your director wants you to go ahead with the Maori touring show you were talking about. I think the Arts Council will fund it."

Alexander swallowed. "Well, thank you. I don't know what to say."

"You might hear rumors about the shadow minister, you know, the photos with the girl, what was her name?"

"Kathy." Alexander nodded. He had deliberately forgotten about the photos, his betrayal.

"Apparently his wife saw them and is filing for divorce. He is resigning his post. I am sure there will be more repercussions. I wanted you to hear it from me first."

"Thank you, I think. But I already heard."

"You did? How?" Catelin caught his pipe as it fell from his mouth.

Alexander finished his Scotch and savored the sharpness at the end, coupled with Catelin's reaction. "Oh, spy stuff. Sources and rumors." Alexander shrugged. He had a flashback to Tsara's termination of their long friendship. He would have to get used to betraying his friends and sources, now that he was a spy. A shiver went through him.

"It does have a bite, doesn't it?" Catelin observed. "And we will never talk of this again."

TURN THE PAGE FOR AN EXCERPT FROM
THE JADED WIDOW
THE FINAL NOVEL OF THE *JADED* TRILOGY

PROLOGUE

When the petite blonde thrust the cattle prod into the bartender's rear for the third time, he emptied his bladder and bowels over her shiny, black, high-heeled shoes. He hung naked from a hook in her late husband's garage workshop, his hands secured with rope and his wrists dripping with blood. An oily rag was taped in his mouth so he couldn't scream; a rope was tied around his legs so he couldn't kick. Michael Donnelly kept his distance, holding the chain that suspended the body.

Known as Babs to her tennis club friends, Barbara Turner was the widow of Terry Turner, the victim of a gigantic explosion on the Southern Motorway a year ago. The police had closed the investigation, ruling that an unregistered truck had accidentally blown up, killing a number of people in a petrol station, including Terry and his henchman, John Eustace, two of the most feared underworld figures in New Zealand. On the same afternoon, the police had suffered the death of five of their officers and a number of others injured in a shootout on the other side of the city with a Maori gang over a truckload of marijuana. There were no survivors from the gang.

"Shit." Barbara stepped away from the smelly liquid around her. She wore a tight black mini-dress and blouse adorned with a long string of pearls. Her hair had been in a bun but had come loose. Her trademark thick blue eye makeup now ran down her cheeks.

"Take him down. You know what to do." She stomped her heels and looked at her feet then at her younger brother. "Shit. He ruined my shoes."

Michael released his grip and the bartender crashed to the floor. The chain made a screeching sound as it wrapped around the bartender's head. Michael stepped back and checked his brown brogues, his pressed khaki pants and blue shirt, then the lifeless body. He looked out of place in the large garage workshop behind what was now Mrs. Turner's Used Car Sales Emporium on Great South Road in Ellerslie. He had played center for his Auckland Grammar rugby Second Fifteen and filled out his blue blazer with his wide chest. His eyes had no life: anyone looking into them would see nothing. His ambition and sadism were hidden by his respectable veneer. He looked like a retired rugby player with a broken nose and cauliflower ears, but he was an accountant and played with money, not balls.

The only sound in the garage was the squeak of the hook that rocked back and forth. Fluorescent lights hung from the open-beamed ceiling. Some of the tubes flickered, creating a macabre scene.

He scrapped his shoes on a pile of sawdust nearby. The workshop hadn't been cleaned in months. Dirty rags littered the floor which was spotted with grease and oil stains. Tools hadn't been put back in their place but lay scattered over work benches or on the ground. Tool chests were left open, half-empty. There were no vehicles on the three ramps. A lifeless body covered in chains lay on the dirty floor.

Michael turned to his sister. "No trace?"

"No hands or face, right? Our people will know he's gone. That's all we need. You know the place under the bridge?"

"Got it." Michael smiled, pleased he no longer had to defer to John Eustace, who was known as Big John. He had towered over Michael, who wore elevated shoes to reach five feet eight inches. Big John had not kept his dislike for Michael a secret.

Michael ran his own investment firm and was the money manager for his sister's enterprises, including the legitimate car lot, the laundromats, the massage parlor in Newmarket and the strip club on Karangahape Road called the Gold Club. Neither sibling was new to the late Terry Turner's legitimate and illegitimate enterprises they inherited. Both had remained in the shadows. And Michael had created a series of companies and trusts to hide the ownership of their businesses, except for the used-car lot they now occupied late at night.

Oz, the bartender, had arrived from Sydney three months ago. The Gold Club's manager, Peter Green, hired him right off the boat: Oz was a fast and skilled barman, could mix drinks and serve more people than anyone else in the club, and he didn't annoy the strippers.

He had taken a week off work recently. A bad case of flu, he claimed when he phoned in sick. Over that week the receipts from the two cash registers at the club's long bar showed a doubling of income when Michael tallied all the earnings and compared them to the previous weeks. Michael went to investigate and worked out that the second cash register was used only by Oz, who must have pocketed the cash.

So Michael and Barbara made a surprise visit to Oz's flat in Grey Lynn. When he opened his front door Barbara didn't wait for an invitation but marched in. When Oz complained, Michael punched him in the stomach, hard. Fast with his fists and legs, he was overcompensating for his size—and for being John Eustace's replacement in his sister's eyes. He secured Oz's hands behind his back with rope and threw him into the back of his Jaguar XJ6. Barbara took her time getting back into the car. She held up a fistful of twenties and looked in the rear-view mirror. "How much did you steal?" she shouted as she drove away.

Oz mumbled. His face was pressed into the backseat as Michael twisted his wrist and arm.

"I reckon he stole about $200 a night. He worked for us, what? Three months. So that's about $20,000. What did you do with the money?" Michael gave the bartender's arm an extra twist.

"I'm sorry," Oz mumbled, then started to sob.

"Shit! Don't let him ruin the leather, Michael. This is a fucking new car."

.   .   .

"Maybe he can float back to Aussie where he came from," Barbara said as she left the workshop. "Knew we should've checked him out further. Probably fled Sydney for doing the same thing."

Michael went to the back where there was a locker room to change into Wellington boots and overalls, gather a few sharp tools and a handful of large plastic bags. Oz had confessed to spending the stolen cash on heroin. The money had gone to a drug dealer Michael supplied, an irony lost on the siblings.

·   ·   ·

Michael dumped the bags into the trunk and looked at the moonless sky. He could feel drops on his face. By the time he had turned into Karangahape Road it was teeming with rain. He drove past the Gold Club. The liquor license allowed it to stay open till 3 A.M. but at 3.30 it still looked open.

At Jervois Road he turned right down the hill. His wipers could not keep his windscreen clear. He stopped at the bottom of Curran Street, which ran underneath the Auckland Harbor Bridge, and turned off his lights. Despite the hour he could hear the occasional sound of traffic overhead. The tide was going out as he opened the trunk and carefully pulled out two black plastic bags. He carried them onto the rocks, using a concrete slab for balance. At the water's edge he opened up the smaller one and threw the contents into the water. Crabs and fish would eat the fingers before daybreak. He opened the other plastic bag and threw it as far as he could into the water, like one of his long rugby passes. There was just enough light for him to see it sink. Before he climbed back over the rocks he saw headlights approaching. He kept still, as he knew any movement might show in the driver's peripheral vision. He should be invisible in the rocks with the rain coming down. The car passed slowly, and Michael resisted the temptation to peek over the wall and see if it was a police car. He was glad he had shut the trunk and the lights were off. When he sensed the car had gone he peered over the wall and saw he was alone again.

The larger bag was more difficult to handle as he dragged it out of the trunk. He lost his footing a couple of times on the slippery rocks before he managed to get the bag into the water. He found his footing and pushed the bag deeper until it picked up the current. He watched until it was lost in darkness. The rain was now a sheet of water as he climbed back onto the pavement.

He looked at the huge steel girders of the harbor bridge. Rain was hitting him vertically as he scanned the dark water, the empty road, the noise of the wind and cars above. He let the rain wash over his face and opened his mouth to taste the water. He took deep breaths and could savor the air, the smell of the saltwater. He felt so alive and in control. It was a feeling he had never experienced before, far more powerful than smoking marijuana with his sister or his favorite girl at the Flamingo Paradise.

Dripping wet, he climbed into his Jag and wiped the water off his face. He drove under the bridge, followed the road to the roundabout, turned right by the boathouse, and headed back to the city along Westhaven Drive. He switched his lights on after he saw there were no cars ahead. He prayed the worn and soaked overalls he wore would not stain the cream-colored leather seat of his Jag. Barbara would get upset.

With his wipers at full speed, he thought about his sister and what she would be doing now. Since Terry was killed she hadn't had a boyfriend. When he was fourteen and Barbara sixteen, she had seduced him one night when their parents were out. They had continued this secret affair for several months until she broke it off and found an older, unrelated boyfriend. Michael was furious and jealous at the time. But then he was no longer a fourteen-year-old virgin, had experience in how to please a woman and a huge boost in confidence. He wondered if he could ever regain that sense of intimacy with his sister, but discounted the idea as a fantasy not worth considering. He knew this little secret would always bind them.

With Big John no longer visiting their key businesses, Michael had seen a dramatic fall in revenue. On his sister's insistence, he reluctantly started to visit the strip club, the massage parlor and the other cash businesses they ran. He had to drop in unannounced late at night, which entailed a change of habit for him. He liked to get up early, go for a run, have breakfast and then head to his office in Newmarket and start his work day, looking over figures, his investments, and the companies he controlled. He was not used to dealing with people who were not smart, used drugs, did not respect themselves, and operated in the hours of darkness.

Once he had gotten used to his new hours he started to be hands-on in a way the women at the Flamingo Paradise and the Gold Club came to fear. Big John Eustace had been a sadistic enforcer, but he knew the value of his property and never went too far in his perverted pleasures and violent outbursts. Terry Turner was a shrewd businessman and did not take kindly to tampered merchandise and ruined investments, as he had once explained to Big John in the presence of his sister's small and annoying brother.

1

Alexander borrowed the small white government van from the National Art Gallery where he was the exhibitions curator. He was in the suburb of Ngaio and parked on Kenya Street facing back into town, a mile away from the house he was going to visit. In a tracksuit, he looked like he was going for a late-night jog. With his six-foot three-inch frame he took long strides and kept an easy pace as he turned right onto Crofton Road. There were no vehicles on the road, no pedestrians out this late. He struggled to run up the hill and had to stop to gain his breath. Too busy at work, he had not worked out in months. He turned the bend and came to a long driveway almost hidden with trees and shrubs. Then he saw the trade unionist's house: there were no outside lights on. He walked towards the front door.

At the steps, he stopped to listen. His breathing had returned to normal. The house was dark, silent. He put on leather gloves. As instructed, he found the front-door key under the second flowerpot to the left. He slipped the key into the lock and carefully opened the door and eased his way inside, keeping the door slightly ajar and the key in the outside lock for a quick exit. He stepped inside and stopped when a small white Scottish terrier came running up to him, growling.

Alexander eased his body down to the carpet and put his right hand out. The dog stopped, looked at the tall stranger and slowly walked up to his fingers. Was the dog going to bite him or bark? Either way he would run, and the dog would probably chase him down the street. He hadn't been briefed about the dog, and his three previous trips to surveil the neighborhood had failed to identify any pets, other than the exotic tropical fish he knew to be in the large illuminated aquarium in the living room.

Alexander stroked the dog behind its ears and it rolled over. He rubbed its stomach and waited for the dog to respond. He kept one eye on the corridor that led to the bedrooms. If his new best friend behaved, he would have time to complete his mission.

The other union job had been easier. His boss Richard Catelin, the Permanent Under-Secretary for the Department of Internal Affairs, had given him a file with a photo of Dougie McLeish, the charismatic secretary of the Trades Council, and a photo of his famous 1956 Chevrolet Bel Air. McLeish always drove his shiny red car to government meetings. In the file was a photograph from the *Dominion* newspaper of McLeish by his vintage car, beaming his wide worker's smile. McLeish was to appear at a critical meeting the next day with the Prime Minister: if the talks failed, the Seamen's Union, the Drivers' Union and the Harbor Board Workers had planned a mass march from the Inter-Island Terminal to Parliament. Alexander had crept up to the car parked in McLeish's driveway. At 2 A.M. all the houses on the street were dark. Wearing leather gloves, he knelt down by the left rear bumper and turned the metal knob at the top of the tail light. He had been briefed on how to open the hidden fuel cap. It wouldn't budge. He had to use both hands to force it to turn before he could pull back the light fitting and find the fuel cap. The hinge made a loud squeak and he thought it would wake up the neighborhood. He kept very still and only his eyes moved to see if any curtains moved. He held his breath. When he realized no one had heard him, he went back to examining the open tail light. He was relieved there was no lock on the fuel cap as he twisted the cap off and placed it in his pocket. He took a plastic funnel from his jacket with his other hand and started to pour water from a large plastic bottle he produced from his other jacket pocket. Once emptied, he replaced the bottle with another and poured that into the tank. A car cruised past, and Alexander froze. He wondered if it was the police but didn't look. Once the street sounded deserted again, he took his last water bottle out of his jacket and poured it into the tank. He put the bottles and funnel back inside his jacket, secured the cap and closed the tail light without the hinge making a sound. He backed out of the driveway on his knees before he got to the street. No curtains moved, no lights went on, no dogs barked. He stood up and walked to his white van he had parked around the corner. He drove to his apartment in Thorndon after throwing the funnel and water bottles into a garbage bin in the city.

Next morning McLeish's prized car stalled at the end of his street. The photographer, hoping to get a shot of McLeish driving from his house, instead caught him kicking his tires and pulling at his hair. That was the photo on the *Dominion*'s front page that mirrored the unions' frustration with the National government's position on no new wage increases. The talks were a failure and the unions marched on Parliament.

Now the Scottish terrier rolled over and went to check its water bowl in the kitchen allowing Alexander to ease up to the large aquarium that separated the living room from the open kitchen. He took a bottle out of his jacket, undid the cap, and made a small gap at the top of the metal cover to the aquarium so he could to pour its contents into the tropical water.

A gust of wind blew the front door open then it slammed shut. The dog jumped and started to bark. Alexander heard noises from a bedroom, someone was getting out of bed. He eased the metal top back into position and, gripping the bottle, made himself as small as possible behind the aquarium. Heavy footsteps came down the corridor in slippers that made a slapping sound. If the man turned on the lights and searched the house Alexander planned to leap up, push him over, grab the door and run as fast as he could. He heard the dog greet its owner and footsteps to the front door. Then a grunt. A light went on in the hallway. If the heavy man found the outdoor key in the front door, he was screwed.

NOTES

The Tear of Tane: Henry Lotus told Dr. Mel Johnson this story in *The Jaded Kiwi*:

"Once upon a time, before Maori came here, Tane was the god of the forest. But the forest was in danger. Bugs were eating the roots of the trees, and unless something was done, the forest would die. Tane called all the birds together and asked for their help. The kiwi was a bird of paradise and lived in the treetops. It was the most beautiful bird in the forest and very proud. When Tane told all the birds what was happening, none of them wanted to help save the forest. Tane was in despair. None of the birds would volunteer or even offer a suggestion. There was silence in the forest."

"Well?" Mel asked.

"I'm pausing for dramatic effect. So, seeing none of the other birds were going to do anything, the kiwi stepped forward and said he would go and live in the undergrowth and eat all the bugs and save the forest. So the kiwi became a fat, flightless bird eating bugs at night. It lost all its bright colorful feathers. Tane was so moved by what the kiwi did, he shed a tear. Tane had never cried before. The tear fell to the ground and turned to greenstone and was lost for hundreds of years until a Ngapuhi, a tohunga, found a piece of pounamu on the forest floor. It was black and covered in moss. No one would have recognized it. But the tohunga picked it up and knew it was the Tear of Tane. He cleaned it and put it around his neck. And with the power the pendant gave him, he was able to guide his leaders to victories over other threatening tribes until the Ngapuhi were feared and respected throughout Aotearoa."

Hikoi: The Maori Land March that started in the Far North and finished in Wellington, 600 miles later on October 13, 1975 at the steps of Parliament with 5000 people, led by Whina Cooper.

The Order of Lenin was the highest award given to civilians. It was a running joke in some western spy agencies that just one special medal of the Order of Lenin was kept in the Kremlin. It was pinned on the lucky recipient, a photo was taken of him or her (for possible future blackmail purposes), and then it was returned to a nameless draw until the next lucky recipient was flown in.

Network of helpers: any good spy in a foreign country will recruit volunteers to assist in a number of benign tasks such as lending a brand-new Datsun, keeping watch on the neighborhood or looking for specific people and cars. The Soviet had sympathizers and members of the local Communist Party to thank for such an enthusiastic cadre of watchers and volunteers unknown to the local police and intelligence service.

Toi te kapa, toi te mana, toi te whenua: a Maori proverb which loosely translates as "Without language, without mana, without land, the Maori way of life would not exist." The proverb was the title of a work by Ralph Hotere, ink on watercolor on paper, 1972.

AUTHOR'S NOTE

The Jaded Spy is a work of fiction. Events, locations, people, places, times and dates have been imagined. Elements of the story might appear familiar, or bear a passing resemblance to a distant memory, a faded recollection, incidents that might have happened, but not as depicted here. Dates have been changed, locations of trees and shrubs have been manipulated and there was never a metal table and chair in that interrogation room in the Auckland Central police headquarters, nor the voluminous office space of the mythical Permanent Under-Secretary. Much as there were glorious pipi and mussel beds in Hokianga harbor, the Wilsons' house, marijuana plantations and other details are the product of the author's imagination. The castle on Castle Street is real but never, as far as I know, contained a Soviet safe apartment. The author, in a cameo appearance at the art gallery opening, never studied for a Ph.D. on Tristram Shandy.

Other parts of the story that appear implausible or outrageous are true. Captain Cook did sit in seat 1A. He was a wonderful traveling companion, even if he didn't use his seat belt. The Captain did have a full police and army escort to the gallery. "The Two Worlds of Omai" exhibition at the Auckland City Art Gallery went without a hitch. No persons as depicted in the gallery actually worked there.

Their characters, like all the people in the *Jaded* series, are fiction.

And this echoes the fact that the novel is but a cock-and-bull story.

BIBLIOGRAPHY

KGB, the inside story of its Foreign Operations from Lenin to Gorbachev. Christopher Andrew & Oleg Gordievsky. Sceptre, 1991.

The Second Oldest Profession: Spies and Spying in the Twentieth Century. Phillip Knightley. Norton, 1980.

The Trial of the Cannibal Dog: the remarkable story of Captain Cook's encounters in the South Seas. Anne Salmond. Yale University Press, 2003. (John Maynard was my counterpart at the Auckland City Art Gallery. As Exhibitions Curator during "The Two Worlds of Omai" exhibition he received the Captain Cook painting I escorted to Auckland with police and army protection. He recommended Salmond's book as valuable background and it is an outstanding story of Cook in the Pacific. John is nowhere to be seen in any shape or form in the novel, but he did provide valuable recollections.)

The New Zealand Wars, and the Victorian Interpretation of Racial Conflict. James Belich. Auckland University Press, 1986.

Two Worlds: first meetings between Maori and Europeans 1642-1772. Anne Salmond. Viking, 1991.

The Two Worlds of Omai. Auckland City Art Gallery, 1977. Catalog notes: John Tarlton, Eric Young, E.H. McCormack, David Simmons.

The Globalization of Supermax Prisons. Rutgers University Press. 2013. Edited by Jeffrey Ian Ross. Chapter 9 *The Emergence of the Supermax in New Zealand* by Greg Newbold. Greg provided valuable insights, descriptions and history to Rawiri's time in Paremoremo otherwise known as 'Parry'. Any mistakes are mine, not Greg's.

Many websites were used to research events and locations for this novel, but mention should be made of https://timespanner.blogspot.com, and also how helpful Lisa Truttman has been in providing background information, including use of the historic aerial photograph site: http://retrolens.nz.

PLAYLIST

Bohemian Rhapsody, Queen

Maggie's Farm, Bob Dylan

Who'll Be The Next In Line, The Kinks

A Time For Everything, Jethro Tull

Fat Bottomed Girls, Queen

Gnossiennes No. 5, Erik Satie

The Sweeney Main Theme

The Stranger Song, Leonard Cohen

Master Song, Leonard Cohen

Too Much Between Us, Procol Harum

The Train Kept A Rollin', The Yardbirds

Shapes of Things, The Yardbirds

2120 South Michigan Avenue, The Rolling Stones

As I Went Out One Morning, Bob Dylan

Gymnopedies No. 1, Erik Satie

If You See Her, Say Hello, Bob Dylan

Eight Miles High, The Byrds

Pictures At An Exhibition, Promenade, Modest Mussorgsky

Mental Notes, Split Enz

Time For A Change, Split Enz

School, Supertramp

Crime Of The Century, Supertramp

A Case Of You, Joni Mitchell

Melody, The Rolling Stones

I'm Gonna Wash That Man Right Out Of My Hair, The
Sound of Music

Love Is A Drug, Roxy Music

Can't We Be Friends? Frank Sinatra

I'm Not Like Everyone Else, The Kinks

I Tried to Leave, Leonard Cohen

Land, Patti Smith

Call it Something Nice, The Small Faces